'I recently saw [...] iting tutor that one sh[...] ory. I thought it was p[...] d this short story ['In [...] it has great command on what can be [...] peech and alternating voices; it builds up character steadily, but, more importantly, shows how someone can be constrained and altered by a relationship that has gone wrong – and then how they can move toward healing. A very well-crafted piece of writing.'

Una McCormack
New York Times and USA Today bestselling author

'To create a believable *voice* is essential. This means being in control of your fictional narrator's vocabulary, style, and sensibilities. A great example of this is 'Wimbledon to Wood Green', the competition winner. It achieves something very difficult in fiction, which is to sustain a voice without error. Someone once said any piece of writing is as good as the worst line in it. Writers who concentrate on editing often achieve better results than those blinded by the temptation to dazzle. One misplaced line could have destroyed 'Wimbledon to Wood Green', but the writer doesn't let us down.

The voice of Rog, the narrator, is pitch-perfect, all the way from "Oh, hullo. Is that Stew? It's Rog. Yeah, that's right. Rog Molesworth." To "Stew, for the last time, are you still there?" Remarkably the whole story is told as just one end of a telephone conversation – technically a very tricky exercise. It requires a lot of clever footwork to signal to the reader what Stew is saying at he other end of the line: as in "Yeah, I heard you got married. Chip told me. Nice girl, he said." The success of this story is the way the author has allowed Rog to reveal himself, while apparently trying to say something else. I particularly enjoyed the section in which Rog tries to claim he hasn't been peeking at a workmate's 'schlong' in the toilets at work.

"Ha, what a joke! The truth is, I never went near the urinals when he was there – he always stood in the middle and with his bulk it was hard to squeeze in."

Rog's inability to be honest with himself shines through as – eventually – does his affection for Stew.

One of the rewarding aspects of stories like this is that they have a core, something serious or even profound, which makes us feel that they are worth reading: a diamond-edge, which stays with us after the story is told. A case in point is the moment Rog recalls – ironically – being honest with Stew:

"Anyway, I repeat, it was embarrassing and I shouldn't have said it. But what I want you to know is this. You're the only person I've ever said that to. I've never said that to anyone else. Ever. Nor, I think, will I ever say it to anyone again."

We can't help thinking at this point that this is the only truth in Rog's sad monologue.'

Jim Kelly
Best-selling crime writer

'Twenty-four stories, between seven and twenty-one pages long, the title story, 'Festival', being the longest at twenty-nine pages, all of them concerning gay males. But the same topic or location need not indicate a lack of variety (think of Joyce's *Dubliners*, Turgenev's *Huntsman's Sketches* or Sherwood Anderson's *Winesburg, Ohio*) and it certainly does not in this case. The range is wide and so is the time span.

The stories cover all age groups. In the first story, 'The Horses', a boy is intrigued by his elder sister's latest boyfriend. The second story, 'You Farzan, Me Duane', is more than a schoolboy crush and separation. In 'Vagabond' a teenager on a sea-side holiday with his parents has a holiday from them in the sand-dunes. And so on up to middle age. The wife's away for a weekend, so what's happening down at the pub? Or ... Let's have a birthday treat and invite round a bit of rent – and who should turn up? The last story 'Coda' is coping with the loss of a long-term partner. It is not necessary to read the stories in strict order. Each one is self-contained. But the dove-tailing of the age groups is quite telling. Something unfolds.

Not all the stories are approached from the angle of the gay man. In 'Tracking James' a mother spies on her son; she's on the lookout for 'tell-tale signs'. In 'Late Call' a father, ex-army, worries about his artistic son. In 'A Canterbury Tale' a nephew (who happens to be gay) is taken in his Uncle and Auntie's car for a historical guide of the city. The Auntie pops off for a chat with her sister and the Uncle breaks off the guided tour, drives to a distinctly shady part of town and visits his lady love, leaving the nephew in the car to ponder the goings-on of the heterosexual life style.

The stories are told in a balance of first and third person, and in a variety of forms. 'Roll-Top Desk, Bottom Left Drawer' is a letter sent but not delivered. 'Wimbledon to Wood Green' is a breathless going nowhere phone call with a distinct sub-text. 'Paris, Vienna, Rome' offers snapshots of various rail travellers, with connections and cards to shuffle. A counsellor prises out the story in 'In the Chair'. Things are not what they seem; this comes over in the couple of amateur theatre stories, including the title story. In 'Liar' a man deliberately adopts different names.

Throughout there is a cross-cultural concern. 'You Farzan' and 'Hassan' feature foreign students. Educational and class divides also feature. The jilted party in 'In the Chair' tells the counsellor that the dominant partner was into 'culture' and wanted to go to the south of France to see the mountain that Cézanne so often painted. The culture-vulture enthuses, but the one made out to be philistine climbs the mountain, enjoys the view and in a sense gets closer to Cézanne. In 'Chance' a man, getting over an affair, is on holiday on the English Riviera. He is bored and wonders why he didn't travel abroad. In a pub he meets a carpenter who is in the resort to do a job. He is married and far from home. They talk about music, books, family history (the carpenter's father is Polish) and stay the night together. In the morning the carpenter has left. But he is traced, via the Polish connection.

An absorbing and varied collection, casting new light, from angles askance.'

John Dixon,
author of *The Carrier Bag and Other Stories*

Festival

Les Brookes is the author of two novels *Such Fine Boys* and *Small Town Blues* and a non-fiction work *Gay Male Fiction Since Stonewall*. He lives in Cambridge, UK.

To Diarmuid and George

with love

Les

Festival

Les Brookes

Copyright © 2022 Les Brookes

All rights reserved

The characters and events portrayed in this book are fictitious. Any similarity to real persons, living or dead, is coincidental and not intended by the author.

No part of this book may be reproduced, or stored in a retrieval system, or transmitted in any form or by any means, electronic, mechanical, photocopying, recording or otherwise, without express written permission of the publisher.

ISBN-13: 9798776983917

Cover design by Phil Bales

For Abdullah Surani

Table of Contents

The Horses 1
You Farzan, Me Duane 8
Vagabond 17
Paris, Vienna, Rome 27
Beryl 37
Cinderfella 47
Liar 68
Hassan 87
In the Chair 105
A Canterbury Tale 114
Moving On 129
Festival 142
Chance 171
Balloon 185
Tracking James 194
Late Call 203
Freewheelin' 212

Requital 220
Pennine Winter 229
Wimbledon to Wood Green 240
Weekend 247
Roll-Top Desk, Bottom Left Drawer 258
Revenant 267
Coda 277

The Horses

Sandy Hill swung his satchel round his neck and trailed home from school, studying his feet, humming to himself and carefully avoiding the gaps in the paving-stones. But as he was passing the newsagent's a thunderous roar broke into his daydreams and he glanced up. A big shiny motorbike had drawn up alongside.

'Hello, young man,' said a set of smiling gnashers.

'Oh, hello,' said Sandy.

It was Don, his sister's current boyfriend. He liked Don, who had silky brown skin, a gold ring in his ear and slick black hair that hung in curls round his neck. Today he was wearing a summer shirt outside his jeans, a shirt with palm trees on it. It was open to the waist, and a small silver medallion nestled in the hairs of his chest.

'Fancy a spin?'

Sandy smiled and nodded.

'Well then, climb aboard.'

It was hard getting on. He was only little, after all. Don gave a hand, then guided Sandy's arms around his waist. They sped along Chapel Street, crossed the Iron

Festival

Bridge, then turned into Dockside. Don's shirt billowed like a windsock in the summer breeze. His waist felt warm, the muscles of his stomach taut. Sandy pressed his nose into the shifting cord of his knobbly spine.

They pulled up at the café on the quay. Sandy was delighted. He'd hardly ever been to a café. Don lifted him onto an outdoor wooden bench – a bench so high that his feet scarcely touched the ground. Then he went off and returned with two thick red mugs and a packet of ginger snaps. The mugs winked at the brim with white bubbles. Sandy took a mouthful, and Don, leaning forward with a laugh, wiped the froth from his lips.

'How's that sister of yours?'

Sandy shrugged.

'Tell her I'll be round tonight, as arranged.'

Sandy nodded and swung his feet in the wide space beneath the bench. He gazed about in wonder. The little fairground at the end of the quay twinkled. The roundabout turned merrily, the swingboats flew high and higher, the helter-skelter rang with tiny shouts of delight. He lifted the heavy mug to his lips and took another mouthful with a loud sucking noise. More froth stuck to his lips. He looked up and grinned at Don, who had crossed his legs and was drawing deep on a cigarette. Don grinned back. He had such a friendly face, with creases that turned upward like smiles. His medallion winked in the sunlight and curly grey smoke drifted lazily from his mouth.

Strains of music floated across the dock. Sandy glanced again at the fairground. Then, sticking his nose deep in his mug, he watched the ash on Don's cigarette grow long and longer until it dropped off into a metal tray full of dog-ends.

The Horses

Don had seen his glance. 'Drink up,' he said, stubbing out. 'Let's go take a look.'

The noise of the fairground grew as they approached. The site was crowded with children, mothers and dogs. Tiny tots stood on tiptoe thrusting coins at the man in the sweet stall, and babies in pushchairs, clutching monstrous cornets, smothered their faces in ice cream. Further off, a couple of louts in a swingboat were trying to swing over the bar. The centrepiece was the roundabout, which they watched for a while, the music from the big jumping box blasting their ears. Sandy gazed up and read the sign as it revolved: *The Golden Galloping Horses.* How splendid they were! What teeth they had! What flashing eyes and flaring nostrils!

The roundabout slowed gradually and finally came to a standstill. Some people rushed forward. Don tucked his hands under Sandy's shoulders and, stepping aboard, lifted him onto a saddle. Then he leapt off and stood at the side, smiling. The music started up again, even closer now – in fact, right next to Sandy's ear – a noisy, clattering march with deafening cymbal-crashes. Sandy held on tight to the golden pole with spiral flutes, and soon his horse began to move, dipping slowly at first and then rising again. Don slid from sight, to be replaced by a gliding parade of smiling faces and waving hands. But then, there he was again, smiling and waving too. The horses were dipping and rising more quickly, the faces in the crowd whirling past like gusting leaves. Don flashed by so quickly, it was difficult to catch sight of him. Sandy held on even tighter, the horses galloped faster, the music grew louder. It was thrilling – so thrilling that he thought he might be sick. But then suddenly it was over, the horses

Festival

eased to a rolling canter, and there was Don again, lifting him to safety.

After that they strolled about and Don tried his strength on the punchball machine, but he didn't score too well and they had a good laugh about that. Don drew some strips of chewing gum from his shirt pocket and offered one to Sandy. Then they wandered into the amusement arcade and took turns shooting the balls on the pinball machine. Sandy gasped whenever there was a buzz and flash of lights, but they failed to scoop the jackpot and turned to each other with a smile and a shrug. They had better luck on the mechanical claw, which came close to grasping a small pink teddy bear several times, and on the fourth attempt, under Sandy's control, delivered a miniature box of sweets.

'Well, what a champ!' said Don, as they hurried back to the bike. 'And now, young man, we need to get you home – pronto!'

Ten minutes later he dropped Sandy outside his front door and sped off. Sandy spotted his mother peering through an upstairs window as he trailed up the path. She seemed to be frowning. No, she *was* frowning. He smiled at her, but she didn't smile back. A faint buzz of alarm ran through his body. He went to the back door and hesitated on the step. There was a fishy smell in the air and he recalled that it was Friday. He could hear someone talking on the radio. He let himself into the kitchen, and his father, who was sitting at the table reading a newspaper, looked up sharply.

'Hey, young man! What's this? Where have you been?'

Sandy was suddenly scared. There was going to be trouble. Big trouble. Trouble for Don, trouble for both

The Horses

of them: the blame would stick to *him* too. He was afraid to open his mouth. He thought desperately of something to say. Something to save them both. But before he could speak his mother flew in.

'Was that Don Pearson?'

Sandy nodded.

'I thought so. That wastrel. What's *he* doing, bringing you home at this time?'

Sandy stared at her solemnly. 'We went to a café.'

'A café?' his mother exploded. '*What* café?'

Sandy gulped. 'The one by the dock,' he said hesitantly, his voice sinking to a whisper. 'You know, near the fair.' He flushed pink, as if confessing to something shameful. 'I had a ride on the horses.'

His mother closed her eyes and shuddered. She looked so strange – so grey in the face – he thought she must be ill.

'I've never heard the like! Snatching up children in the street.' She turned to his father. 'That's it! He's not to set foot in this house again.'

His father flung his paper aside with a snort. 'Don't worry, he won't!' He leapt up and paced the room. 'In fact, I've a good mind to call the police.'

Sandy was studying the floor. '*Look* at me,' said his mother. 'What have I told you about coming straight home?' He raised his eyes and shrugged. She flung a glance at his father and shook her head. Then she turned back to him. 'Oh, I don't know, my boy! What *are* we to do with you?' She pointed to the door. 'Now go to your room.'

He climbed the stairs very slowly, and every step seemed to bring him lower. The warm feeling in his tummy had gone stone cold. How strange life was. It

Festival

flipped you over like a pancake. People were funny too. You couldn't understand them. He reached the landing, stopped and glanced at his sister, whose door was ajar. She was lying face down on the bed.

'Hi,' he called softly, and she looked up, her face tear-stained, her mouth in a sulky pout. 'Don said he'll be round tonight.'

'What?' She sat up. 'You saw Don? Where?'

'On his bike. He took me to the café by the dock. I went on the horses.'

She gave him a painful smile, snuffled a bit and blew her nose into the little cotton hanky she kept tucked in her sleeve. She was wearing the skirt she wore to school, but he spotted her new red dress draped over a chair.

'They won't let me out. He'd better not come to the door.'

Sandy gaped in alarm. 'No, they'll go bonkers.'

She pulled a long face. 'I'll listen for his bike and speak to him from the window.'

He nodded, then showed her his box of sweets. 'I won these. Want one?'

She stared at them with a frown. 'No, thanks.'

In his room he tossed his satchel aside and sat on the edge of the bed, dangling his feet. Wastrel. What did it mean? Don was fun. He had a big smile and strong brown hands. What was all the fuss about? It had been a nice treat and now it was spoiled. Everyone was angry and mean and miserable. He put his ear to the door. There were raised voices in the house and he wondered if the meal would be ruined. Ah well, he hated fish anyway. He tipped some sweets into his palm and tried one. They were little animals made of jelly. He thought

The Horses

he'd save some for Don. Would he see him again? He hoped so. He'd keep a lookout.

You Farzan, Me Duane

All that summer he wore shorts. Brief cotton shorts, pale yellow and snug around the arse. His legs were the colour of charcoal and amazingly hairy. Too hairy, I thought at first – like shaggy black rugs. But within days they'd worked their magic on me and I was devoted to them. He always sat next to me in English and rubbed his knee against mine. I still remember the tickle, the electrifying thrill of it. Miss Webber often smiled at us, I recall, as if she was in on the secret. His father was a visiting professor and they lived in a large house they were renting in Wood Lane.

When the holidays arrived, he and the family went off to France for two weeks. It seemed an eternity. I felt dull, empty, forsaken. Were they planning other trips? Would they be away all summer? How would I survive until September? My family had no plans. I sat around indoors, reading a gloomy novel set in a death-haunted sanatorium. Then a postcard arrived, postmarked

You Farzan, Me Duane

Rennes. 'Too much bloody walking, the sea is freezing and we've been drenched by thunderstorms.' It seemed wrong to take delight in his misery, but my heart sang.

The day after their return there was a knock at the door. I was alone in the house and stuck my head through the upstairs window. It was a bright August morning. He grinned at me from the doorstep and pointed at his bicycle propped against the fence. I tore downstairs and yanked him in. We sat in the kitchen drinking thick brown coffee from giant mugs while he rattled on about the holiday. I didn't hear a word he said, though. I was too busy basking in the warmth of his big white smile.

I fetched my bike from the shed, checked the tyres and we headed for the spinney up on the hill – always our first port of call. He rode a little ahead of me in his comically awkward fashion, head tilted slightly, feet splayed heavily on the pedals. Though athletic in other ways, he was ungainly on a bike – an effect of his height, I think. But awkward or not, his shaggy legs, his tensed muscles and taut buttocks were lovely to behold, and I drank in the view.

At the spinney we propped our bikes against a tree. No reason to chain them. Who would steal our jalopies? We followed a path to the pond, sat on a log and threw stones into the water. We did this in silence for some minutes, before I turned and glanced at him. Some bits of dry twig had fallen into his hair. I reached out, brushed them off and combed my fingers through his black curls. He laughed, pushed me backwards onto the grass and leapt astride my chest. He pinned my arms to the ground and I lay there giggling like a schoolgirl. Then he dug his fingers into my ribs until I shrieked.

Festival

'We should go away for a few days,' he yelled as we freewheeled downhill into Newton. 'I've got a tent.'

It had to be the coast, and Cromer was the obvious choice. Trains ran to Cromer and there was camping in the area. We stuffed clothes into panniers, a few provisions into rucksacks and strapped the tent and sleeping bags to the racks. On the day of departure, we tore onto the platform just as the train was about to leave. It was no more than a couple of old wagons, but cosily picturesque. We threw our bikes into the guard's van and sat side by side in the carriage, munching apples and watching the sunlit fields roll past. We grinned at each other, his knee rubbing against mine.

The first site was full, but we were directed to another – a farmer's field with just a few tents and a primitive washroom in an old barn. The ground was rock hard. We smashed at the pegs with a small rubber mallet and fell about laughing. Eventually we crawled inside and lay there, hands behind heads, gazing at the dizzy blue canopy in a thrill of quiet delight at our snug little abode.

After a spot of lunch, we rode into town, where the seafront was breezy, though baking in the sheltered places, and hordes were strolling the promenade and lazing on the beach. A Punch and Judy show had drawn a crowd of kids and parents, and a sign above the entrance to the pier was advertising some variety entertainment at the Pavilion Theatre. We stared at it blankly, since the names of the performers meant nothing to us. But the pier itself, suspended over heaving brine and battered by strong waves, had a certain end-of-world appeal and we spent some time

You Farzan, Me Duane

peering over the edge at the rusted, barnacled pillars. Then we polished off a couple of ice creams and lost money in the amusement arcade.

The cove that we found in the late afternoon, after a short cycle ride, was not quite ours. There were some other couples there, sunbathing on the rocks, and a family were paddling at the water's edge. The so-called beach was a thin strip of shingle. We changed into bathing gear beneath our towels and hobbled into the shallows, the cold making us shriek. 'Aaaaagh!' Farzan yelled. 'Worse than France!' But he was the first to take the plunge, diving headlong into the deep with a sudden thrash of disappearing legs and then leaping up again like an ecstatic dolphin, a halo of beads spinning from his wet hair. He gave a great gasp of shock, then a bellow of laughter. I was standing up to my knees, shoulders hunched, shivering and hugging my chest. He beat the surface with his arms and sent a spray flying towards me. I shrieked and laughed and gazed in wonder – he looked so gorgeous, his eyes bright with elation, his hair plastered to his scalp, water cascading in torrents down his face and chest.

We pedalled into town for supper and found a steak bar in the high street, cheerful, bright, bustling, and just the ticket. We went for the mixed grill, and sat grinning at each other and playing hangman on a beer-mat while waiting for it to arrive. It came on a couple of large oval platters, accompanied by paper napkins and sachets of sauce. Our eyes flew open and we tucked in with ravenous delight. It was, quite simply, the best meal I've ever had. Nothing I've eaten in fancier places has ever come close. In my pantheon of great meals it holds a unique place, retaining an elusive magic that grows

Festival

stronger and more bewitching with every year that passes.

The joke came to me as we were eating, by the way. It's a bit of a cheat, though. I mean, I'm not Duane, am I? I'm Greg. So I kept it secret at first, thinking it silly. Also, I wasn't sure he'd get the reference. But when, towards the end of the meal, I changed my mind, he was tickled pink. 'Oh yeah,' he hooted. 'Maureen O'Sullivan and Johnny Weissmuller.'

We returned to the tent with some bottled beer. The moon was full and bright, the sky clear and pricked with stars. A small group, sitting round a fire in a corner of the field, was singing softly to a couple of strummed guitars, but otherwise the deep quiet was broken only by the faint murmur of voices. We pulled our beds from the tent and squatted on them. And there we sat, lifting beer to our lips, listening to the sounds of the night, feeling no compulsion to speak. Secure and comfortable, we simply communed in silence. And shortly the singers switched to a new tune. The Bee Gees were big that year. We grinned and hummed along. *Ah, ha, ha, ha, stayin' alive.*

It was warm in the tent, so we left the flaps open, stripped off our shirts and lay on top of the beds in our shorts. Through the gap we could see the moon and the profile of trees against a pale sky. Moths and fireflies hovered round the entrance. I gazed at the scene for a while, my hands clasped behind my head. Then, drowsy from the beer, I must have drifted off because when I next looked the flaps of the tent were closed. I glanced at Farzan, who was sleeping. The air was still warm, though slightly cooler now. So I turned on my side and snuggled into the sweater I was using as a pillow.

You Farzan, Me Duane

I woke to the feel of his arm around me, his chest pressed to my back, his nose buried in the nape of my neck. Taken by surprise, I started. 'Hey, it's only me,' he whispered and licked my ear. I half-turned with a small gasp of delight and he drew me closer, hugging my waist. And there we lay, quite still, for several minutes, though my heart was beating wildly and I could feel the heave of his chest. Then his hand slipped into my shorts and grasped me firmly. I was rigid. As stiff as a guard on parade. I leaned back against him with a moan and he laughed quietly in my ear.

After a while, with sudden boldness, I turned on my back, slipped out of my shorts and smiled at him. He smiled back, then slowly removed his own and knelt beside me. I stared at him, mesmerised. His body was not quite new to me – I'd seen him in the showers. But never this close, the thick hairs of his chest and groin almost brushing my face. Nor this big – in his present state, huge as a horse. He leaned forward and kissed my nipples. Then, kneeling astride my head, he gently swung his resplendent gear just inches above my spellbound eyes. I gazed up at his loins and arse and felt the dark growth of his fuzz tickling my nose.

When the moment came, he spat on his hand and smeared me with a gummy finger. The entry was painful, but after the initial thrusts I groaned with delight. Wriggling beneath him, I spread my legs wider with every push, riding hard with the motion, willing it to last for ever. But it was soon over. I watched his face buckle, felt the violent shudder of his release. Then, breathing deeply, he slowly withdrew and, leaning forward, massaged me with firm strokes. I responded instantly, bursting high over his chest in fulsome

Festival

splendour, and breaking – or so it seemed to me in the lush technicolour of my imagination – like some great tropical flower from its pod.

He gazed at me in wonder for a few moments. Then, swaying a little, he fell forward onto my body and we rolled across the tent, glued together by jizz and rocking with deep laughter.

There would be no more summers together. And somehow, in some secret part of me, I knew. For all that autumn change was in the air and I sensed calamity long before the bombshell came.

It came on a Monday in early January. As I passed through the school gates I saw him sitting on the front steps. He looked serious, deep in thought, a bit dazed. I sat down beside him.

'We're going home,' he said. 'My father's been recalled.'

I nodded and stared at the ground. The news simply confirmed a long-held fear. For weeks our television screens had exploded with the austere face of someone called an ayatollah. Farzan had sometimes spoken about his country – its customs, politics, religion – but I had taken very little in. I was a dizzy creature and the place was just too far away. Ayatollahs meant nothing to me. Until then.

'I'll write,' he said. 'And we'll be back.'

'No you won't,' I said.

They were gone within a week. The house in Wood Lane was suddenly empty. In the raw winds of February I sometimes strolled past and gazed through the windows at the bare boards and walls. It was April before anyone moved in – a smart young couple with a flash new car. I watched the furniture arrive with seething resentment. Meanwhile there was school to think about, exams, the future. Everything was changing. The May elections, for instance, brought an insistent, half-familiar voice ringing over the airways. Until that moment, with next to no interest in politics, I'd scarcely noticed the rise of Margaret Hilda Thatcher.

Not a word from Farzan. I grieved in secret. The summer came and I started to ride out to the spinney for old times' sake. Then an envelope flew through the letter-box. Inside, a postcard of the Azadi Tower and a photo of the lad himself in yellow shorts. 'Hey, it's only me. How are you, buddy? Stayin' alive, I hope. I'm doing just fine. Going to university next year. Miss you and the rides. Drop me a line at the above address.' The above address was not too decipherable. I dropped a line, but nothing came back. Not sure about the post over there.

That was an age ago. I work for a London theatre now and live with Richard. And it's good, very good, don't get me wrong. But it remains an echo. An echo of rocks and coves and country lanes, of French fries and bottled beer and strummed guitars, of summer nights and the Bee Gees. I live, to be honest, in a kind of weird, buried hope. A hope that one day I'll just turn a corner and walk slap-bang into him. And he'll say 'Hi, buddy' and we'll stand there for ages just grinning at each other. Then we'll dodge into the nearest place and order a mixed grill and shoot ketchup over everything and yak our silly heads off for hours, his knees grazing mine.

The field at Cromer has changed, by the way. There's not a tent in sight now. Just a couple of chestnut

Festival

horses that push their noses over the gate and nibble grass from your palm.

Vagabond

It's a nice little room, right at the top of the building, with a dormer window and a glimpse of the sea across roofs and chimney pots. The only single in the guesthouse, according to the landlady. She's a dumpy little thing, with a bustling manner and a false smile. When they arrived last Monday she showed them round, and Robbie saw his mother run a finger along the window sill – one of her many embarrassing habits. 'No points for cleanliness,' she commented later.

He stands in front of the mirror in his new swimming briefs. They look good. He admires again the three bands of colour – green, orange, navy – and slaps his belly. Not bad; flatter than last month; the workouts are starting to show. Turning to the side, he surveys his figure in profile, runs a hand along the line of his chest, and then strikes a pose, a crooked arm placed against his pouting rump.

There's a knock at the door. He pulls on a T-shirt and sticks his head out. His mother and father are pacing the narrow landing.

Festival

'We're off,' his mother says, pressing some money into his hand. 'Have a nice day and we'll see you at dinner.'

Half an hour later he saunters out of doors in shorts and sandals and a blue check shirt that he bought from a market stall just last week. In the small rucksack lolling from his shoulder there's a bar of chocolate, a bottle of squash and a copy of *Special Friendships* by Roger Peyrefitte, which his parents have been staring at with puzzled frowns all week but have so far failed to comment on. It's a lovely warm day, slightly sultry, though softened by misty sunlight and a bloom of alpine clouds. A family is playing cricket on the beach and some small children are paddling near the water's edge, but it's too early for the crowds; they'll come later. At the mid-point of the prom some men, pottering about on a stage laden with cables and speakers, are rocking the area with great blasts of amplified music.

Further on, he stops off at the Dolphin Café, pleasantly situated on a grassy slope with a view of the sea. He joins the queue, then sits on the terrace with a pot of coffee pretending to read his book, for he's easily distracted in such a setting and watching people on the sly is a favourite pastime. The couple at the next table with raised voices, for instance – are they quarrelling, or simply talking? And the old lady with the faraway smile – is she happy, lonely, or just a bit cracked? Then the two men near the railing are lovers, that's clear. Look at the way they're gazing at each other and touching hands. It won't last, though – the younger one is far too cute and will soon be tempted away.

In the small aquarium, shoals of tiny luminescent fish shoot around like shards of coloured glass or glide carelessly past the mouths of alarming sea-monsters. A sluttish octopus pulses gently on a rock and a shy lobster waves antennae at gazing visitors. The place is dark and smelly, like a damp cellar, and he emerges from its sea-green gloom into brilliant sunlight with great relief.

He skirts the edge of the golf course, turns into a sandy lane, and regains the beach at last, but now much further west, away from the town. The beach here is backed by high dunes, and he scrambles up the side of one, his feet sinking into the soft sand. At the top he gazes around in a small thrill of delight – the view of the coastline, the surrounding cliffs and the sparkling sea is exhilarating. Time, then, for a picnic. He sits down cross-legged on the sand, reaches into his bag and breaks off two squares of chocolate.

After a while he uncrosses his legs, lies out full stretch on his back and closes his eyes. The sun is warm on his skin and he drifts into a state of mellow dreaminess. He sees a swimmer emerge from the sea and come striding up the beach towards him, a young man with streaming locks of blond hair. The swimmer stands over him, smiling, and shakes himself from head to foot like a dog. Drops of cold water splash onto Robbie's body. Then they lie facing each other, their noses touching, and he licks the salt from the swimmer's face.

He sits up, embarrassed by the bulge in his shorts. Stupidly so, it seems, since there's no one around, is there? Well, not evidently ... But wait, who's that, in a tight black thong, peering at him from behind the next dune? And further off ... Is he still dreaming, or is that two more figures, similarly attired, looking keenly in his direction? He gazes round. No, he's not dreaming – the

Festival

place is alive. There are busy, thong-clad figures everywhere, straining their necks and keeping a sharp lookout, appearing and vanishing like bobbing meercats.

He does nothing at first – just sits and watches, his stomach fluttering, his blood tingling. His first impulse is to get up and walk away, but then a reckless, itching curiosity takes hold, and after a while he rises and wanders warily towards what seems to be the centre of the action. He gets no further than the next hillock, however, for on the other side he stumbles on a wondrously exotic sight – a truly fabulous, heart-stopping vision, reclining on a straw mat in a deep declivity. The person, a hill of pink flesh, has green lips, black fingernails and a luxuriant mane of strawberry-blond hair. Wearing what seems to be the lower half of a red polka-dot bikini, she's lying on her side – for 'she' is surely the pronoun – her head propped on one arm, her body bent into a paunchy S-shape. Slim shades, in a stylish white frame, cover her eyes; but she removes them on seeing him approach.

'Hullo, sweetie,' she says.

Robbie freezes. Stares fixedly at her, in a silent dither. How to respond? Something tells him not to respond at all, that to make any response would be playing with fire. Tells him to walk on past, giving her a wide berth, or perhaps beat a quick retreat. But that would be rude, and Robbie's been raised to be polite. In any case, he's torn. To snub her, to pass with an air of aloofness, would be to miss a rare chance. He's not sure if she holds the secret to life, but certainly it's not every day that you come face to face with someone so thrillingly other. So he smiles and, despite the dryness

Vagabond

in his throat, manages to return the greeting in a rather weak voice. 'Oh, hi there,' he says, hating himself instantly for sounding so feeble.

'Now there's no reason to be shy.' She pats the sand beside her. 'So tootle over here, plonk yourself down and talk to Mamma.'

Robbie hesitates, his mind racing, his face screwing up. 'Well,' he stutters, 'the thing is, I was just ...'

'Passing through?' She smiles knowingly. 'Listen, child – no one here is ever just passing through. So do as I say, step this way and park that exquisite little tush of yours right here beside me.'

Robbie wrestles with a spasm of revolt; he's not used to being spoken to in this manner. Still, the invitation is not to be lightly turned down; there's real strength and command behind it. So, with a smile and a shrug, he moves forward and drops onto the patch of burning sand beside the mat, collapsing gracefully into a cross-legged position, while keeping his distance at a good yard and a half.

She reaches forward and dangles a hand, as if inviting him to kiss it. 'It's Letitia, by the way.' Robbie takes hold of it tentatively and shakes it a few times, in a manner close – or as close as he can manage – to a normal handshake. 'And you? Who are *you*?'

'I'm Robbie.'

'En*chan*tée.' Letitia breathes the word through puckered green lips as if blowing a kiss. 'Now, Robbie, tell me. You're slim and lithe and lightly tanned. Did that come naturally or have you been working on it?'

Robbie snorts and dissolves into giggles.

'Because,' she continues, patting a fleshy midriff, 'I'm seeking a little more shapeliness myself, so any

Festival

tips are welcome.' She looks severely at him as if to reprove his laughter, flaps a dismissive hand and wriggles into a more comfortable position. 'But enough of me. What about you? Tell me *all* about yourself.'

'All?' giggles Robbie.

'*All!*' she thunders.

Robbie, straightening his face, shrugs. 'Well, there's not a lot to tell, really.'

'Oh, my lambkin, what a fib! You know as well as I do there's *everything* to tell.' Robbie smiles, a flush spreading over his cheeks. 'So out with it, vagabond. Beginning with where you live, what you do, and what brings you trolling this way into my depraved hollow.'

Robbie grins. 'Okay. Well, for a kick-off, we're just down on holiday.'

'We?'

'Mum, Dad and me ... from Maidstone ... I'm still at school.'

'Still at school? Oh dear Lord, forgive my trespasses.' She crosses herself. 'So Mum, Dad and you, that's the bundle?'

'Yeah, I'm an only child.'

'An only child ... I knew it.' She lifts her eyes to heaven, as if raising a prayer for only children everywhere. 'Well, as for me, although one of six, I'm no one's child. Not now. Not since becoming a drag queen.'

'A drag queen?'

'I work at the Prince Regent, my sweet. Nightly at nine.' She throws Robbie a bold look, and her eyes widen. 'So I guess that tells *all*?'

Robbie grins and nods.

'And the life of a drag queen, let me tell you, is

always hard, but sometimes harder than others. I mean I've worked some places, but this is the living pits. Here the vestibule is miniscule, my dressing room a mere cupboard. No room to flounce a frock or punch a boob. And as for the audience, I'm speechless.' She shakes her head. 'Now don't get me wrong, I love a rude audience. Or at least, a certain type of rude audience. A cheering, sneering, jeering audience. An audience with attitude. I need the banter, the repartee. What I can't abide is a crowd that ignores you, that turns its back and jabbers.'

Robbie smiles, and there's a pause. Groping for some response, he reaches into his bag. 'Eh ... there's a bit left, I think ... Ah, yes ... Going soft, though ... I mean, would you like some chocolate?'

'Chocolate?' Letitia stares in horrified disbelief. 'Heavens, no, sweetie! Chocolate is poison. I'm an ar*tiste*, remember.' She slaps her midriff again, and flicks a loose strand of hair from her face. 'But now, to resume ... where was I? ... Ah, yes ... Life is hard, as I say, but who am I to complain? It's hard for all of us.' She fixes him with a searching look. 'Isn't that right, Robbie?' Robbie casts his eyes downward. 'So tell me about school. Do you have friends?'

Robbie shrugs.

'Now look, lovie. We all need friends. Only children especially. So get out there and find an amigo or two. And when you come this way again I want to see you hand in hand with a doe-eyed Puerto Rican.'

After dinner he tells his parents he's going for a stroll. They eye him curiously. The three of them usually take a stroll together, often returning to the hotel to read their books for an hour. Normally they're in bed by eleven.

Festival

'On your own?' says his mother.

He nods, and there's a period of bodeful silence.

'In that case, watch your step,' she advises. 'There are some very odd people about. Especially at night. As you know.'

Robbie *does* know. His book is fascinating, but now, half-sick of shadows, he craves the real thing. Up in his room, he hauls on his jacket and surveys himself in the mirror. Then he skips down the stairs and slips out into the night.

The promenade is thronged. Everyone is strolling. The purple sky has a gash of deep red where it meets the horizon, and gulls, blotches of ink, swoop around the black arm of the pier. He stands at the railing and gazes, fanned by eddies of warm air. The wrinkled sea, speckled with light, whispers up the sand. He glances to his left. The youth leaning on the railing a few yards away is staring at him. Robbie, turning away sharply, pretends an interest in a group of people hauling a boat up the beach. Then, attempting a nonchalant air, he ambles off in the opposite direction.

At the entrance to the pier he hesitates for several minutes in front of the kiosk. Taking a deep breath, he approaches boldly. 'The Prince Regent?' growls the man, throwing him a funny look. 'Are you sure you're old enough?' Robbie smiles shyly. 'Anyway, Fore Street, off the Parade.'

It's one of those sprawling corner-house pubs, with a weathered signboard and tall frosted windows etched with a decorative design. He lingers outside, watching the entrance. Men, in pairs and groups, come and go, bursting through the door with gusts of raucous laughter. One man, arriving with a friend, sees him hovering and beckons him in with a nod. So, glancing around, as if to be quite sure that no one's watching, he seizes his chance and lopes in behind them.

Inside, he simply stands for a while, taking in the crowded, noisy scene. Hundreds of eyes feast on him, and he feels he's never been the focus of so much attention. But instantly the eyes revert to the far side of the room, where a portly figure in a blond wig and a radiant skin-tight dress is lip-syncing to 'I'm Thru With Love', a song he's heard before though he can't recall where. The voice, too, is familiar. An oval signboard to the side of the stage, propped on a three-legged easel, reads *Letitia D'Amore* in extravagant lettering. He watches the performance in a quiet thrill of excitement, all the while glancing at the man beside him, who seems equally transfixed. 'That's my friend,' he's tempted to murmur, and smiles in proud acknowledgement whenever Letitia's eyes light on him. But has she spotted him? Is he anything more than a face in the crowd? Her gaze, like her smile, is blank, and seems to go straight through him.

After the next number she disappears and a tall man in a T-shirt and bowler strides onto the stage to announce an intermission. Robbie gazes round, and almost immediately spots a familiar face, a face that's smiling at him, though he can't recall where he's seen it before. Then it hits him. It's the boy from the prom, the one who was staring at him. He returns the smile, rather hesitantly, and the boy comes towards him, weaving his way through the crowd.

Up close, without the scowl he'd worn earlier, he turns out to have some appealing features: sharp brown eyes, gleaming teeth and a lean, clean look with just the hint of a spot or two. He looks closely at Robbie, smiling so deeply into his face that Robbie is forced to lower his gaze.

'Saw you on the prom.'

Robbie looks up and grins. 'Saw *you*.'

There's a moment of awkward silence.

'Fancy a drink?'

Robbie bites his lower lip. 'Yeah, okay.'

'So what can I get ya?'

'Get me? Oh, thanks. Eh ... just a coke.'

The boy grins. 'Cokehead, eh?'

He disappears and is gone for an age – for so long, in fact, that when he returns the show is about to start again and Robbie has given him up for lost. He hands Robbie a glass, smiles broadly and breathes something into his ear just as Letitia drifts onto the stage to the opening strains of 'Funny Girl'. Robbie smiles back and then turns to watch the performance, his neck tingling, his face glowing. The song pulls him down, though; it misses the kick of the moment. 'When you're a funny girl,' Letitia croons, 'funny how it ain't so funny.' Gazing at her, he sips his drink and longs for a change of tempo. And in the next number he gets it. Backed by a big syncopated beat, soaring strings and snarling trombones, she squares up to the audience with a fighting stance, feet apart, hands on hips. 'Nobody, no, nobody,' she belts out, 'is going to rain on my parade.'

Paris, Vienna, Rome

8.15 am. A spare window seat? Can't believe my luck. Midweek is quieter, I guess. Still, quite a bustle on the platform. That guard is besieged. He looks patient, unruffled, steady as a rock, but then he's used to handling questions from fretful travellers. Now who's this shooting out of the subway? Nice looker, natty in his sailor suit. And travelling light, just the duffel bag. There he goes, sprinting down the platform. Hey, watch your step, mate! Jesus, that schoolgirl caught a smack. Noisy crowd, those schoolgirls. Who's in charge? That booming woman in the check suit? She certainly looks the part. A form mistress all the way down to her sensible shoes.

The guard's glancing at his watch, surveying the platform. Slamming of doors, there goes the whistle, we're in motion. And how gently we glide past all these gaping bystanders, smiling and waving as if we're performers in a parade. Now there's a familiar face – Lucy Henderson – though she hasn't seen me. How small and lonely she looks, stuck out there on the end of

Festival

the platform. Smaller and lonelier, as the station recedes. And here we go, into the long tunnel. Into the burrowing dark ...

So another interview. And what's the advice? Just be yourself. Jesus, they all say that, don't they? Well, thanks for nothing, all of you. I mean, what *is* myself? Or rather, which of my selves should I be? Still, I need this job. Need it badly, even though there's no part of me that wants to work in a bank. I've got to leave home. And soon. I can't stay kicking my heels here. They've all gone now, the old crowd. And I've lost touch with Joe. I must get to London. I must find Joe.

What chance of that, though? The address is right here, top of this letter. Jesus, the times I've read this letter. I could recite it word for word. *I'm planning a tour of Europe. There are so many places I want to see – Paris, Vienna, Rome – and it would be great if you could join me.* Yeah, too true. And believe me, Joe, I was wild to join you, but it was out of the question, what with having no future and Dad nagging me to get sorted. I wrote back, but you didn't reply, did you? And I would've called, but I had no phone number. I'd give my life to see you again, but chances are you've moved. And where are you now? Paris, Vienna, Rome? ...

Mmm, I love the motion of trains. I love this journey through wooded hills and cuttings, this short stretch of shoreline. I love the sudden rocks and cliffs, the waves breaking on shingle, the sunlit mudflats and stranded sailboats of the Dawlish coast. I love it all. Yeah, I'll look him up after the interview. He doesn't know I'm coming and maybe he's moved, but I'll look him up anyway and perhaps we'll talk our heads off over a drink, just like old times ...

Paris, Vienna, Rome

Old times. Lunchbreak at the Prince William. He was always lively after the first pint, especially when we went with the usual crowd. He'd open up, become almost extrovert, lift his glass: 'Here's to grief!'

'What?'

'Well, there's no happiness without grief, is there?'

'Ho ho, listen to this guy, right little philosopher ...'

Exeter St David's. And it looks like I've got company. A retired naval officer and his wife? Anyway, extremely well turned out, he in his blazer, she in her print frock. And those handsome suitcases. Nice smile she has, very gracious. What's he reading? The Telegraph. Hm, how appropriate. And she has her book. A slim paperback. A thriller, though she's not very thrilled. Keeps gazing out of the window ...

Yes, when I get to Paddington I'll hop on the tube to Embankment, pick up a bite to eat in the Strand, and from there it's a short step to the City. Two o'clock. The dreaded hour. How can I convince them that I want to work in a bank? ...

She keeps smiling at me. I think she's going to speak.

'I think this is Wiltshire, isn't it?'

'I'm not sure, really. Somewhere like that.'

Christ, what did I say? What a dumb remark.

'I love this rolling countryside, don't you? It's so flat where my husband comes from. That's why we chose to move this way on his retirement. What about you? Are you from these parts?'

'Yes, sort of. But I'm hoping to move to London.'

'Oh really? Well, that sounds exciting. I was born and raised in London, but I couldn't live there now. It's not the place I knew as a girl, and I don't want the noise and bustle at my age. But a young man like you, I think you'll love it. The buzz, the social life, the opportunity. Do you have friends in London?'

'Oh yes.'

God, what a liar! Why did I say that? I guess because the truth's pathetic. Do you have friends in London? Not really, but I'm planning to look up someone I knew at college, a guy who's actually my best mate though we lost touch more than a year ago. Sounds pitiful? Well, it gets worse. He was living in Golders Green when I last heard, but he might now be in Paris, Vienna or Rome …

'That's good. It's a lonely place otherwise. We're off to Broadstairs ourselves, for a short break. Staying with friends. Old neighbours actually. We've known them for years …'

11.45 am. Oh dear, I must have dropped off. I hope I haven't been lying back with my mouth all agape like Tom. Look at him. His Telegraph has slipped to the floor. I'd nudge him awake, but he'd be very put out if I did. The indignities of old age, I think they call it …

Where are we now? Looks like we're approaching London. All this ugliness and squalor. Look at that hideous block of flats. Leaking pipes, walls filthy and stained, balconies littered with washing and broken furniture. No, I couldn't live here. They could at least brighten the place with a few window boxes …

The other thing they talk about is coping with retirement. These little phrases the experts use. Everything neatly labelled. Well, we're not doing too badly, in my view. We keep busy. I've got the club and the garden, and Tom has the two days with Brian. But I wish they got on better. Tom can be awkward and cantankerous. Still, it's difficult for him, taking orders from his son when he's used to giving them ...

That young man has gone again. Keeps going to the toilet. Shy, nervous, a bit lonely. I can't believe he'll be happy in London. But they all do it, they all flee the home. I knew Brian was unhappy. Chasing that silly girl to Bombay. I knew from his letters. I can always tell when people are hiding things. Three years to get *that* out of his system. I must have known that he'd come home because I didn't change a thing in his room. His sports gear, his pinboard, his posters. All exactly as he left them ...

Paddington. We've arrived. And there they are, Kath and George, anxiously looking for us. George oughtn't to drive in his condition. He could go at any time. And she's a bundle of nerves. I don't envy her. He's quite a handful. Such a restless man. And stubborn. You can't stop him when he's set his mind on something. I hope we don't have a scene like last time. Not her fault, of course. She tries hard and copes well. She's plucky. I admire her ...

2.13 pm. I wonder where she'll go. She can't move in with him. He's got a wife and three kids. And if she goes to her mother, they'll be fighting like cats within the week. No, she'll almost certainly dump herself on Mark and Sue, and that won't last long. I'd give it a fortnight. Well, I won't take her back, the bitch. Not if she comes begging, crawling on her knees. Who is this bloke anyway, this creep from Finance? Maurice. What sort of fucking name is that? I knew something was going on. All this tearing off to Blackheath for – what is it – life enhancement classes?

Festival

'So fill me in a little more, Mr Mitchell. What exactly have you been doing since you left college?'

'Just bits and pieces, really. I worked for a firm of solicitors for a while, but the trouble was I didn't get on with my colleagues.'

Well, no surprise there. What did they think of *you*? I know what I think. A bit vapid, a bit wet and dreamy, a bit of a sap. You haven't got a hope, chum. Not a chance. Just give me a break and go away. God, I hate these interviews. I've been holed up here for hours and they're still queueing.

'Mr Mitchell, why do you want to move to London?'

'Well, the thing is, I need to change my life.'

Ha, don't we all? My life's not exactly a bed of roses right now, let me tell you. The wife's threatening to leave me for some gorilla she's having a fling with, we haven't eaten a square meal in weeks and the house is in chaos. But let her go. I'll be fine, never fear. It'll take more than this. It's *her* I feel sorry for. Does she seriously think he's going to chuck up everything to follow her? She must be a bigger fool than I thought. She's just a bit on the side. He'll ditch her as soon as he's had enough and then it'll be my turn to laugh. And let me tell you, darling, I'm going to laugh my face off.

'Well, yes, certainly London offers a lot, Mr Mitchell. But it can also be a lonely place. Have you ever lived away from home?'

'Not for long. Just while at college. I shared a house with a group of students. But I'm sure I can cope. I have this friend who lives in London … or at least …'

Oh Christ, will this never end? Do I deserve this? Sitting here for hour after hour listening to some noodle wittering on about his dismal life. This is a

Paris, Vienna, Rome

heartbreaking case. Doesn't know his navel from his armpit. Just look at the way he knots his tie and the state of his hair. What a mess! So why drag this out? No, I'm sorry, chum, you're trying so hard and you're going to be bitterly disappointed, but the time has come to be brutal and release both of us from our misery.

'Mr Mitchell, time's running short and I have a lot more applicants to interview today. Anyway, I'm going to be quite frank. I don't think we can offer you anything at present …'

4.22 pm. Roll on September. I keep sane telling myself that it's only until September. Then she's off my hands for the best part of the day. And it won't be a moment too soon. Some days I think I'll kill her. Today I told her there would be no television until she'd cleared up the mess she'd made in the living room. She ignored me completely until I seized her by the arms and shook her, and then she screamed the place down. Mary Wallace came knocking, the sarky cow, saying she thought there'd been a murder.

And that was it. The highlight of my day. I've scarcely spoken to another soul, except the girl at the checkout and someone collecting for famine relief. Oh yes, and the young man who called at the door an hour ago asking after Youssef. I told him he'd moved and I had no idea where he was living. He looked so upset I thought of inviting him in for a cup of tea. He said they'd been at college together and had been planning to hitch around Europe or something. Sweet young man, nervous as a kitten. Great shock of untidy hair. I wanted to mother him, brush the specks from his coat, straighten his tie.

Festival

To be honest, I'm glad Youssef has gone. Erich is much friendlier, though I didn't expect to get on with a German. Youssef was pleasant enough, but a bit deep. I never felt easy with him. And then the way he left so suddenly. He mentioned a girlfriend once or twice, but I never met her. She has a nice place, apparently, down in the Fulham area, and I think he might have moved in with her, though he never let on. He said he'd look in for his post sometime, but he never has. I'm still holding a couple of letters for him ...

4.38 pm. Ah, what a drag! Missed it by minutes. Just my luck. And with time to kill, what was the choice? Sit in the bar and drown my sorrows on a lethal dose of gin, or lounge in the buffet with tea and a sticky bun? I guess the buffet won on points ...

Still, at least it's warm and cheerful in here. A bit crowded, though. I was lucky to find a seat. So here I go again, killing time in a station buffet. The hours I've killed in station buffets. I could kill an hour counting them ...

Look, the truth is I didn't stand a chance. He seemed to take an instant dislike to me, and I can't say I took a shine to him, the supercilious bastard. Fill me in a little more, Mr Mitchell. Pacing the room, cracking his knuckles, like he had a sore head or something. And the way he kept staring at me, like he was trying to spook me. I couldn't think straight, couldn't think at all. Ah well, look on the bright side. I don't want to work in a bank anyway ...

No, no, I must stop this groping for comfort and face the facts. Like where to go from here and will I ever get my life together? Where *are* you, Joe? Paris, Vienna,

Paris, Vienna, Rome

Rome? And why didn't you answer my letter? I'm sorry I couldn't make the trip. It was the timing. It was all wrong. I wanted to, I really wanted to, please believe me, but everything was a mess. I guess we'll never make it now, and what chance we'll ever meet again? Joe, I need you. Need you badly. Now more than ever. I mean, what's going to happen to me, Joe? What's the future and where *are* you? ...

Ah well, you said it. No happiness without grief ...

Hey, I'm sinking fast. Sliding into the deep black mire. Fast going off this buffet too. Warm and bustling it may be, but there are some pretty odd types hanging about in here, some of them very down-at-heel. That shabby old woman over there seems to be collecting leftovers. And that rat-faced man with the dark stubble seems to be calculating who to tap up next ...

Hello, I've got company ...

Yeah, seems a nice lad. A bit surly, but not bad-looking apart from the cracked tooth and the nicotine stains. Out come the fags. He's lighting up. Haven't I seen him before? Surely he was sitting over there when I came in ...

Gosh, he's smiling now. Offering me a ciggy. I must say he's trying pretty hard to be matey. Ah, go on, force yourself. Share a smoke with the lad. Yeah, that's it. Now, return the smile. Sit back, relax. I wish he wouldn't stare so hard, though. Makes me nervous. And that smile is so sly. I mean, what *is* this, a pick-up? I'm so jumpy I can't think of anything to say ...

Christ, it *is* a pick-up! He winked at me. He definitely winked at me. I hardly dare look, my heart's pounding. I'm turning hot and cold. How could I have missed it? The smiles, the smokes. It was obvious, staring me in

Festival

the face. And what now? Is it my imagination or is he pressing my foot? My hands are trembling, I can hardly hold this cigarette. How old is this guy anyway? He can't be more than sixteen ...

Oh God, I don't believe this, he's groping me under the table. Yeah, squeezing my knee, stroking my thigh. Jesus, what to do? I can't move, there's nowhere to go. But I can't stay here. I guess I could just get up and walk out ...

Oh, for Christ's sake, this is desperate. Kick him. Kick him on the shin. Hard!

Ha, that's done it! That's knocked the grin off his puss. But for how long? He's persistent, this one. I must avoid his eyes. Difficult, though. He won't be ignored. Yeah, he's coming on again. Leaning forward, beckoning. I think he wants to whisper something. What's he saying? It's hard to focus. His hot breath is in my ear. I think he said he's going for a stroll outside. Yeah, he's standing up and leaving ...

So what now?

Hm. Keep cool. Don't move. Wait for a bit, then follow at a distance. Let him make the first move. And be wary. Remember, this *could* be dangerous ...

Beryl

It was a fair-sized gathering. A few friends and neighbours, some aunts and uncles, a couple of cousins. His parents liked to throw a party now and again, and their Hallowe'en night had become a fixture, so by tradition some of the guests had come in costume. Stephen, aged nine, was draped in a sheet with a pair of peep-holes, and Mike, aged thirty-seven, was wearing a vampire mask. As usual, there was a good spread on the table. His mum had made sandwiches and sausage rolls, and Emmy from next door had come with a cake she'd made. It was wrapped in a band of silver foil and decorated with cobwebs in piped icing.

Beryl was there, of course. He'd met her before; she was becoming a regular. But he was never quite sure who she was. He had an idea that Gran had met her at a séance, but this was difficult to ascertain since the family seemed reluctant to admit that Gran attended séances. Gran was a gadabout and belonged to all sorts of clubs, so it was less embarrassing to suggest that she'd met Beryl at a whist drive or tea dance.

Festival

He disliked Beryl, though he'd have found it hard to say why. He just felt uncomfortable with her. Was it that she blew smoke everywhere and smelt of ash? Was it her voice, deep and husky like a man's? Was it her jewellery, which seemed only to highlight her wrinkled skin? Perhaps it was her beady green eyes, or the flash from her gold teeth. Anyway, he always kept his distance when she was around and had never really spoken to her beyond a few brief exchanges.

His mum laid a hand on his shoulder. 'Paul, why don't you give us a tinkle? I'm sure Beryl would love to hear you play.'

'Oh no, please,' he groaned. 'I don't know any party pieces, do I?'

'I wouldn't let that bother you,' said Beryl. 'Play whatever you like. We'll lap it up.'

She nudged him towards the piano, and reluctantly he sat himself down at the keyboard. He knew that she played the piano herself. In fact, someone had told him that she'd once been part of a dance band, and his mum described her as having a nice touch. But he was sure she had no wish to hear him play, that she was simply going along with his mum's idea. His mum was always showing him off, seeking praise from people she looked up to. But why she should look up to Beryl was a mystery.

He glanced over 'Ritual Fire Dance', the piece displayed on the music stand that he'd been practising for the past week. He took a deep breath, slammed into the opening trill and stormed all the way through to the end. In his haste, though, he became a bit unstuck in the final bars. He shook his head, feeling annoyed with himself. He could play the piece well enough when no

Beryl

one was listening. If only he were more confident. If only he could learn to slow down and not take everything at a rush.

The listeners, however, broke into wild applause.

'Splendid,' declared Beryl.

His mum laughed nervously.

'Oh now,' she said, 'be honest.'

'No no, I mean it.' Beryl smiled wryly and her mouth flashed. 'That's coming along nicely. Some parts need a little more work, but he knows that.'

'Well, thank you,' said his mum, appropriating the compliment as if Paul were an exhibit, like a musical toy or trinket box. Then she and Beryl, chatting confidentially, wandered off for a word with Gran. The others, however, were standing around as if for an encore. Well, to hell with that! He jumped up smartly and slunk off to the kitchen, where he helped himself to a ham sandwich. There was no one there, thank God. Or at least until his cousin Rosemary turned up.

'Hello, Paul,' she said with her sheep's eyes. 'That was nice.'

'What?'

'That thing you played.'

'I flunked it – or didn't you notice?'

She giggled. 'Oh, you *are* funny, Paul.'

She was always mooning around him. He wished she'd shove off.

'D'you know Bertolini's, Paul? The coffee bar on the Parade? Me and Sandra often go there.'

'Well, you won't want me barging in then, will you?'

He hastily finished his sandwich and sloped off into the garden. Unfortunately Brian was out there, the idiot from up the road who spent every hour polishing his

Festival

two-seater convertible. He was wearing a skeleton outfit and snogging Marcia, Mrs Pascoe's niece. They broke apart when they saw him and she adjusted her dress.

'Well, well, here he is, the ivory tickler.' Brian swung his hips and snapped his fingers. 'So now, Paul – how about some boogie-woogie?'

Paul frowned. 'Sorry, I don't do boogie-woogie.'

Brian and Marcia brayed loudly. There was an awkward pause, and then Paul, turning smartly, re-entered the house, where his mum was inviting everyone to eat. A slow drift towards the food began and he joined the queue.

After tea, noticing that Beryl had disappeared, he feared another ritual was about to begin. And sure enough, some time later his mum clapped her hands.

'Listen, everyone. The moment has arrived. The moment you've all been waiting for. Yes, I've again persuaded Beryl to do some fortune-telling.'

'Oooh.' A ripple passed through the room, as the guests turned to each other with little gasps of excitement.

'So now, who's it to be? Who's the first victim?' His mum glanced around with a roguish wink at Gran. 'Or should that be volunteer?'

There were some moments of hesitation, then Meg waggled her fingers in the air and gave a little shriek of laughter.

'Attagirl.' His mum slapped her shoulder. 'So off you go. Beryl's waiting for you in the kitchen.'

Meg rose, looked around giddily and scuttled off with a rich cackle, pulling the door behind her. Loud chattering broke out instantly among the guests, who were soon so engrossed that he seized the chance to slip

Beryl

away unnoticed. He bounded upstairs to his room. Fortune-telling! What idiocy! As in previous years, he'd not be drawn in. Besides, he had no wish to be locked up in a room with Beryl. And on Hallowe'en! He sat on the bed, his back to the headboard, his legs extended, and mused for a while before snatching up his book from the bedside table. He'd read another chapter and then go back, by which time the excitement might have faded.

But when he re-entered the sitting room, his mum spotted him instantly. 'Good timing,' she called out. 'Now come along, Paul. Your turn next.'

He froze. 'Look, I don't think so. It's not my thing, is it?'

'Ah, go on, lad,' his dad shouted. 'Don't be stuck up. Don't be a spoilsport. Don't be a wimp.'

Wimp! He hated that word. It was a shaming, bullying word. A word that was always on his dad's lips. But he glanced around the room and every face said the same: *Ah, don't be a wimp.* So clearly there was no ducking out.

He shrugged. 'Okay,' he said after a pause. 'I mean, what the hell.'

'Attaboy,' Gran whooped, and everyone laughed and applauded.

In the kitchen he found Beryl seated at the table. She glanced up with a tight smile. 'Come in, Paul. I won't eat you.'

He sat down opposite her. She gazed at him for a few moments. 'Tell me if I'm wrong, Paul,' she said, 'but I gather that you're a bit sniffy about this kind of thing.'

He shrugged. 'Oh, I dunno ... I guess it's just a bit of fun.'

Festival

She gave him a long straight look. 'It's whatever you want to make of it,' she said.

He studied her intently, never having done so before. Her face was sallow and heavily lined. She had a touch of bright red lipstick and kept drawing deeply on a cigarette. Her hair was wiry and rust-coloured with patches of grey. He assumed it was dyed. He noticed again that flash whenever she opened her mouth. She shuffled the pack of cards, then spread them face-down on the table.

'Anyway,' she said, 'choose.'

He picked one up. Three of diamonds. She stretched out a hand and he gave it to her.

'Again', she said.

Queen of hearts.

'And again.'

Ace of clubs.

She placed the cards face-up in front of her and studied them intently, all the while blowing jets of smoke from the side of her mouth.

'So tell me about yourself,' she said.

'Like what?'

'Like what you hope for … what you want to be.'

He shrugged. 'Oh, I dunno. I'm not too sure, am I?'

'Okay,' she said. 'So what do you like doing?'

'I like reading … playing the piano.'

'Ah, yes.' She smiled indulgently. 'That sultry Fire Dance thing.' Plenty of crackle at the start, her smile said, but not enough blaze in the finale. 'So who's your favourite composer?'

'Liszt'

'Liszt?' She raised an eyebrow. 'And you'd like to make a career in music?'

Beryl

He shrugged again and hesitated. 'Yes ... I'd like to compose.'

'Compose?' She leaned back, fixed him with an arch look and then took another pull on her cigarette. 'Anyway,' she said after a while, blowing smoke rings at the ceiling, 'let me see your palm.'

He held out his upturned hand and she pulled it towards her, studying it closely and sometimes running a finger along the creases.

'So tell me, Paul ... are you happy?'

'Am I happy?' He snorted and shifted. 'Yeah, sometimes.'

'What about friends? ... You *do* have friends?'

'Of *course.*' He frowned and stared hard at her. 'What d'you mean?'

'Okay.' She smiled sweetly. 'So tell me about school.'

'Like what?'

'You're not popular, are you?'

He flinched. 'I don't think I'm *un*popular.'

'I didn't say you were.'

Silence.

She released his hand and turned back to the cards. 'Well, then, let's move on.' She took another draw of her cigarette. 'So tell me, Paul, d'you have a girlfriend?'

'No.'

'Have you *ever* had a girlfriend?'

He squirmed and huffed. 'Hey look, excuse me, but where's all this leading?'

Glancing up, she met his gaze head-on. Her mouth had a little twist at the corner. 'Nowhere ... it seems.'

More silence.

Festival

'Anyway,' she said, pulling the cards towards her, 'here's my advice. I see a future in music. So stick with it. You've got talent. But get out more and try to make friends. Go to the park, join a club, kick a ball around sometimes. And don't always listen to your mum. Do a bit of thinking for yourself.'

He stared at her fiercely, then gave a curt nod. She gathered up the cards and threw him a tough professional smile. He got up and went into the sitting room, closing the door behind him. All heads turned as he entered. He hated it. Being looked at. It was mortifying. He coloured up, felt his face burning. He looked around for somewhere to sit. His mum slapped the arm of her chair, but he shook his head. He slunk to a corner of the room and flopped on the floor.

'Well?' said his mum.

Everyone was grinning at him, teetering on the verge of laughter.

'Well what?' he said.

'Well what have you learned?'

'Nothing much.'

'Oooh.' The room erupted with disappointment.

'Ah, go on,' his mum said. 'Give us a hint.'

He crooked his legs, clasped his knees. 'She didn't say a lot. She told me to stick with the music.'

'I bet she said a lot more than that,' someone quipped, and the room erupted again.

'You go next, Emmy,' said his mum, nodding at her. 'And I hope we learn a bit more from you.' She gazed around, looking pleased with herself.

Emmy, a bit on the stout side, rose slowly, brushed her skirt down and glanced at the others with a titter. 'Ah well, here goes. In for a penny, in for a pound. And

Beryl

I don't want any of you listening with a wineglass pressed to the wall.'

Gales of laughter followed her into the kitchen.

She closed the door firmly behind her.

Chattering immediately broke out in the living room. He stared at the floor for a while and then glanced up, relieved to be no longer the centre of attention. Rosemary, however, was still gazing at him with that moony smile of hers. He looked away quickly. As for the others, they were talking in groups or pairs and he had no wish to join in. He watched the scene for several minutes, feeling quite detached, as if the people in the room were actors on a stage. With no need to interact, he could observe them closely yet distantly, so to speak. And from this point of view, how small, vain and silly they all looked.

He got up, wandered to the piano and thumbed through his copy of 'Carnaval'. He stared fiercely at the passages that had so far defeated him. Tomorrow evening, after school, he'd attack them with determination. At the same time he'd try to finish that rhapsody he was composing. Polish it up till it gleamed like diamond. He'd astonish his mum, astound his teachers and take everyone by storm.

He moved to the window. Across the street, two little witches were standing at the door of Number Eleven. One of them stood on tiptoe and rapped on the knocker. They waited for a while and then passed on. He continued to gaze, and from many windows fat pumpkin heads gazed back at him with blazing mouths and eyes. Some had bared teeth and some were simply smiling, but to him they all looked malevolent. He thought of Beryl – her rusty hair and fags, the flash of gold in her

Festival

mouth, her knowing look. He thought of his family – their grins, their smirks, their eager nosiness. He clasped his hands tightly. So tightly his knuckles began to crack. He filled his chest with air and then expelled it with a loud snort.

His mum glanced across at him: 'Are *you* all right?'

But before he could reply Emmy came crashing through the door. Flushed in the face, hand clapped to her mouth, she was convulsed with giggles.

Cinderfella

Ben gets ready to wince. The Kerslakes have a doorbell that plays 'The Toreador's Song'. He stabs the button and stares at his feet. There's no response, however, and he's wondering whether he can bear to try again when Sally comes to the door and greets him with her usual embarrassing gush. She's dressed to kill, her round figure thrusting at a tight-fitting red dress that shines like tinfoil and froths up into a pink ruff at the neckline. And what on earth has she done to her hair? Rising in tiers, glittering and golden, it looks like a monstrous wig. Her face too: it's unmistakably hers, but somehow transfigured. Awesome to behold, it has the radiance, the remote idealised look of a religious icon. She shows herself off with a quick twirl and a shriek of laughter. Ben is speechless.

'Please excuse the mess,' she trills, leading him into the sitting room, 'but it's been a hectic evening, with no time for clearing up. I don't get home till six, as you know, and then Sonia has to be fetched from Brownies, there are mouths to be fed and Steven insists on a

Festival

bedtime story. Not to mention the time it takes to get all done up for a thing like this.'

Ben, still gazing, says he can quite believe it.

'Now, make yourself at home. If you want a hot drink of any kind, it's all in the usual place and there's some leftover lemon meringue in the fridge. The telly's on the blink, I'm afraid. The man's promised to come tomorrow. Excuse me for dashing off, but there are some last-minute touches.'

She bounces out and Ben sets about making himself at home. This requires effort. The sofa and floor are littered with playing cards, pieces of a jigsaw puzzle and parts of a plastic modelling kit. There's a tumbled heap of children's books in front of the fire, several of them open, displaying torn and defaced pages, and one bearing the imprint of a muddy shoe. He feels resentment growing. He's already sacrificed his evening for them and now he's forced to clear up their mess.

His mother's most to blame, though. She's always doing this kind of thing, jumping in, making decisions for him. He can hear her very words: 'Ben would be delighted.' There was a furious row about it. After all, it isn't the sort of thing boys are usually asked to do. He wouldn't dare breathe a word about it at school. But she got round him in the end, and now he despises himself for being such a pushover. It wouldn't be quite so bad if he were earning himself some pocket money. But no, she insists that taking money from old friends like the Kerslakes is unthinkable.

These thoughts consume him as he clears up, so that he finishes the task feeling hot and annoyed. Then he collapses onto the sofa and sits looking around at the

Cinderfella

sitting room. It's full of ornamental clutter: framed photographs of the children at every stage of growth, numerous souvenir plaques of foreign holidays, a giant pair of Dutch clogs blocking the hearth, and on the mantelshelf a solid antique clock in fancy carving, framed by two sentimental statuettes of tattered old buskers playing fiddle and concertina. He's struck again by the rankness of it all; there seems to be no stopping the Kerslakes.

He reaches into his duffel bag for his library book, which falls open at Chapter Six. It's a novel called *Leap All Civil Bounds*, a title ascribed in the epigraph to Shakespeare. He has no idea why it's called that, but perhaps it will become clear as he reads on. He chose the book on impulse, being attracted to the photograph of the author on the inside back cover, which he studies again. It shows the face of a dark-featured young man with lean good looks, his ironic expression partly concealed by a skein of cigarette smoke escaping from his finger-tips. It's an intriguing face, strong, sensitive, intelligent. The face of someone Ben feels he'd like to meet.

The novel is about a policeman who resolves to track down the killer of a colleague shot in the line of duty. It's a kind of psychological thriller, though it's not easy to read since the story, partly told through the policeman's diary, keeps moving back and forth in time. Ben finds this rather tiresome. On the other hand he's curious to know how things will turn out.

It's also hard to concentrate. There seems to be a row going on upstairs. Peter is booming away and Sally is sounding shrill. Ben thinks he can hear the voice of Sonia too, who has doubtless found some excuse for

Festival

getting out of bed. Suddenly there's an angry shout and tiny feet scamper along the landing. Ben hears a door slam, followed by muffled weeping.

Shortly after this Peter thunders down the stairs and bursts into the sitting room looking irritable. He seems surprised and slightly embarrassed to see Ben. He's wearing a pair of black trousers with sharp creases and his gym-toned chest is encased in a gleaming white singlet. A stripey cotton shirt is draped over one arm. He explains that he's lost a button and is looking for the sewing box. After a frantic search through drawers and cupboards, he eventually finds it. Then, sitting beside Ben, he begins rummaging noisily. Ben, focusing fiercely on his book, hears him huffing and uttering little expletives. This proves so distracting that after a while he's forced to put his book aside and show some kind of interest. Peter, fumbling with needle and cotton, glances at him, helpless and appealing.

'Are you any good at this kind of thing?'

Ben smiles wryly. He's seen this act before; the man plays it so well.

'Not really.'

Peter shrugs. Then, squinting at the eye of the needle, he begins to probe it with the frayed end of the cotton, all the while cursing between clenched teeth and heaving sighs. 'Ah, come on. I bet you're pretty handy with a needle, a chap like you.'

Ben snorts. 'What's that supposed to mean?'

Peter shrugs again, then lapses into preoccupied silence. He succeeds in threading the needle but runs into trouble at the next stage, stabbing himself and tangling the thread. Ben watches with amusement.

'Found a girlfriend yet?'

Cinderfella

'Nope.'

'I dunno, can't make you out. When I was your age I was Jack the Lad.'

Ben decides to ignore this and picks up his book. Peter, sensing a chill in the air, changes tack. 'Anyway, good of you to give up your evening, Ben. We appreciate it. I told your mother so. He's a good lad, I said. A little gem.'

He reaches across and squeezes Ben's knee. Ben catches a whiff of cologne and looks up briefly with a bleak smile. He knows it well, this insinuating flirtatiousness of Peter Kerslake. It makes him squirm, and he's determined to resist it. The man is far too confident of his power to charm and manipulate, the cocky beggar. There's no denying his dark good looks, though, and Ben finds himself sneaking glances at the fuzz of black hair sprouting over his vest.

'A little gem,' Peter repeats with slow deliberation, as if Ben hasn't heard. But this approach is clearly failing, and shortly he tries a new one. 'So what've you got your nose stuck into?'

Ben lifts his book and Peter squints at the title with a puzzled frown.

'It's Shakespeare.'

'Gawd Almighty.'

'The title, I mean, not the book.'

'So what is it? Poetry? Stuff like that?'

'It's a novel.'

'A novel?'

'Yeah, a sort of thriller – but complicated.'

'Looks too deep for me, whatever it is. D'you know, I haven't read a book in years. To be honest, I have trouble getting through the Daily Twaddle these days.'

Festival

'It's here!' Sally yells down the stairs.

Ben looks up in wild surmise.

'The taxi!' Peter gasps.

He snaps the thread with his teeth, seizes his shirt and tears off.

It's all confusion for the next few minutes. The driver bibs his horn three times, then rings the doorbell. The house resounds to 'The Toreador's Song'. The Kerslakes rush frantically up and down the stairs, calling to each other in urgent voices. It might be an air-raid. Ben opens the door and smiles. The driver is a heavyweight with a busted nose and the no-nonsense look of an ex-boxer.

'This your taxi?'

'Sorry to keep you waiting. We're having a few problems.'

The man draws on his broken-backed roll-up and eyes Ben suspiciously. Ben smiles again but fails to lighten the mood. Then, just as the tension is becoming unbearable, he hears movement behind him and is relieved to see the Kerslakes descending the stairs. The undignified scramble of the previous half hour has been put behind them and they now carry themselves with an air of regal serenity. Sally has turned up the collar of her fur-trimmed cape and Peter is flaunting his unbuttoned overcoat and white silk scarf. The driver looks them up and down with weary disgust, flings his cigarette butt into the middle of the lawn and trudges off down the path. Sally totters after him and Peter turns to Ben.

'All's quiet on the western front, but if there's any trouble, knock 'em on the head with a mallet.'

He waves goodbye and climbs in beside Sally. There's an extravagant slamming of doors and the taxi

Cinderfella

moves off with an angry jerk. Ben watches till the tail-lights vanish and the purr of the engine fades into the night.

Back in the house, he can almost feel the silence. It's so striking that he simply sits for a while listening to it. He picks up his book, but finds it hard to read. His thoughts keep wandering off. He can't stop thinking about the Kerslakes. What an absurd couple. How did such people evolve? He tries to imagine them in their younger years. Perhaps they were once normal. Perhaps marriage changed them. Marriage is a weird business. People get warped by it. Look at his parents.

He sees his life stretching before him. What should he do with it? His mother would like him to keep studying, but he's sick of school, and in sharp contrast to Charles Mottram, the head boy, who's already constructed a detailed plan of his life, he feels no interest in any kind of career. His one source of inspiration is Toby Fenton, the drama teacher, on whom he has a secret crush, and it's true that after being taken to see *Twelfth Night* at Stratford and *Three Sisters* at the National he did talk for a while about becoming an actor. But everyone greeted the suggestion with horror, and his mother called it 'an absolutely mad idea'.

More recently, feeling an urge to travel, he'd tried to persuade his friend Paul to join him on a working holiday in France. He'd read an article about some young people who'd gone to help with the grape harvest. But this turned out to be another of his mad ideas. Paul listened politely, asked a few questions and never mentioned the subject again.

He's startled out of these thoughts by another blast

Festival

of Bizet. A caller? Who could it be? He gets up, goes to the door and finds, to his delight, a resplendent young man standing on the step beaming at him. The vision is clad in leather from head to toe and holds a crash helmet under one arm. Fresh-faced and bright-eyed, he has a brush of black hair that springs up straight from his gleaming brow, giving him a look of electrified astonishment.

'Sorry to disturb you, but I'm looking for the seven stars.'

The voice is warm and husky. Ben stares in wonder and bemusement. The situation feels theatrical, like some strange echo of a myth or fairy tale. Indeed, it brings to mind *Twelfth Night*, that play about shipwrecked mariners with boyish good looks fetched up on the Illyrian coast.

'Er ... excuse me ...'

'It's a pub. The Seven Stars? It's around here somewhere.'

'A pub? ... Oh yes, of course ...'

They smile at each other. Ben shrugs. There's an awkward pause.

'Well, don't let it bother you, I'll try somewhere else.'

'Eh, hold on ... I'll look in the phone book.'

The young man nods. 'Cheers, mate.'

His smile, like his gear, is an absolute knockout.

In the hall, he stands gazing at the floor as Ben searches in the directory.

'Ah yes, it's in Acre Street. Down to the junction, turn right, first left.' Ben draws a sketch map, tears the sheet from the pad and hands it over.

The young man flashes another smile.

Cinderfella

'Brilliant. Thanks a lot.' He glances at his watch. 'Sorry, can't hang about. Promised to meet a mate half an hour ago.'

With a thumbs-up he turns and trudges off.

'Have a good evening,' Ben calls after him, trying not to sound tragic. But does a forlorn note creep into his voice and hang in the air? Anyway, the young man comes stalking back.

'Hey, what about you? Fancy a drink?'

'I'd love one, but I'm baby-sitting.'

'Baby-sitting?' The young man stares in horror. But just then Steven appears on the landing, yawning and rubbing his eyes. They glance up. 'I see. And here comes the baby.'

'Well, one of them,' Ben sighs.

'You mean there's more?'

Ben nods painfully.

'Who's that?' demands Steven, frowning.

'None of your business, Mr Security.'

'Anyway, I'm not a baby, I'm six and a half.'

Steven descends and sits on the bottom stair gazing at the visitor.

'This is Steven,' says Ben.

'Hi Steven, I'm Henry. Nice to meet you.'

Steven stares at Henry, then spots the crash helmet. He stands up, straining as if to catch sight of something over the hedge. Ben and Henry turn to each other with splutters of laughter.

'Hey, come on, I'll show you,' Henry grins.

Ben and Steven, the latter in dressing-gown and slippers, follow him into the street, where they find a powerful machine, loaded with gadgetry and gleaming like new.

Festival

Steven, amazed, pats the fuel tank and Henry lifts him onto the front seat.

Ben whistles. 'Wow, great set of wheels! So I guess you've travelled a lot.'

'Not yet, but I've got plans.'

'Me too,' says Ben.

'Oh really?'

'Well, just one specific plan, actually. I'd like to take a working holiday in the south of France. You know, knock about in the sun. They say it's easy to find work in the harvest. I've been reading about it.'

Henry looks interested, and Ben, thrilled to find someone in tune with his thinking, feels an urge to confide everything.

'Snag is, I've no one to go with.'

Henry considers this for a moment, then breaks into another smile. 'Ah well, stick with it. Someone'll turn up.' He glances again at his watch. 'Hey, look, I must go.' He lifts Steven from the front seat, gets astride his bike, snaps on his helmet. 'Anyway, thanks again. Hope you get to France.'

He nods at them both, raises his arm in a farewell salute and roars off into the night.

'Who's that bloke?' Steven shouts at Ben, trying to get above the roar.

'Keep your voice down,' says Ben. 'You know who he is. He's Henry.'

'But *who* is he?'

'He's just a caller.'

'What's a caller?'

'Oh, Steven, give me a break, please.'

They return to the house. Ben closes the front door in a kind of trance. What a strange, dreamlike episode.

Cinderfella

But a few moments later he comes to earth, feeling flat and dispirited. Already the dream is fading, the prince has vanished, and he's here, forced to sit at the Kerslake hearth while the fun is happening elsewhere. He feels a surge of his old resentment.

Steven tugs at Ben's sleeve with a pleading look. 'Can I have some milk?'

Ben, staring stonily at him, makes him wait for an answer, keeping him in suspense for so long that the corners of his mouth begin to droop. Then he marches into the kitchen and fills a tumbler with milk from the fridge. Steven follows at a respectful distance, takes the tumbler in silence and begins to drink, glancing warily at Ben. But before he's finished sounds of movement warn that Sonia is awake and soon she appears at the kitchen door.

'I heard voices,' she says.

Ben raises an eyebrow. 'Story of your life. Right little Joan of Arc.'

'I thought it was Mummy and Daddy.'

'It was Henry,' says Steven.

'Who's that?'

Steven shrugs. 'A caller,' he mumbles, lingering over his last inch of milk.

'Get a move on,' says Ben, frowning at the offensive sucking noise. He turns to Sonia. 'I suppose you want some milk too.'

'No thanks, yuk!'

'Well, in that case I think you should both go back to bed.'

'Can I show you my Brownie Scrapbook?' pleads the expert strategist.

'I've seen it many times.'

Festival

'Not the new stuff.'

'Sonia, not now!'

But she's away to the sitting room and when she returns she thrusts a pink folder with a stencilled cover into Ben's hands. He submits, silently turning the pages until he comes to some drawings and newspaper cuttings of Sunhill Camp, followed by captions in Sonia's childish hand. She points out her friend Debbie in one of the photographs and begins to tell a tall tale in which she and Debbie get chased by a bull. Ben cuts her short.

'Yeah, all very interesting, but it's way past your bedtime.'

'Can't we just –'

'No!'

Sonia and Steven look hard at Ben and see an irresistible force. They turn glumly and trail out of the kitchen. Ben follows, but they make such slow progress that he begins to urge them on, pinching their bottoms and chasing them up the stairs. They leap into bed, shrieking with laughter. He tucks them in, turns out the light and for a short while stands listening on the landing. He hears them whispering, but after a while they fall silent. They seem to have settled and he steals away.

Back in the sitting room he takes up his book and tries to read. But it's difficult to pick up the threads. He can't remember who Jim is or why the policeman wants to speak to him. He reads a passage several times, then tosses the book aside. A mood of listlessness takes hold of him. His life is so circumscribed he might as well be in prison. How nice to be independent like Henry. How nice to *go* where you like, *do* what you like. Will it ever

Cinderfella

be the same for him? He can't imagine it. His mother will always be around, reaching into every corner, checking every item, chronicling the motion of his bowels and even trying to take over his friends.

Friends. Cue for a fantasy. Ben, leaning back, decides to relax and indulge. The scene is a seaboard hotel on the Riviera, the balconies shaded by palms, the paint on the shutters cracked. A gentle breeze is ruffling the curtains and two men are lying on a bed in shorts, their sleeping heads and pulsing chests dappled with sunlight. Occasionally a distant voice is heard calling from the beach, but otherwise nothing disturbs the stillness. Slowly they come awake and turn to each other. One of them reaches out and pulls the other close. Their mouths are soft, their breath is hot and sweet, their bodies rub together ...

The fantasy builds to a point where Ben can no longer ignore the muscular serpent sprouting from his crotch, whose needs are now desperate. He marches to the bathroom, bolts the door. Glancing round, as if to be sure he's alone, he unzips his jeans, shuffles his pants to his knees and stares at this furious blind thing with its drooling slit. The sheer strength of its neck when he grips it takes him by surprise, and the ensuing tussle is tremendous, though it lasts no more than a few minutes. At the climax he falls back, heaving, exhausted. The battle's over, the thing slain. It shrinks to a ruin of its former self, a pathetic punctured worm shuddering in its throes.

Suddenly the telephone in the hall rings loudly. His heart leaps into his mouth. Jesus, who the fuck! Scrambling to his feet, he hauls his jeans over his haunches, but when he reaches the phone and lifts the

Festival

receiver he's quite speechless and can manage no more than heavy breathing.

'Hello, who's that? Is that you, Ben?'

Oh God! 'Hi, Mum,' he croaks.

'So *there* you are! I mean, where have you *been*? I almost rang off.'

'Eh, slight accident ... tripped over the carpet.'

'Hm ... a likely tale.'

'Oh, thanks.'

'Anyway, look, it's nothing serious. I just popped some washing into the machine and couldn't help noticing that one of your socks is missing. Have you any idea where it might be?'

'Eh, one of my socks? ... Well, no, not really.'

'Just as I thought. Well, that's a shame. It's one of that blue checkered pair. You know, the ones Marion gave you last Christmas.'

'Uhuh.'

'Well, don't let it worry you. It's not a calamity. I just thought you might shed some light, but vague as ever, I see. Now, what about the children? They're not giving any trouble, are they?'

'No.'

'Are you sure?'

'Not a peep.'

'Don't take any nonsense from Madam Sonia. She needs very firm handling.'

'I know.'

'So when are Peter and Sally getting back?'

'Around midnight, I think. They weren't sure.'

'Well, you'll remember to come in quietly, won't you? Mr Sutcliffe is on earlies this week. And don't forget to bolt the door. There was a report of a burglary

Cinderfella

in the paper just this evening ... Hello, are you still there, Ben?'

'Yes, Mum.'

'Well, that's all I've got to say. Pity about that sock. Keep a sharp lookout. It's sure to be lying right under our noses. Bye for now, dear.'

'Bye.'

He replaces the receiver and stands for a while, silently smouldering. She's getting worse, going clean off her head. Life's becoming unbearable.

Minutes later he slumps back onto the sofa, feeling weary and depressed. A dog is howling outside. It sounds lonely and pitiful. He closes his eyes and sinks into a slough of melancholy. His thoughts turn to Henry. He sees him at the Seven Stars with a glass of foaming beer, laughing and joking with his friend. He sees the gleaming teeth, the warm crease of his face. Will they meet again? Probably not. That brief encounter is the full works, all they'll ever know of each other.

Struck again by a sense of loss, he gets up and moves to the window. It's a clear, still night. A full moon, hanging high and bright over the houses, stares down wanly, casting cold light over the gardens. The tall firs across the street reach up as if straining for the stars. Cats are prowling, crouching in shadow, watching with keen eyes. Young laughing voices ring out loud and clear on the cold air. They lift his mood slightly and, feeling an urge to shake off his despondency and sense of isolation, he goes to the door, opens it and stands on the step, sniffing the chill spring air. There's a scent of newness everywhere that makes him breathe deeply. Young life is pushing upward, struggling free of the

Festival

earth. He feels a stirring inside him, a quickening of the spirit, a sense of sharing the same process. He too is at the beginning of life; he too is on the verge of a great adventure. He sees it stretching before him with a mixture of fear and excitement.

But it's not warm enough to stand on the step for long. So, with a last lingering look at the brilliant sky, he goes inside and makes another attempt to read his book. Shortly, however, he hears something in the distance. It sounds at first like the faint whirring of an insect, but it soon becomes unmistakable. It grows louder, then stops. He waits in a thrill of expectation, but minutes pass and nothing happens. He goes to the window and reaches for the curtain, when another chorus from the bullring shatters the peace. He quickly composes himself and approaches the door in a flutter.

Henry, on the step, beams his knockout smile. 'Hello again.'

Ben smiles back. 'And so soon.'

'Yeah, can't stay away.'

'So no luck? Back to the drawing board?'

'Found the pub. Spot of bother, though.'

'With your mate?'

'Didn't show … or got tired of waiting.'

'Oh,' says Ben. 'That's a shame.'

Henry shrugs. 'Anyway, thinking about those grapes has whetted my appetite.' He holds aloft a bottle. 'Fancy a foretaste?'

His eyes glisten like the wine.

Ben grins. 'You'd better come in.'

Shortly after midnight a diesel cab draws up outside the house. Ben, still drowsy from the wine, rouses himself

Cinderfella

from his torpor. He's been dozing since Henry's departure an hour ago, his book abandoned on the coffee table. Thank God it's the weekend and he can sleep in. He sits up, stretches every limb, and shakes his head to clear the fuzziness. Outside, there's a burst of noisy laughter and door-slamming. The Kerslakes seem bent on letting the street know of their night on the town. Sally, first through the door, looks flushed, unsteady, giddy with excitement. She stares at Ben for a few moments, a wild gleam in her eye, and collapses giggling into an armchair. Peter strolls in behind her. He too looks more than a bit tight. He unwinds his scarf slowly, removes his jacket and drapes them over the back of a chair. Then he falls back onto the sofa with a sigh and closes his eyes. Ben looks around, bemused. Sally, like her husband, seems to have drifted off.

'Good time?'

'Fabulous,' she murmurs.

Peter grunts in agreement. 'You can't beat that place. The waiters know how to treat you. They have … oh, what's the word, Sal?'

'Finesse.'

'Finesse, that's it. Anyway, just the six of us, seated in a circle.'

'Yes, good food, great company.'

Peter gives a snort of amusement. 'Mind you, cost an arm and a leg.'

Sally's eyes fly open. 'Don't speak of money, Peter.' She fixes him with a fierce look. 'Not on our anniversary.'

A short pause. Peter's lips twitch wickedly. 'Talk of great company reminds me that you and Derek had a cosy time tonight.'

Festival

'I've always liked Derek, Peter, but strictly as a friend. You know that, so don't insinuate. Anyway, who are you to talk? You were all over Angela.'

'All over Angela? My dear woman, she was all over *me*. But perhaps that slipped your notice.'

Ben shifts nervously. 'I think I'll be getting along now.'

'Oh, sweetie,' says Sally. 'I'm so sorry. We're neglecting you, and we haven't even mentioned the children. Anyway, thank you *so* much. How have they been?'

But before he can reply, the door flies open and the children burst in. 'Oh my darlings!'

Sonia goes straight to Mummy and flings her arms round her neck. Steven climbs eagerly onto Daddy's lap, crushing his testicles. Daddy sits up sharply.

'I hope you've been good,' says Sally.

'Yes, we have,' says Sonia, throwing Ben a challenging look.

'We only came down once,' says Steven.

'Then you both deserve a big, big kiss.'

It's a brisk ten-minute walk home. Ben cuts across the common, a place that's reputedly dangerous at night, though his mother's warnings have made him avidly curious about the men who loiter here. He's therefore disappointed to find that there's no one about. But in general he's feeling buoyed and heady. It's been a great evening. His new friend has a smart new bike, a set of shiny leathers and a smile to die for. They polished off the wine, discussed France, swapped phone numbers. It feels like a breakthrough.

He gets home at twelve-thirty and finds his mother

Cinderfella

watching television. She's waited up for him, as expected.

'Something to drink?'

'Yes, but leave it to me.'

She follows him into the kitchen and hovers, constantly relaying scraps of news. 'Your father went to bed early with a headache. He's overworked and sickening, I'm sure of it.'

He flinches. There you go again, alert to any hint of illness. Always eager to tuck us up, prescribe a dose of this or that. Perhaps he turned in early, mother dearest, to avoid your nagging presence.

'Did Peter and Sally enjoy themselves?'

'They were pretty pie-eyed.'

'Well, no surprise there. Never slow to hit the bottle, those two.'

He carries his coffee into the sitting room. She follows hard on his heels. He falls back into an armchair, snatches up the evening paper and begins to flick through it. She sits opposite him.

'I've still not found that sock, you know. I've hunted high and low.'

He ruffles the paper. There's a pause. She drums her fingers on the arm of the chair. 'Anyway, on a different note, I've been thinking.'

Oh Christ, run for cover!

'I mean, wouldn't it be a good idea to speak to Mr Naylor now about where you might apply next year?'

He looks up, his mouth set. 'No, it wouldn't.'

'I don't see why. There's nothing to stop you putting out feelers, surely?'

He puts the paper down. 'Mum, we've been here before.'

Festival

'Ben, you're a bright lad. I don't want to see you waste yourself.'

'I won't waste myself.'

'So what will you do with your life? What have you got in mind?'

He throws her a bold look. 'With my life? No idea. For the moment I plan to go to France.'

'To pick fruit and live in haystacks?'

'To help with the grape harvest.'

'Oh, for heaven's sake! That's not a plan, that's a whim. Anyway, who will you go with?'

'A friend.'

'Oh really? And will I get to meet this friend?'

'Not if I can help it.'

She frowns, eyes him closely, clicks her tongue. 'Well, that's very nice, I must say.' She gets up, plumps the cushions. 'Whoever she is, Ben, I hope she's decent.'

He throws her a withering glance. 'Oh, more than decent, Mum. This guy's divine. So rest easy. There's no chance I'll put him in the club.'

He flings the paper aside, leaps up and strides from the room. He takes the stairs two at a time. He reaches the top just as his mother comes into the hall. She calls to him. 'What on *earth* are you talking about? I can't think what's got into you. Have you been drinking?'

He shoots along the landing, dives into his room and shuts the door. Then he stands with his back to it, as if to hold off intruders. His heart is pumping, his breath comes in short bursts. Bright moonlight is falling on the bed, the desk, the bookcase. Shadows are playing on the walls. He stands in fuzzy confusion, taking in the calm of the scene, trying to settle himself.

Cinderfella

Earlier this evening he'd been feeling so good. It's hard to believe it now. It wasn't just the wine that was intoxicating, it was the rap, the being with someone who knew how you thought and felt. That was something special. For a couple of hours he was truly alive. Can he get it back, that feeling? It's already fading, slipping from his grasp. Oh God, he *must* get it back. It's urgent, vital. He *has* to save himself.

After a while his chest stops heaving and he moves to the window. The branches of the sycamore are swaying in a light breeze and a pair of cats are eyeing each other on the shed roof. Parked cars are lined up head to toe like sleeping vagrants. He pulls the slip of paper from his back pocket and stares at the number. He'll write it in his book, then memorise it. His life depends on it. France is the goal. France is the key. Everything will come together in France. He must end this confinement, this world of shadows, this living in limbo.

He lifts the latch and throws the window wide. Resting his arms on the sill, he leans into the night. Something brushes his face. Something tremulous and hairy. He gazes up at the moon. A handful of stars are defying the city glow. He remembers the three sisters. He murmurs, 'France! France! France!'

Liar

Until he was sixteen Daniel believed so strongly in the inventions of his exuberant imagination that he was scarcely aware that they *were* inventions. At a stretch you could call them innocent untruths. Then one day, in his sixteenth year, he *lost* his innocence.

It happened at his sister's wedding. His cousin Prue was there with her new boyfriend. He'd never liked Prue. Her cool superiority and quiet irony got under his skin. But the boyfriend was a different matter. Now *he* looked promising – an absolute stunner, in fact. Tall and straight, bristly blond hair, shapely neck. Daniel wandered over to have a word.

'Hi, Dan.' Prue had that twist in her smile. 'Meet Nigel.'

Daniel gripped the hand that was thrust at him. It was warm and hammy. Prue had landed herself quite a catch.

There was an awkward pause. Then she broke the silence. 'So, Danny Boy, what've you been up to?'

Liar

'Oh, nothing much. What about you?'

'Not a lot. Nigel and I went riding yesterday.'

'A first for me,' said Nigel. 'Never been in the saddle before.'

'Oh, really?' said Daniel. 'I went riding last year. Great fun.'

'Last year?' said Prue, her eyes narrowing.

'In Spain. I was there on holiday. You remember. With my friend Brian and his family.'

'Oh, well,' she said. 'Behold the broncobuster.'

Daniel smiled, though a shiver ran through him and for a moment he felt a trifle queasy. His moment of lost innocence had arrived. Previously he'd believed in the things he'd made up. Or almost. Not this time. This time he was conscious of what he'd done. He'd lied. And he knew why. He'd lied to impress Nigel. Moreover, the deception had worked. Nigel *was* impressed. Nigel was looking at him with admiration. Yes, at *him* – the guy who rode horses in Spain. Of course Prue was still appraising him with those diamond eyes and that twisted smile. But then, Prue was Prue. He'd never liked Prue.

So when the moment passed, he dusted himself down and waved goodbye to innocence without a qualm. On the contrary, he felt pleased and excited: he'd broken through. And from then on he stopped believing in the creations of his imagination and started making conscious use of them.

Well, just for fun, of course.

But his next little falsehood went embarrassingly wrong. It happened when he ran into his neighbour Trish one afternoon on the way home from town. She was a little older than him and went to a different

Festival

school. She'd been swimming and was teaching herself to dive, she told him. So he saw his chance and seized it. The temptation was too great. Dive? Oh, he could dive. In fact, he could high-dive. She looked at him and her eyes popped. Wow, she said. Then a few days later she saw him at the pool. He was swimming breaststroke, slowly and leisurely, in one of the side lanes. She called out to him and waved. Filled with sudden panic, he struggled in vain to think of some way to dodge her. Eventually he swam to the steps, climbed out and hobbled towards her, clutching a leg.

'Touch of cramp.'

'Oh, that's a shame. I was hoping you might show me a trick or two.'

After that he was more guarded. He learned not to leap at every opportunity; to restrict himself to the kind of inventions that were less easily tested against reality. The occasional slip sometimes got him into difficulty, of course; but in the main he enjoyed himself. There was a lot of fun along the way.

Then one evening, shortly after his twenty-first birthday, he greatly extended his inventiveness. It was the evening of his first visit to the Queen's Head, a bar off Princes Street in Edinburgh. He was now a history student and about three hundred miles from home. He glanced around, noted the dress of the clientèle, and felt immediately reassured that this was the bar where he'd find what he was looking for. No one paid him any attention, however, which caused him some concern. Was he the wrong shape? Did he look too shy and nervous? Had he used too much deodorant? He sat sideways on his bar-stool, hoping to be approached, his

Liar

fist wrapped tightly round his beer glass. Then, turning in the other direction, he caught the eye of the man on the next stool.

The man smiled. He was roughly Daniel's age, or perhaps a little older, and wearing a dazzling white shirt and black trousers creased to a knife-edge. A dark jacket was draped over his knees. He looked like an off-duty waiter. He offered Daniel a cigarette, and Daniel, who didn't smoke, took one because he thought it would look cool and friendly.

'Hi,' said the man. 'I'm Glen.'

'Hi, Glen,' said Daniel, 'I'm Lloyd.'

Glen nodded and they grinned at each other.

'Nice place this.'

'Yeah,' said Daniel, glancing round.

'I just dropped in. Never been before.'

'Oh really? I took you for a regular.'

'No, I work for a brewery down south. We're on a promotional tour.' Glen's face clenched as he drew deep on his cigarette. 'So what about you?'

'I'm a musician,' said Daniel. 'A jazz trumpeter.'

Glen raised an eyebrow and gave a low whistle. 'Wow, tell me more.'

'We're a group of six. On tour. We had a gig here on Thursday. Next stop Berlin. Then Frankfurt, Stuttgart, Milan.'

Glen looked dazzled and Daniel could see from the gleam in his eye that this new image had considerably increased his allure. A few more questions followed, though nothing that invention couldn't handle, then a pause. Glen seemed dumbstruck.

He bought Daniel a drink and they considered where to go. Glen was staying in a small hotel with a group of

Festival

colleagues; there was no chance of going there – they'd have to sneak in, which was potentially embarrassing. Daniel was equally doubtful about taking a guest back to – a spurt of ingenuity here – the house in Leith that he was sharing with other members of the group.

Which left Glen's car. So they drove to Carlton Hill.

The workout was brief – a bare twenty minutes – but explosive and spectacularly messy. And when it was over, they cleaned up using a towel that Glen drew from a holdall on the back seat. Then they reassembled themselves and smiled at each other.

'Mm, nice to meet you, Lloyd,' said Glen, zipping up. 'A trumpeter, eh? Well, if you hadn't said, I should've known. Boy, can you blow.'

Judging the moment was the crucial thing, Daniel decided. In the right place, at the right time, you could invent without consequence, become your own creation. So in the next few years, among strangers and casual acquaintances, he tried on a series of guises. At a café in Prague, for instance, in the company of a wide-eyed American that he chanced to meet, he became Robert, a hip young aristocrat, now wandering Europe in Byronic self-exile after a spectacular falling-out with his father, Lord Beauchamp of Belmain.

On another occasion, while dancing with a shirtless black youth at a disco in Bermondsey, he became Cameron, a mountaineer recently returned from a trip to the Andes, a guise that worked passably well in the flickering lights of the disco, but less well the next morning when he crawled bleary-eyed from the youth's bed and stumbled into his pants, the puniness of his frame cruelly exposed.

Liar

These brief adventures gave him quick shots of excitement and pleasure, although he sometimes forgot earlier lessons and became overconfident, pushing invention too far and straining credulity to the limit. On these occasions the telltale sign was an odd look that came over the face of his listener, a hint of scepticism conveyed by a slight tilt of the head or knitting of the brows. But, ever alert to danger, he learned to negotiate these tricky moments, always backing off, heading for the door or slipping under the wire before being rumbled.

Then, a few days short of his twenty-fifth birthday, he met Keiron.

It was the chanciest thing. He was simply strolling home from a party in the small hours when he found himself passing an all-night food store. He almost gave it a miss, but then decided to drop in and pick up some milk. He was now living in Streatham and working in a bookshop, having abandoned teaching, to which, as he cagily replied to all inquiries, he was 'temperamentally unsuited'. On entering the store, he glanced at the signs and made straight for the area of the milk. The place seemed empty, but in the middle of an aisle he came across a man reaching for something from a top shelf. The man was tall and lean, and wore his blond hair in a ponytail. He filled his jeans as if poured into them, and his brown arms extended from a slim white T-shirt. He turned and smiled as Daniel approached, his hazel eyes enormously enlarged by a pair of rimless glasses. Daniel's heart skipped a beat.

'Milk?' he inquired, returning the smile.

'Straight ahead,' said the man.

Festival

Daniel, previously in a hurry, now dawdled, glancing around and inspecting the shelves for items he didn't need, so that, by a mixture of accident and manoeuvre, he and the man arrived at the checkout together. The man indicated that Daniel should go first, and on the other side Daniel turned, smiled and raised a hand in salute.

Out in the street he stopped to tie a shoelace, then sauntered along until he heard someone pounding up behind him.

'You forgot this,' said the man, smiling and holding out a carton.

Daniel clapped a hand to his head. 'Ah, thanks. Always doing it.'

Not true, of course, but he had, as we know, a tricky 'relationship with the truth.

They strolled along together.

'I'm sure I've seen you before,' the man said. 'D'you live around here?'

'A couple of miles over there,' said Daniel, pointing vaguely. 'Sorry, I'm a bit heady. Been to a party.'

'A couple of miles?' The man stopped outside a tall tenement building. 'In that case, come in. You need reviving. A black coffee perhaps? Some other stimulant?'

It was a spacious apartment, tastefully furnished, with a scattering of rugs over bare wooden floors. Plants and ferns sprouted everywhere, and the plain white walls were adorned with charcoal sketches of people and landscapes. Daniel, invited to sit, flopped back on the sofa and listened with closed eyes to the smoky rendition of 'Night and Day' that the man had chosen to fill the silence while he busied himself in the kitchen.

Liar

'I'm Keiron, by the way,' Daniel heard him call out.

And quite spontaneously it flew from his lips, 'I'm Dexter.' The appeal of the name at that moment, the chance to try on new guise, was simply too good to pass up.

Keiron returned with two mugs of coffee and joined Daniel on the sofa.

'Nice place,' said Daniel, glancing around.

'Bit of a climb, but I like it. Found it through a colleague. I'm in advertising. Small firm in Camberwell. How about you? What do you do?'

'I'm an actor.'

'Really? Wow, tell me more.'

'I've not done much. Mostly theatre. Bits of film and television. Toured with a company last year. Played the butler in this drawing-room comedy thing.'

'Terrific. And what currently? Where can I see you?'

'Ah well, that's the problem. I'm resting at the moment.'

'I see. Waiting for the call.'

'Yeah. Got an audition, though. Next week.'

The conversation, steered by Daniel, now switched back to Keiron's line of work, and then moved on to travel. Keiron had recently journeyed by train from Toronto to Vancouver, stopping off to visit some cousins in Edmonton, and he showed Daniel the stunning pictures he'd snapped while passing through the Rockies. They discussed books, music, films, declared a hatred of sport, and finally, just before the hands of Keiron's clock touched four o'clock, confessed to a love of soap opera.

At which point Daniel's drooping eyelids closed and his head slumped backwards.

Festival

Keiron drew up beside him and placed an arm round his shoulders.

'Two miles?' he said. 'What's the point? Why not bunk down here?'

Seven hours later, sitting opposite each other in the kitchen, they chomped into toast and marmalade while swigging black coffee. Keiron peered closely at Daniel, who was feeling happily consummated but rather worn.

'Busy night.'

'Yeah.'

'So how d'you feel?'

'A bit wrecked. Thank God it's Sunday.'

They smiled at each other.

'So what's the programme for today? Preparation for your audition?'

'Perhaps.'

'Anything in particular?'

'Oh, you know – I have this repertoire of pieces I dip into.'

Keiron reached across the table and took Daniel's hand. 'Hey, Dex, you will stay in touch, won't you?' He pushed a strip of paper across the table. 'That's the phone number. I'd love to see you again. Honestly.'

When he got back to his room that afternoon, Daniel lay down on his bed. Faint strains of music reached his ears from the room below and from time to time the shouts of drunks in the street. He thought about Keiron, about how warm and sweet his kisses were and how good the night had been. And did he really mean that about wanting to stay in touch, or did he say that to all his guests? He wondered if they'd ever see each other

Liar

again. He fervently hoped they would and regretted now that he'd pretended to be an actor called Dexter. For what chance did he now have with Keiron, given the web of deceit he'd spun around himself? Perhaps he should just come clean and put the record straight. But would that be wise? Would Keiron still like him if he confessed to being a fraud? He'd assumed a casual encounter – a stupid miscalculation.

Fortunately, in the distractions of the following week – his twenty-fifth birthday, the temporary loss of his house keys, his mum's lamentations at failing the driving test for the fifth time – he had little opportunity to worry about any of this. In fact it was Saturday before he realised, as he sat over breakfast in the café across the street, that he was in a rage to see Keiron again. So he reached for his wallet, took out the strip of paper and stared at it. He'd call that morning; no time like the present, and to hell with the risks. Confession was for later. Rejection was the worst that could happen and he knew all about *that*.

Back in the house he took a deep breath and dialled. The ringing lasted a while, then someone picked up.

'Hello.'

'Keiron?'

'Yeah.'

'It's Dexter.'

'Dexter? Well, dang me, I was just this minute thinking about you.'

Daniel's heart rose.

They arranged to meet at the Green Man, a pub near Keiron's place where there was live music every Saturday night. The place was noisy and crowded, but since they arrived at roughly the same moment, they

Festival

found each other instantly. There was no chance of finding a seat, though, so they propped themselves against a wall and swigged pints of lager.

'Hey,' said Keiron, pressing a mouth to Daniel's ear, 'how did the audition go?'

'Eh ... not too well ... I screwed up.'

'Ah, that's a shame. Can't wait to see your next performance.'

After that they began to see each other regularly, often meeting at a prearranged spot, but nearly always going back to spend the night at Keiron's place. Keiron, not surprisingly, was curious to see where Daniel lived, but Daniel, fearing that some incriminating evidence would come to light, always made some excuse: his room was a mess, the mattress was lumpy, the neighbours were noisy. His dread deepened too, as his fondness for Keiron increased; and of course the more they saw of each other, the more his guise became unsustainable.

One night, for instance, during a meal in a restaurant, Keiron asked him what he did with himself between contracts; and although they were still at an early stage in their relationship, he put the question in a surprised tone as if he'd just realised how little they knew about each other.

Daniel hesitated for a moment and then said quietly, 'I work in a bookshop.'

'Oh really? You never said. Where exactly?'

'Oh, it's a small place in Peckham High Street called Barnett's. You won't have heard of it.'

Keiron looked taken aback. 'Well, well. I don't know why I didn't ask before. I guess I assumed you were living on benefit.'

Liar

He made no further comment, but a fortnight later he turned up at the shop. Daniel, checking some deliveries at the time, heard someone cough behind him as if to attract his attention. He looked round and the shock of seeing Keiron made him freeze.

'Hey, it's only me. It's not a ghost.'

Daniel smiled and quickly rallied himself. He took an early lunch break and they went for a bite to eat at the pub up the road.

'Shouldn't you be working?'

'I've taken a few hours off.'

'To come and see me?'

'Yeah. Thought I'd look you up. Fancied a little rendezvous.'

'And no problem finding the place?'

'None at all. I mean, what's this about the shop being small? You work on the third floor.'

That night, lying in bed, Daniel considered the options. Break it off or drop the mask? Neither was easy. His attachment to Keiron was now so strong that to terminate it, especially without honest explanation, was unthinkable. On the other hand, to fling off the guise of Dexter, to reveal himself as a poseur, would be not only excruciating but perhaps disastrous. Still, the second course of action was clearly the right one. The time had come, however painful, to end this pretence.

So the next day he called Keiron and proposed that he come over at around nine that evening to see him.

Keiron cheerily agreed. 'In fact, why not come earlier? Say, about seven? I'll cook us a meal.'

This was so unexpected that Daniel hesitated, thrown off balance.

Festival

'Okay,' he said, trying to match Keiron's enthusiasm. 'Sounds great. Love to come.'

He spent the rest of the day in a state of high tension. How to break the news? How to word his confession? He considered many different ways and rejected them all. He could think of no way to own up without sounding ludicrous, clumsy, false, flippant or too solemnly self-mortifying. Consequently, as the hour drew near, he realised that he'd have to rely on his instinct. Hence his greatest fear, as he stood poised to ring Keiron's doorbell, was that his moment of disclosure would come in a rush of stuttering incoherence.

Keiron greeted him warmly and admired the bottle of Burgundy that was thrust into his hands. He then led him into the flat, where Daniel, unprepared for the candle-lit splendour, gasped at the gleaming display of cutlery all lovingly laid out on a spotless white tablecloth.

'Wow! You've really gone to town.'

Keiron nodded proudly.

'Look, I must get back to the kitchen. So choose some music and take a seat.'

Daniel couldn't settle, however. Instead he wandered around the room, lifting and replacing objects and chewing anxiously at the corner of his thumb. He must not let this surprise event weaken his resolve. He was here for a purpose; he must not be deflected. It was simply a matter of choosing the moment.

So when?

Now, or later?

Well, it had to be later – the wine would assist the flow.

Liar

And with that calming thought, he dropped into an easy chair and let the strumming of a Spanish guitar wash over him.

Keiron was full of apologies for the meal. The melon he'd chosen for the starter was under-ripe, and the main dish – the tagliatelle with porcini and goat's cheese – was something he'd knocked up in a hurry. As for the blueberry tart topped with ice cream, that was certainly delicious – for which praise was due to the freezer in the local food store. Daniel countered with lavish compliments.

In any case they ate voraciously and the conversation just rattled along. Keiron wanted to know more about the bookshop and the odd types who came to browse. 'Ah well, there are so many.' Daniel's gallery included Dr Lorna Fiedler, who came every day with a list of titles but had never been known to buy anything, and old Mr Hesketh, who sat snoring all afternoon in the easy chair of the biography section. And what about Keiron's office? Any characters there? 'You must be joking.' Keiron's rundown of colleagues included expansive accounts of Dave, the coke-snorting philanderer of Graphics, and Marcia, the dragon of the tearoom, who was hated by just about everybody.

By this time they were enjoying themselves immensely. They'd polished off a bottle of wine and started on a second, and were laughing wildly in bursts of flushed abandon. Indeed, Daniel was having such a good time that all thoughts of his mission had vaporised in the headiness.

But then Keiron said something that brought the conversation to a halt.

Festival

He said, 'So tell me about the types you meet in the acting profession.'

Daniel, who'd just taken a mouthful of wine, spluttered slightly, put down his glass and stared at Keiron as if he'd just been slapped in the face. At any other time, his powers of invention being almost limitless, he'd have risen to the challenge magnificently. But this was not any old time, this was now. He had to end this charade before he was found out, or greatly increase the risk of losing Keiron. Keiron, who was now more precious than any amount of fun you could have with disguises. Keiron, who was now smiling at him across the table, with a face open and guileless.

'Hey, Dex, you okay? You're looking a bit strange.'

Daniel shook his head to clear the wooziness. Then he fixed Keiron with a serious expression and swallowed hard. 'Keiron, I've something to tell you. It's why I rang this morning.'

'Something to tell me.'

'Yeah, something important.'

Keiron raised an eyebrow. 'Okay, that's fine. I'm listening.'

Daniel swallowed again. 'The truth is …'

Ah yes, bring it on. The truth. What an innocent little flower, and how scruffily he'd treated it. But then, innocence – he lost that years ago. He passed a hand over his eyes and looked down at his plate; his vision had misted over. How had it come to this? What a fool he was. Why had he been so careless with something so fragile? His confession was about to turn messy, he felt it in his bones. He'd lived in a tangle of untruth for so long he'd lost the knack of talking straight. And along

Liar

with everything else, he'd now lose Keiron.

'Dex, are you sure you're okay?'

'I'm fine.'

'Well, go on, I'm listening.'

Daniel shifted, dashed a tear from his cheek, looked up. Ah, what the hell!

'Look, the truth is ...' His voice sank to a mumble. 'I'm not ... Dexter.'

There was silence for a few moments. Moments that felt like aeons. Then something astonishing happened. Keiron threw back his head and began to shake. The attack was gentle at first and seemed to begin in his lower abdomen, though it soon spread to his chest and eventually grew to a spasm that seemed to rock every limb in his body. Daniel could do nothing but stare. He liked to amuse people, but preferred to be in control.

The seizure eventually died, and Keiron, all spent, his mirth reduced to a few blips, reached across the table and took Daniel's hand.

'No, you're not. You're Daniel. Big deal.'

Daniel stared even harder. Had he heard correctly? Wine can corrode the wiring in the brain, can't it? He poked his ear with a finger.

'So you know.'

Keiron nodded warmly – with such fond indulgence that it somewhat eased Daniel's confusion – and they continued to gaze at each other.

'Well, what can I say? I mean, when did you ...'

Keiron sat back with an arch grin. 'Ah, come on, I've known all along. Since that first night, actually. You left your wallet open beside the bed with your name displayed in a plastic window. I could hardly resist a peek, could I?'

Festival

'I see.' Daniel gave a dazed nod.

Gripping the seat of his chair, as if someone might snatch it from under him, he focused on Keiron as a way of grounding himself. He felt hopelessly bemused and immensely foolish. At the same time an odd sense of relief flooded over him. He reached for his wine and took another gulp. The door was now ajar; there was no holding back. He felt strengthened; he must push on.

'Well, there's something else. Perhaps you know this too.' He lifted a hand to quell the tic in his face. 'The fact is ... I'm not an actor.'

'Not an actor?' Keiron sat back, richly self-amused. 'Dex, you're a natural – born to stride the boards.'

'Oh God, you know what I mean. I've never been that side of the footlights.'

Keiron shrugged, a smile flickering on his lips. 'You'd be very good though.'

'Keiron, be serious. It was all a pretence. And I'm sorry, so sorry, honestly. I deceived you like I deceive everyone. I pretend all the time. I can't help myself.'

'Well, don't beat yourself up. We all have disguises.'

'But I'm different – I'm pure fake.'

'Oh, come *on*.'

Daniel wriggled in anguish. 'And you knew, didn't you? You *knew*.'

'I suspected a dash of make-believe.'

'So why didn't you say? Why have you led me on?'

'Look, Dex – or is it Daniel? – I like you whoever you are, whoever you want to be. It's not my role to drag the truth out of people. Life isn't a law court.'

Later, they sat entwined on the sofa, listening to the bluesy murmurings of a jazz trio while reaching from

Liar

time to time into a box of mint creams. The slim red candles, now reduced to waxy lumps, were still burning, but otherwise everything had been cleared from the table and the door closed to drown out the noise of the dishwasher.

'So Dex or Daniel?'

'You say it makes no difference – you like me whoever.'

'I do.'

'In that case, Daniel.'

'So should we lay Dexter to rest?'

'I think we should.'

A long period of silence, filled only by the bounce of the bass player's solo break.

'I shall miss him though,' Keiron murmured. 'Couldn't we compromise? Resurrect him from time to time?'

'I don't think so ... I don't need him now.'

'Well then, bring him back just to show that you *don't* need him. That he has no power over you. That you can call him up, entertain him graciously and wave him goodbye.'

'Hm ... have to think about that.'

In the silence that followed they turned half an ear to the music. The piece was winding up; the trio had reached the restatement.

'Anyway, resurrect him? How do you propose we do that?'

'Well, we could go to see a play. Mix with the luvvies. Feel the call.'

Daniel, sensing mockery, swiped him on the arm. 'Yeah, we could. But I thought you didn't like theatre. I mean, is there anything you fancy?'

Festival

Keiron suppressed a grin. 'Oh, I don't know. Perhaps one of those drawing-room comedy things? You know, with a butler?'

Daniel pushed him onto his back, knelt aside his chest and began to pinch the flesh around his ribs until he was shrieking hysterically and begging for mercy.

'Look I'm sorry, I'm sorry, I'm truly sorry!'

'You bastard! You sly toad! You fucking tease!'

They finished up on the floor, yelling and giggling like schoolboys. And while they were rolling there, oblivious to everything except themselves, the track faded out on a series of ascending notes atonally spaced.

Hassan

Ricky always sat in the front row for lectures. It was essential to look diligent, especially if you were not too confident about your written work. He always smiled at the lecturers and rushed forward to help if they dropped something. Today the lecturer was Professor Collimore, the respected Conrad scholar, whose topic was *Heart of Darkness*. Collimore was a large, imposing figure with a mass of curly red hair, a bushy moustache and rumpled, purplish face. He had a bluff, outspoken manner and was sometimes downright rude to students who irritated him. Ricky, who also attended his tutorials, was thoroughly intimidated by him and therefore especially keen to offer a nervous smile whenever their eyes met. This happened quite frequently. The smile, however, was never returned. Instead, it was greeted by a kind of mad glare.

He was therefore struck with dread when the professor approached him at the end of the lecture and asked him to come to his room to discuss something.

Festival

His mind flew back to his last submission, an essay on Yeats that had not yet been returned. He could scarcely remember what he'd written, only that he'd been very unhappy with it. He had a vague memory of a long rambling introduction and a feeble, perfunctory conclusion. He got up and waited at the front of the hall while the professor spoke to some students. Collimore dealt with them briskly and then, with a beckoning glance at Ricky, gathered up his books and stalked off. Ricky trailed miserably at his heels, as if heading for the firing squad.

Ricky knew the room. He'd sat there on many occasions. It was, as ever, in a shocking state. Collimore fought his way over piles of books and papers to his desk. Then, with a sweep of his hand, he invited Ricky to sit. Ricky glanced around in dismay. The only spare seat was already occupied by a stack of files and essays. So, removing them cautiously, he placed them on the floor and took a seat. Collimore unloaded his briefcase and fussed around for several minutes, snatching up memos and tossing them aside with snorts and grunts. Indeed, for a while he seemed unaware that Ricky was in the room. But then, in a flash, he swivelled round and fixed him with that familiar hard stare. Ricky flinched, but managed to hold steady and force a smile. And to his great relief the professor's face brightened.

'So now ... Ricky ... how *are* you?'

Ricky shifted and shrugged. 'Eh ... okay ... I guess.'

'Good.' The gaze intensified. 'Yes, one of my better students.'

Ricky blinked. Can he mean *me*? He glanced over his shoulder, convinced that someone had appeared at the door. But no. He turned back.

'Is it the essay, sir?'

'The essay?'

'Eh ... you know ... the Yeats?'

'Yeats? ...You've written on Yeats? ... Anyway, no, no ... nothing to do with Yeats.'

Ricky gave a weak smile and inwardly levitated.

'No, the thing is I've a proposition to put to you.' Ricky stared. 'Yes, I need some help. Someone to work part-time. Filing, handling post, bit of copy-editing, that kind of thing – a personal assistant, if you like. It's for just a few hours a week, but you could work them whenever suits and fit them round your studies. I thought you might be interested. Most students need some extra cash.'

Ricky gaped. 'Eh ... you mean here, sir ... on campus?'

'No no, at my house. It's no great distance. You could walk or cycle.'

Ricky was silent. Then, with a gasp of amazement: 'Eh ... well ...'

'Gosh, you look overcome.' Collimore leaned forward and squeezed Ricky's knee. 'Look, no need to decide now. Think about it and let me know.'

On Ricky's first visit Collimore showed him around. His house was only slightly less chaotic than his room on campus. He had a study on the first floor where he worked and slept, but his office was on the ground floor. This would be Ricky's base. There was a desk, a computer and several filing cabinets. Collimore gestured vaguely at the sprawl of books, files and papers lying on every surface.

'Start by tidying up and getting some order into the

place. Then take a look at these drawers. The filing needs a good deal of attention, but be sure to put things away where I can find them.' Ricky glanced around and nodded. 'Is that okay? I'm upstairs if you want me. Oh, and there's coffee or whatever in the kitchen if you need refreshment.'

Collimore disappeared, and Ricky scratched his head. Where to begin? He opened the drawers of the cabinet labelled 'Twentieth Century' and noted the tabs on the suspension files: Eliot, Joyce, Woolf, Hemingway, Auden, Fitzgerald and so on. Another cabinet was labelled 'Nineteenth Century' and a third 'Miscellaneous'. So that was a relief – there was some kind of system here. He stroked his chin. What next? He surveyed the books, files and papers littering the room and decided to sort them into separate stacks. That would at least give the room an orderly look, and might suggest, if Collimore should stick his head round the door, that he'd accomplished something.

This operation took about fifteen minutes. He then started on the filing. But just as he got under way the phone rang. He made no attempt to answer it, however, since he presumed that Collimore had an extension.

Suddenly a voice rang out. 'Get that, somebody, I'm busy.'

Somebody? Ricky couldn't recall seeing anyone else in the house. It must mean *him*. His scalp creaked. He hesitated, filled his lungs, lifted the receiver.

'Hello.'

'Ronald?'

Ricky gulped.

'Who's speaking, please?'

'It's Milton Gregory. Is that you Ronnie?'

'No, this is Professor Collimore's assistant. He's busy. Can I take a message?'

'Assistant? Jesus, things are moving up around here. Anyway, yes. Tell him I've managed to make progress with regard to Beckett in Galway. Speak to him later.'

'Beckett in Galway.'

'That's it. Spot on. Bye for now.'

The line went dead. Ricky replaced the receiver and stared at the phone in bemusement. Then he wrote 'Beckett in Galway' on his pad. But, oh God, what was the name of the caller?

After an hour he stopped and took stock of the situation. The work was proving even more difficult than it looked. The books were relatively easy to put away because the shelves, though crowded and muddled, were arranged in rough alphabetical order according to surname. It was the papers that were giving him the headache. He couldn't decide where certain items should go. Perhaps the solution was to create a file for the homeless. The vital thing, though, was to make a note of where everything was and any changes he'd made. But first – he glanced at his watch – what about a break for coffee?

The kitchen was at the back of the house, and as Ricky approached he caught the sound of movement and the smell of cooking. Hesitating at the door, which was slightly ajar, he peered through the crack. Someone was preparing a fishy meal. Someone tall, slim, very dark, wearing a white T-shirt and cook's apron. He was chopping something on a board with keen concentration, but on hearing Ricky approach he glanced up and fixed him with a look of intense

Festival

curiosity. He was about Ricky's age. There was a hint of fuzz on his upper lip and his hair was cropped to a circle on the crown of his head. His eyes were as black as midnight and shone like alabaster.

'Hi,' he said, breaking into a smile.

'Hi,' said Ricky, hanging back. 'I'm Ricky.'

'Hassan.' The youth pointed to himself. 'Come in. You want tea? Coffee?'

'Eh ...' Ricky slid through the gap. 'Well ... if I'm not ... you know ...'

'Over there.' Hassan waved his hand at some jars, smiled again and turned back to the chopping board. Ricky filled the kettle.

Nothing was said during the operation, but as Ricky was about to leave, Hassan sprang forward to open the door for him, and Ricky felt the air envelop him in a faint, sweetish aroma. Back in the office he sat puzzling over it. Was it jasmine?

He saw no more of Hassan that day, but in bed that night he flirted with its brief delights. Those eyes, that crown of black hair, that breath of heady fragrance! He rehearsed the name mentally and sometimes murmured it aloud. Hassan, Hassan.

On his next visit, two days later, Collimore introduced him to the computer and explained some of the tasks he wanted him to perform. First, to look through the inventory of everything he'd published, checking for errors and omissions. Next, to read through the chapters of his current book, checking for typos and other minor errors. After which, there was the index. Had he ever compiled an index? No? Well, they could talk about that later. For the present there was plenty to get on with.

Hassan

Collimore swivelled round and fixed Ricky with the same hard stare that he often produced during lectures. Then he smiled, leaned forward, and in a gesture that was becoming habitual, squeezed Ricky's knee. Ricky, mesmerised, studied his expression, and in a flash the word *leer* came into his head. It was not a familiar word, one that he'd much thought about or used, but he felt that he could now add it to his vocabulary. It had acquired meaning.

Left alone, he pondered the situation. What was he getting into? He thought anxiously about the demands of the work. Was he up to the tasks ahead, the standards required? True, he was attentive and reasonably literate, but there were plenty of other students just as qualified. So why had *he* been chosen? Had he caught the professor's fancy? It certainly looked that way and he smiled to himself. After all, he could scarcely return the sentiment: the professor was a gargoyle. But calling up that image made the smile fade on his lips: being pursued by a gargoyle was not a pleasant prospect.

Now Hassan: that was a different story. Yes, the professor had an eye.

And with that thought the door opened and Hassan entered bearing a round metal tray, on which stood a mug of coffee and a chocolate biscuit on a small china plate.

'Mr Ricky ... milk, no sugar ... yes?'

Hassan was always there, cooking, sweeping, cleaning. Ricky sometimes glimpsed him returning from the shops with bags of provisions. His presence lightened the burden of the work, the fear Ricky had that he might fail. Indeed the prospect of catching sight of him, of

Festival

exchanging a few words, however brief, made each visit a thrill. The words *were* brief, though; Hassan was shy, his English endearingly limited.

'Where are you from, Hassan?'

'Tangier.'

'And your family?'

'Big family.' A wide smile, spread of fingers. 'Four brothers, two sisters.'

'Wow, lots of mouths to feed.'

So Ricky was charmed but frustrated. There seemed no moving beyond these meagre exchanges, no way to get to know Hassan better; and for several visits nothing changed. Then one day Ricky strolled into the kitchen and was greeted with an even bigger smile. Hassan had made something special and pointed proudly to a plate of finger-shaped pastries. Would Ricky like one? They were very popular at home. Ricky nodded keenly, and the two of them grinned at each other as they bit into the almond-paste cigars. But it was a messy business; crumbs flew everywhere and they ended up dusted with icing sugar. Ricky looked down at his bespattered jeans and spluttered with laughter. Then, raising his head, he gazed at Hassan and saw the flash in his eyes. Hassan closed the door and put a silencing finger to his lips. He brushed the dust from Ricky's clothes, and with the cushion of his thumb gently flicked away the crumbs clinging to Ricky's mouth. Ricky submitted in quivering wonder.

Delicacies appeared at every visit after that, and a recurring favourite was baklava, though Ricky had a special fondness for a small flower-shaped cookie made with sesame and honey. The professor was scarcely seen. He emerged from his study only rarely, sometimes to make himself a snack, sometimes to check on Ricky's progress. He never greeted Ricky on arrival, having passed that duty to Hassan. Meanwhile, in the kitchen, the two young men munched away and brushed each other down with careful hands and glittering eyes.

It was on a Friday in mid-March, when Ricky had been working for Collimore for about three weeks, that Hassan opened the door looking unusually relaxed. He was wearing a light blue shirt that threw his dark features into striking relief. The apron was missing and there was no flour on his hands.

'Hi, Hassan. You look cool. Not working today?'

'Professor away. In Galway, for weekend.'

'I see.' Ricky nodded, quietly absorbing the news, and hung his coat on the hall stand. 'So you're on holiday.'

'Holiday, yes.'

Hassan took him by the hand and led him into the kitchen. Ricky chuckled.

'Hey, hold on, Hassan. No holiday for me. Some of us have to work.'

'Not now. Work later. Come.'

Still gripping him, Hassan led him through the kitchen to a room at the back of the house, a room that Ricky had never entered and scarcely knew existed. For a while he stood and stared in amazement. It was breathtaking – a riot of pattern and colour, a scene out of Eastern fantasy, romance and myth. Rugs of elaborate design covered the floor and the walls were decorated with richly embroidered art. A bed beneath a sumptuous counterpane projected from one wall and a low wooden table with filigree carvings stood beside a brilliant red sofa strewn with gold cushions. Something was burning in a little bowl on a shelf and the air hummed with that sweet aroma that Ricky associated with Hassan.

'Wow, what can I say, Hassan? It's simply fabulous.'

Ricky's eyes circled the room and came to rest on two photographs in decorated silver frames that stood beside the bowl on the shelf. He stepped forward to take a closer look.

'Your family?'

'This, mother and father. Here, brothers and sisters.'

Ricky nodded. The parents, with lined faces and flecks of grey in their hair, looked grave and dignified, but the children, all younger than Hassan, were crushed together in a yowling, jostling pack. Ricky smiled and was about to comment on their unruly appearance, when he felt Hassan's hand reaching for his own. Their fingers interlocked, and he continued to gaze at the photographs for a while, trying to master his excitement, his heart floating in airy suspense. Then he turned. Those dark eyes, like wet polished stone! He gazed at them in a trance, sank into their depths, and his mouth, inching forward with robotic slowness, hovered at a narrowing distance until it brushed tremblingly against those dusky brown lips.

So Hassan knew the score. But what did Ricky know? Ricky, who some years earlier had stared at his first leakage and thought himself wounded; who puzzled and panicked over the draw of boys; who always looked away when certain eyes met his; whose secret scrapbook was his sole experience; who had dreamt of this but had never imagined it would happen.

Hassan

Not a problem. Leave it to Hassan. Hassan, who preferred the goatskin rug to the bed; who knew the arts of holding off, of slowing down, of changing roles; who had tested all the pleasure points and explored the charm of even ears and toes; who was as thrilled by Ricky as Ricky by him; who wanted this to be the summit, the shuddering triple-forte climax of their lives.

For Ricky, every aspect of Hassan was a surprise and a delight. The perfect compact symmetry of his chest; the sprout of bushy hair that crested his rump; the delicate veined intricacy of his cock; the fulsome wetness of his tongue. Even his disfigurements captivated: the warty protusion on his left arm; the patch of scaliness on his knee; the scar on his thumb, gained from a cooking accident, which Ricky sucked with assiduous care as if it were still raw and in need of treatment.

They floated in a bubble. For Ricky, Hassan was an inescapable, all-consuming presence, and time an absence, the hours away, dancing elsewhere. In his office the phone rang several times, and voices – calm, brusque, hesitant – left messages.

That night, back in his room, he lay on his bed in dreamy surrender, replaying the scene with ecstatic recall. But he fretted all weekend, and when he turned up for his next visit he approached the house with dread. How to explain his lack of progress on the book, not to mention the missed calls? The professor, deep in his customary wild-eyed distraction, seemed not to notice, however, and made no inquiries.

Instead, during his one brief appearance, he moved his chair next to Ricky and spoke about the finer points of indexing, illustrating his comments with reference to one of his own books. 'Now look here. That's what I mean. D'you see?'

Ricky, feeling an arm snake round his waist, kept his eyes fixed on the page, his limbs frozen, and Collimore, after some further comments and a departing pat on the thigh, stumped off up the stairs.

In the kitchen, Ricky and Hassan faced each other with shy smiles. But as Ricky leaned forward to kiss him, Hassan held him off with a raised palm. There were pastries, of course – those cookies of sesame and honey that Ricky loved best – and they brushed each other down in the usual way. But now they touched with hands that knew too much, that itched to cast off constraint. And constraint was necessary: the professor was back. So was this forever? No, said Hassan's eyes, glittering with promise; there would be other chances. But for the moment they must wait.

The Easter break came, then the new term. Spring broke one day in late April. Ricky, after finishing work on the book, grew more confident and was given additional work. Life at the house assumed its old pattern of coffee and pastries, finger fondling and whispered endearments. At night, Ricky made love to the absent Hassan, and each visit rekindled his desire until he thought he'd go mad with frustration. He studied the professor's diary for any hint that he might be off on another trip, but it was difficult to make sense of the man's hasty scrawl.

Then one afternoon, after hours of slogging away at an essay in his room, he arrived at the house feeling low. Hassan opened the door and instantly hurried off saying he had something to attend to. Ricky went into the office, turned on the computer and sat staring blindly at the screen. He'd certainly learned a lot since starting to work for the professor, but the workload was heavy and beginning to interfere with his studies. Nor did he really need the money. Hassan had become the main reason to be here, the dallying in the kitchen the highlight of the week. Yet meeting him, under the constraints of the situation, was becoming increasingly painful.

He'd been asked to look at a piece that Collimore had written for a journal and note anything that might need attention, but he found it hard to focus. His mind kept flying back to his troublesome essay. It was in dismal shape and had to be submitted by noon tomorrow. His heart slumped as his brain stumbled around in a fog. Was he good at anything? He felt a sense of failure creeping back. And what about Hassan? Hassan played with him, but was otherwise distant. He felt like a toy, a diversion. Nothing was satisfactory. He ached for the euphoria, the transport of that vanished hour.

Then, at his lowest point, he heard laughter in the kitchen. He got up and, moving to the door, peered through the crack. It was Hassan and Collimore. They were enjoying a joke together. Collimore was biting into a pastry and Hassan was brushing him down. The image burned itself into Ricky's mind like a brand. He turned away, a gush of resentment sluicing through him.

He avoided the kitchen that day, and after a couple of hours pulled on his coat and went home. His room was on the first floor of a student block a few streets from the campus. He sat at his desk and mulled things over. There was no going on; he had to give it up. Perhaps tell the professor at his next visit, or even write

Festival

to him. He'd say he was not up to the task, that it was interfering with his studies. Yes, write; he could explain himself better in writing. He turned to a clean page in his pad and gnawed on his pen, but the words wouldn't come. He wrote a few lines, then threw them away. They were false. Did he really want this? Giving up the work would mean never seeing Hassan again. He got up and wandered around in a daze. Then he lay down on the bed. He thought he was feeling a bit unwell. He put a hand to his brow. Yes, it was definitely hot.

He woke suddenly, shivering from head to foot. But whether from cold or feverish heat was not clear. The duvet had slipped from his bed and he could scarcely muster the strength to haul it back. His head was dull with pain, his back and legs ached and it was a struggle to switch on the lamp. He glanced at his bedside clock and stared in disbelief. Half past five? Oh no, he'd been sleeping for hours! Since eight the previous evening! Oh God, what a disaster!

He gazed at the ceiling, his mind floating restlessly. His essay; it was due today; he had to finish it. But how? How? He couldn't lift his head from the pillow. And then his letter to the professor; he had to finish that too; he had to explain his decision. He'd agreed to put in some hours this afternoon, but what if he was too ill? He had to call or leave a message; he *had* to. It would look bad if he simply failed to turn up; it would ruin his good name.

He swung his legs off the bed and got unsteadily to his feet. It was like lifting a great rock, an immense boulder that overpowered and crushed him. He sat down again and fell backward, his head smashing into the pillow. No, there was no dodging the fact that he was ill. Very ill. He had to rest; rest was the thing. If he could just rest a while, he might wake up in a few hours feeling much better, even fully recovered. That would leave time to contact the professor and finish his essay.

He snapped off the lamp.

Oh God, what timing! ... If he could just ...

He drifted into near-oblivion as the first stirrings of the morning broke the silence in the street outside his room: a passing dustcart, a barking dog, a rising clatter of feet, a blur of voices in greeting and conversation. Then the slow build-up of rush-hour traffic, human and motorised, growing to a continuous low-level roar. Meanwhile, the sky, full of sailing white cloud, began to clear, giving way by late morning to an expanse of blue through which the smiling sun climbed to its zenith and then sank blazingly to earth behind trees and chimney pots.

He woke in the violet glow of twilight, staring at the ceiling in a haze. Then he recalled that he was ill. Very ill. But he'd slept; he'd slept for hours and hours. Had it helped? He put a hand to his head. Perhaps a little. He glanced at his clock and groaned. It was too late now to finish his essay; too late to call the professor. He was failing on every front: in his job, in his studies, in life. Everything was a mess; he wanted to give it all up. But how to explain himself; it was too much, too much. He staggered out of bed. His mouth was dry. He needed water. He crept to the wash basin and filled a glass from the tap. Then he undressed, tossing his clothes to the floor, and climbed back into bed. He lay awake. The sky darkened and night came on. His consciousness

Festival

flickered, his soul shrivelled. He seemed to be losing his hold on life. Hamlet's speech came to mind: *To die, to sleep* ...

He woke to a soft knocking on the door, but was too surprised and dazed to make response. It came again. Hello, he called in a weak voice. Hello, came a faint echo. And after a pause a dark profile appeared, framed in a strip of light. Then a shadowy figure slipped in and closed the door.

Ricky, in sudden alarm, struggled to raise his head from the pillow. Someone was kneeling beside his bed, stroking his hand. Someone with a familiar aromatic presence. Too amazed to speak, he simply stared, peering fixedly into the gloom. The presence chuckled quietly and placed a hand on his brow.

'Hot.'

Ricky reached out to touch the looming face. It drew nearer and nuzzled his hand. Ah, he knew those lips, so soft, so precious!

'Hassan, I can't believe ... how did you find me?'

Hassan grinned and tapped the side of his head.

'Easy.'

Ricky fell back onto the pillow. 'Oh Hassan, thank God you're here ... I'm so glad, honestly, so glad, but you must keep away ... I'm ill ... I'm very ill.'

'Rest now ... don't speak ... you want water?'

'Eh ... perhaps ... just a little.'

Hassan filled a glass and lifted it to Ricky's lips. He took a few sips and for several minutes they simply gazed at each other with rueful smiles.

'Hassan, does the professor know you're here? Did he send you?'

'No, no ... professor is ill.'

Hassan

Ricky's eyes widened. Then he started to giggle. And instantly Hassan joined in. They giggled convulsively – giggled and giggled and giggled – becoming helpless and silly like children. And it wasn't quite clear why. Was it the notion of that intellectual powerhouse, that awesome force of nature, being knocked flat by a bug? Or was it just the thrill of seeing each other again?

Hassan pulled a small plastic box from his bag, removed the lid and flashed the contents before Ricky's eyes. A fragrance filled the air. Sesame and honey! Ricky smiled, reached out, then shook his head.

'Oh Hassan ... I *can't* ... I'm so sorry ... I just *can't*.'

Hassan climbed onto the bed and lay beside him. He slid an arm round his neck and drew him close, cradling his head. Ricky smiled faintly and began to shake with quiet laughter. And with the laughter came a blurt of tears. How strange life was. It dragged you this way and that. It raised you to the sky, it cast you into the deepest pit, and sometimes it was difficult to know whether you were up or down. Last night he'd been all for throwing up the work. But now? Where was he now? Was it a blessing that he'd failed to write to the professor? Hassan had come to his room. He could come again, and away from those watchful eyes, they could throw off restraint and perhaps regain that blissful hour they'd known on that memorable burning day.

Hassan kissed his brow and slipped from the bed.

'Hassan ... don't go, please.'

'Professor is ill ... come tomorrow.'

'Oh, Hassan ... stay a bit.'

'Rest now ... come tomorrow.'

Ricky squirmed, then yielded. 'Okay, tomorrow. And Hassan, thank you. Thank you for coming.'

Festival

Hassan blew a kiss from the door, then, drawing it softly behind him, he vanished. Ricky, plunged into cruel darkness, groaned and pitched about in desolation. Oh God, what hours lay ahead! The lowest, deepest pit. Would daylight ever come? Would Hassan return? Oh Hassan, Hassan, come back, please, I beg you …

In the Chair

So let's return, Michael, to that hotel in Aix. Had you been to France before?

No. I'd never been anywhere. It was Dominic's idea. To mark our year together.

And you say there was a picture of a mountain in the dining room?

Yes. A reproduction. So I went to take a closer look and Dominic came up behind me. He murmured something in my ear. Something in French. I shrugged. He knows I don't speak French.

'It's one of a series,' he said. 'He painted it many times.'

I shrugged again.

'Cézanne,' he said.

'Says Anne?' I chuckled. 'Says Anne who? Queen Anne? Anne Boleyn?'

He said, 'Cézanne, the painter, you dork.'

You dork?

Yes. I guess that tells all. Everything you need to

Festival

know about us. I'm not sure what attracted me to Dominic. He's not really my type. He has sleek blond hair and a square jaw, but I've never been one for the classic look. He picked me up, so to speak, in the salon where I work. He made a booking every month and always chose me to groom his locks. Then one day he suggested we go for a drink. So we went to the Mayflower and three months later I moved in with him.

Despite the misgivings?

Yes.

So why did you succumb?

I think I was flattered by the attention. He's a good bit older than me. Thirty-something and super-confident. He had a very expensive education and works for the BBC. Arts and culture or something. The night I walked into the flat I was awestruck. The room wallowed in plush furniture, potted plants and subdued lighting. It was all glass and faced a balcony over the river. It was the reverse of the shabby hole I shared with the gang. I treated everything with caution, trod on eggshells. I felt small, out of my sphere. He poured the drinks, then played some music. A lush piece, all swoony strings and flutey bits. I felt sure I'd heard it before but didn't like to show my ignorance.

Go on.

Well, it was like that for the whole year. I never shed my caution, never relaxed, never really settled, if you know what I mean. I seemed to spend the whole year, just like that night, hunched on the sofa, trying to shield my ignorance. It was Dominic, as I say, who arranged that week in Provence. I had no reason to celebrate our first anniversary.

So why did it last that long?

In the Chair

As I say, it was partly the lure of the glamour. He bought me gifts – clothes, flashy cufflinks, an expensive watch – which, even at the time, seemed wrong, a form of bribery. I knew I shouldn't take them. I could see they were a kind of trap, but I didn't know how to refuse. To be honest, I was afraid of him.

He bullied you?

He never struck me. Never laid a finger. But he had flashes of anger and would sometimes sulk for days. He could make me feel guilty, as if I was rejecting him. Is that bullying? Of a kind?

Absolutely classic. What else? Did he criticise you?

All the time. He didn't like my clothes, my music, my way of speaking. He found fault with my cooking and even my table-laying. He often invited friends and colleagues to dinner and would signal his disapproval of something I'd prepared – though in a more subtle way than if we were alone.

In what way?

Well, he'd ask the guests if the soup was seasoned enough, or add knobs of butter to the vegetables. He'd frown at things I said. Sometimes he'd replace the bottle of wine I'd brought to the table.

Did you ever complain?

Not really. He always had an answer. Or he'd retaliate. I complained once that *he* made all the decisions – about where to eat, which films to see, what telly to watch – and he replied with a list of grudges against me.

He kept a scorecard?

Yes. You could never get the better of him.

And was it the same in bed?

Eh ... I'll skip the details. But yes, he always took

the lead, and I was afraid to refuse him. As I say, he held grudges. He played on guilt.

In general, did you feel inadequate? That it was your fault?

Yes. All the time. I tended to keep my mouth shut, especially when we had guests. I thought I had nothing interesting to say. That I might let him down, show him up. And then he was always commenting on how I looked. He implied once that I was putting on weight, though I knew I wasn't. I mean, my weight scarcely changes. It doesn't need to. If anything, I'm underweight. But I stopped eating for days, until someone at work said I was looking skinny and undernourished.

Worst of all, I suspect him now of planting evidence of my failure. On several occasions it looked as if I'd left the oven on when I was quite sure I'd turned it off. Or that I'd failed to buy something from the shop when I was certain I had. Or that I'd left the front door off the latch when I was convinced I'd locked it.

Did you look for support? What about your friends?

He didn't like them. He was rude to them if we met them in town or if I brought them home. He complained if I spoke too long on the phone. I used to make calls in secret. He was madly jealous. He didn't like me going out alone and questioned me if I spoke to complete strangers.

Were you flattered by his jealousy?

At first. Until I realised how scary it was, how fanatical.

Was he jealous of anyone in particular?

Yes. Of my friend Terry. We've known each other since school. But we weren't lovers back then. He was

In the Chair

just my best mate. We went everywhere together. He'd been around forever. He's the most unassuming guy you could meet. So quiet and easy-going I didn't even realise he was keen on me. I took him for granted. Assumed he'd always be there.

Did you confide in him?

No. Not in anyone. I pretended to be fine. I told no one the truth. It was too embarrassing. I felt isolated. Ashamed.

Okay, Michael. So let's return to that hotel and that picture in the dining room.

Yes. So when he'd finished lecturing me, we gazed at it for a while and he suggested that we climb that mountain. It was an easy climb, he said. There were several routes up and spectacular views at the top. Okay, I said, though I didn't want to go. I didn't want to climb at his pace and listen to his commentary. I mean, to hell with scrambling over rocks and studying a map. He was always poring over maps. I wanted to stroll the town. I wanted to sit in a café and read a book, but I knew if I objected it would hang like a thundercloud over the whole week.

So you gave in? You went?

Yes. But here's the strange thing. It wasn't the experience I'd expected at all. It wasn't a wearisome trudge. I didn't feel burdened or confined by it. Quite the reverse. I felt liberated. It was a turning point.

In what way?

Well, we walked for an hour and came to an abandoned priory – or part of it – an old restored chapel that's now a refuge. And from there we climbed to the mountain's most famous monument – a cross standing nineteen metres high on a ledge of rock. It was a glittering day, and for a long while we stood on that spot looking down on the rolling plains of Provence. It was thrilling. Absolutely breathtaking.

Yes, no doubt – but in what way a turning point?

Well, I don't know. I guess mountain-tops are clarifying, aren't they? Especially on a crystal day. I mean, looking down, you see life in all its dazzling profusion. You see its wider reaches, its larger aspect. I scanned the rolling landscape. I looked northward to the Alps and southward to the sea, and thought of life going on in towns and villages, in ships and ports, in cities across the globe. And gazing around, I had a flash of intuition. I'd been living in a tunnel, I realised. I'd begun to doubt my intelligence, my value, even my sanity. And suddenly I knew what I had to do. I had to take action. I had to seize the moment. Get my life back.

Get your life back? No small challenge, then. At the summit another peak appears. So did you act instantly?

No. But a seed had been sown. Something was stirring. A shift had occurred and change was in the air. We returned to London. To life as before. To the criticism, the jealousy, the bullying. I felt the walls closing in again, the curbs tightening, the shackles chafing. Then came the critical moment, the crunch. I returned from work one night to find him reading my emails. I'd suspected him before, but never caught him at it. I'm still not sure how he gained access.

And what was his reaction?

Oh, predictably weird. He looked at me boldly, with no sense of apology at all.

He said, 'I see you're still writing to Terry.'

I said, 'It's up to me who I write to. It's no bloody business of yours. Get off my laptop.'

In the Chair

'Sometimes,' he said, 'I think you like your friends more than you like me.'

'Is that surprising?' I said. 'They're not snoops. They respect my space.'

He said, 'Hey, calm down. You need to realise I do this out of concern. Because I care.'

I said, 'I need to realise, do I? Funny, isn't it, how you seem to know more about my needs than *I* do.'

He heaved a great sigh and shook his head. He looked deeply offended and stared at me as if to say, how could you accuse me? Have you gone quite mad? Then he threw up his hands and came towards me, reaching out as if to stroke my face. I knocked his arm away, gathered up the laptop and marched into the bedroom. I threw all my things into a wheeled suitcase, snapped on my jacket and emerged minutes later, dragging the trolley behind me.

He followed me to the door. 'And where do you think you're going?'

'Somewhere out of your reach,' I said.

'You're being very silly,' he said. 'You have a nice home, lovely things, a man who dotes on you.'

'I don't want to be worshipped,' I said. 'I want to be loved. D'you know the difference?'

He said, 'If you leave, that's it. I won't come after you, nor will I have you back.'

'Oh well,' I said, 'thanks for the bonus.'

And did he follow you?

Yes. Onto the landing. He came up and hauled me back by the shoulder. But I didn't look round. I simply slammed my arm behind me and stepped into the lift. Then I turned, and as the doors closed I saw that he was doubled up. I'd accidentally socked him in the groin.

Festival

Oh, splendid! Bull's eye! ... But are you quite sure it was an accident?

Well, you're the mind-reader, you decide.

Anyway, outside I made straight for the tube. I thought I'd try the old pad first. The gang are a bit dippy, but decent enough. I paused at the knocker, though, wondering how the hell to explain myself. Anyway, Sean came to the door, and I was glad, because he's the best of the bunch. He was eating a sandwich, but his jaw froze when he saw me.

He said, 'Christ, Mickey, what's this?'

'Sean,' I said. 'Can I have a word?'

He waved me in. We sat in the kitchen.

'I just need a few days, Sean. Till I find somewhere.'

'Okay, mate, leave it to me.' He patted my knee. 'I'll speak to the others.' He's a good old boy is Sean.

So you'd broken out and found a refuge?

Yes. But it was only when I moved in with Terry the following week that my year with Dominic came into focus. I mean, I can see it clearly now, but when you're in a tunnel – to state the obvious – you're in the dark. Your view changes only when you emerge.

Or perhaps when you climb – and height, distance, vision fuse in a blaze of insight.

Yeah, nice one. I'll go with that. For me, the moment came then. On a peak in Provence.

So have you spoken about all this to anyone else?

I've talked it through with Terry many times. 'We thought you were happy,' he said one day. 'We envied you. We thought you'd got it all. The champagne, the caviare, the man.'

'I lied,' I said. 'Even to myself. The truth was too shaming.'

In the Chair

So where are you now, Michael?

Still adjusting. The past hovers, but recedes a little more every day. I've not spoken to Dominic since, though I see him every month. He still comes to the salon, but he books with one of the others. My chest tightens when he's there, though he never speaks or looks in my direction. If he's hoping to unnerve me, he can think again. My skin hardens with every appearance.

And Terry? Tell me about him.

Well, he's the sweetest guy. How come I didn't realise? He's the pearl I overlooked. The flower beneath the foot. I owe him so much. Him and all my friends. And that includes the mountain. I often think of that rocky pile. I read about it all I can.

That picture, by the way, is in the Courtauld. So I took Terry along. I'd never even heard of the Courtauld, let alone been there. Neither had he. I think he thought I was getting a bit above myself.

Anyway, we found it on the first floor. And it was only then, standing in front of it, that I told him why I wanted him to see it. He was amazed.

'You *climbed* it? And what did you see?'

'The light,' I said. 'It streams everywhere. Over every hump and rise, into every dip and crevice. It rolls over the great plains. It lifts the top of your head off. It's like standing on the roof of the world and then floating off into space.'

He looked at me as if I was having a rush to the head.

Which I was, of course.

'Hm,' he mused. 'Sounds great. Almost as good as a spliff. We must try it together sometime, though just now I'm gagging for coffee. How about you?'

A Canterbury Tale

'You should always breathe through your nose,' declared Uncle George, swerving to avoid a cat streaking across the road. 'The hairs act as a filter.' He glanced at Peter with a smirk. 'Besides, you don't want to catch flies, do you?'

A rich guffaw, followed by a series of shoulder-shaking spasms.

Peter, gazing through the windscreen at fields of cows and sheep, responded with a humouring chuckle. It was only Tuesday and he was already well acquainted with the man's bossiness and bluff egotism. This day trip to Canterbury was likely to prove a trial. His uncle and aunt were an embarrassingly odd pair, and their clothes – *his* floppy fedora, *her* showy cape and white crocheted stockings – tended to provoke titters. He glanced over his shoulder. Aunt Bea, on the back seat, was placidly knitting a cardigan while reading an article entitled 'I Married a Serial Killer'. She looked up and smiled. Her sallow round face, with its dull eyes and extra chin, was quite without wrinkles and almost

A Canterbury Tale

entirely devoid of character. It was a lazy face, slow and complacent. The face of a spoiled, well-fed, not too bright child.

At the next set of traffic lights a motor cyclist drew up beside them and threw up his visor. 'Oy, mate, where's yer L plates? For the past mile you've been drifting about like a fart in a wind tunnel.'

Uncle George, staring pop-eyed at him, flushed purple. 'You young –' he spluttered just as the lights changed and the cyclist sped off. Then 'hoodlum!' he yelled, thrusting his head out of the window and stalling the car in his rage. Instantly the queue behind broke into a cacophony.

Several stumbles later they reached the other side, where, to his relief, Peter spotted a sign: 'Canterbury 5.' Gripping the seat with white knuckles, he raised a silent prayer.

'When I was your age I was eager for adventure. I started to work in the bank here in Britain, but when an opportunity arose in Canada I grabbed it with both hands. Canada was a very young country then, with lots of space to flex your elbows. And boy, did I have some sharp ones.' Another rich guffaw: Uncle George had recovered from his brawl with the motor cyclist. 'So I worked tirelessly and quickly rose to the top. Oh yes, I was madly ambitious. A go-getter, if you like, though I can't say I care for the term. Anyway, the day they made me manager was the proudest of my life.'

Peter, who had heard much of this before, tried to compose his face into an expression of interest. They were at a café in the high street, Aunt Bea having insisted that she needed some refreshment before taking

Festival

a tour of the Cathedral. She was currently visiting what she called, coyly and perhaps appropriately, the little girl's room. They had not yet ordered, since she always paid a visit on entering and was always gone for a quite baffling amount of time, causing Uncle George to explode on every occasion with his now-familiar outburst of 'Where *is* that woman?' Peter could see that he was building up to it again, the waitress having been twice dismissed with a brusque wave of the hand.

'I'd been courting Bea for a year or more before leaving Britain, so as soon as I had a place of my own and enough money I wrote and proposed marriage. And I was amazed at how readily she accepted. After all, it was no small step to leave her family behind and join me in Canada. And times were hard then, you know. It was just after the war. We went through some rough patches. It's not the same today. We were pioneers, you might say.'

Peter nodded and fiddled with the salt cellar. Uncle George glanced around tetchily for Aunt Bea.

'Anyway, after retirement, I'd have stayed on. But Bea, she was all for coming back.' He lowered his voice. 'To be honest, she never really settled over there. And there was no choice about where to retire over here. It had to be near her family in Kent, didn't it? Which was fine with me. I mean this is a very nice part of the world. I love Herne Bay, and as for the bungalow, it's a perfect Shangri-La.' He paused, glanced around. 'Oh look, this is insufferable. I mean, where *is* that woman?'

A few minutes later Aunt Bea arrived, her face aglow from newly applied lipstick and skin cream, her frizz of salt-and-pepper hair freshly raked. She smiled at them.

'Have you ordered?' she said, dropping onto a chair.

A Canterbury Tale

'Of *course* not,' growled Uncle George. 'We don't know what you want, do we? Besides, we assumed you'd been abducted by pirates.'

Aunt Bea turned to Peter. 'Our little joke,' she smiled, with sweet composure.

They'd hoped to join a conducted tour, but they were too late for the ten-thirty and the next was not until twelve.

'Oh, what a shame,' sighed Aunt Bea.

'Fiddlesticks,' snapped Uncle George. 'It's not a problem, *I'll* conduct us.'

He led off with a brisk turn of the heel and the others followed, Peter smiling to himself. Uncle George had a tendency to pose as an expert in all manner of things, though his knowledge was often found to be faulty. His shelves were packed with history books and he declared great respect for what he called 'facts'. He boasted that there was scarcely a work of fiction in the house. Fiction, he claimed, was just a pack of lies. He made an exception, though, for the Alice books of Lewis Carroll. Clever, very clever. They made you think, and there was truth in every word the man wrote.

'Now, what you're both keen to see, I know, is the spot where Becket was struck down. Well, we'll come to that shortly, so possess your souls in patience and let's start at the beginning. Saint Augustine, the first Archbishop, came to Britain from Rome in 592 AD –'

'597, actually,' said a boy who was passing. 'It tells you that on the chart over there.'

Uncle George stood for some moments in offended silence, as if he could scarcely believe that he was being interrupted. 'Anyway,' he continued, 'be that as it may,

Festival

the point is that he'd been sent by Pope Gregory the Great to convert the people of Britain. Gregory had seen some slaves for sale in the city market, and when he asked who they were, he was told they were Angles. Not Angles, he replied, but angels.'

'Isn't that story apocryphal?' remarked a woman to her friend as they passed.

Uncle George took a deep breath and closed his eyes, and when he opened them it was to confront a starchy church official who had stepped forward from a gloomy recess.

'I hope you won't mind my asking, sir, but if you're going to give a commentary, could you please keep your voice to a reasonable level. This is, after all, a place of worship.'

Uncle George gulped and, when he'd recovered, nodded assent with a look of fierce resentment. The official responded with an acid smile and walked off.

'So then, let's move on,' proposed Uncle George in a pointed whisper. 'And as we pass along please take note of the vaulted arches and these magnificent windows of the high Perpendicular ...'

For lunch, they ate at a quaint little place in a side street that specialised in traditional English fare, a place where Uncle George and Aunt Bea had eaten on so many occasions they were greeted as old friends.

'Now the plan for this afternoon is this,' said Uncle George between mouthfuls of roast beef. 'I'll drop Bea off at her sister's place and then take you to see the ruins of the Castle. How does that sound?'

Peter nodded in bemused agreement.

A Canterbury Tale

'After which, there's the Abbey. But that will depend on time.'

'Dolly and I have some catching up to do,' said Aunt Bea. 'And anyway I've seen enough old ruins to last me a dozen lifetimes.'

She tittered naughtily and Uncle George harrumphed.

Dolly lived a short drive away in a stone cottage with a small front garden. They dropped Aunt Bea at the gate.

'We'll be back at around five,' said Uncle George.

'No hurry,' she said.

They drove to a car park, then headed for the Castle on foot, Uncle George striding out like a giraffe, so that Peter struggled to keep up.

'Don't expect too much. It's just a shell now. The original was a motte and bailey, begun by William the Conqueror. The stone keep came later, in the reign of Henry the First. For years it was used as a prison, but by the seventeenth century it was already a ruin.'

Peter, breathless, scampered at his heels. 'I guess you've been before.'

'Oh, many times. But don't let that bother you. I'm always glad of any excuse to avoid an afternoon at Dolly's. An hour with that cackling pair and I'm close to murder.'

On entering the castle grounds, they strode around the gardens, surveying the scene and stopping now and again for Uncle George to expand on some point of historical note. A narrow gateway led into the keep and, after a brief inspection of the ground floor, they climbed the only tower with a staircase.

Festival

'This castle was one of three – the others being at Dover and Rochester – built on the main Roman road from Dover to London, a vital route that had to be well defended. Dover was by far the largest and most important, of course – in fact, the largest castle in England …'

Peter gazed around and, lulled by the ever-rolling stream of commentary, drifted into a trance. It was a relief to be free from the tension between uncle and aunt for a while, even if his uncle's current briskness was faintly disturbing. True, he was a man of familiar restless energy, but the insistent breakneck speed of this visit was exceptional and puzzling.

'So now.' Uncle George glanced at his watch.

Peter, snapping out of his daydream, tried to look bright and keen. 'Yes, so now, what? On to the Abbey, perhaps?'

'Well, if time allows. But before that, I'd like to visit a friend of mine. Someone I always look up when I'm in town.'

Peter nodded, his curiosity aroused. 'Okay. That's fine by me.'

They picked up the car and drove a short distance out of the centre. Peter glanced around in surprise. They were surrounded by tall blocks of flats, the buildings shabby, grey and featureless, the balconies hung with washing, the walls sprayed with graffiti and defaced by ugly streaks from overflow pipes. They pulled up in a bare forecourt, full of weeds and cracked paving-stones and strewn with fag ends and sweet wrappers. There was scarcely a soul about, except for a very old woman leading a small child around and two youths sitting on a doorstep apparently rolling joints. Uncle George

A Canterbury Tale

straightened his tie in the rear-view mirror and passed a hand through the sparse remains of his hair.

'I'll just go and check things out,' he said. 'I shouldn't be long, but the radio's there if you need it. Or perhaps you've got something to read?'

Peter hesitated. 'Eh ... yes, I've got a book here somewhere ... I think.'

'Good.'

Uncle George smiled, walked smartly across the forecourt and vanished up a staircase. Peter watched him and then sat staring ahead for several minutes in puzzled reflection. What odd behaviour. What was going on? Oddest of all was that nothing had been said about the friend. Not a word. It was hard to imagine what sort of friend it could be, living out here in this desolate place. Insofar as it was possible to imagine Uncle George having a friend, given his testiness and solitary habits, the kind of person that came to mind was a whiskery member of a book club or historical society, some old buffer in baggy cords and a chain-stitch cardigan smoking a pipe. Not the sort, in other words, that you might expect to find lurking in the smelly stairwells of this sinkhole.

A man in a grubby zipper jacket and torn jeans went by. He had a hard, unshaven face and was holding a black mastiff to his side on a leash. He stopped for a moment and peered into the car with a scowl. He was an alarming sight and Peter flinched. But fortunately he didn't hang about, and when he'd gone Peter got out and stretched his limbs, sensing that it was perhaps safer outside the car than in. He could hardly go far, though, since it would be fatal to leave the vehicle unlocked and he had no keys. So after a while he got back in, turned

Festival

on the radio and found a music station. A DJ was interviewing a rock band. He listened for a while, feeling too edgy to pay much attention, then snapped off and picked up his book. But, still uneasy and nagged with curiosity, he again found it difficult to focus. He also felt a wave of resentment. It was surely very inconsiderate of Uncle George to leave him hanging about in this awkward situation.

The City and the Pillar, the cover claimed, was a worldwide bestseller. It was not a book to flaunt, though, and certainly not in front of parents or his aunt and uncle. Stumbling on it in the library, he'd been intrigued by the blurb: 'Jim Willard is haunted by the memory of a romantic adolescent encounter with his friend Bob Ford.' On reading that, he'd felt a surge of interest and a compulsion to read more. Here was a character who embodied his own experience. So he was disappointed to find his affinity waning: he simply couldn't warm to Jim, who seemed aloof and arrogant.

But he pushed on, and when, some chapters later, he glanced at his watch, he was amazed to find that he'd been reading for forty minutes. He was also alarmed. What on earth had happened? Ought he to abandon the car, whatever the risk, and go in search of his uncle? He began to imagine all manner of scenarios. Was he in trouble? Mixed up with some shady character? In debt? Being blackmailed? He got out of the car and cast his eyes about for any sign. But apart from a small boy flying about on a tricycle, there was not a soul in sight. The youths on the doorstep had disappeared.

Then, as he glanced around, he heard his name being called and turned to see his uncle hurrying towards him

A Canterbury Tale

in the company of a young woman. They approached with wide smiles of apology.

'Sorry about the delay, old chap.' His uncle looked flustered. 'Yvonne, this is my nephew Peter.'

She was slim and pretty, a blue-eyed blonde with a pale oval face, a delicate nose and the faint suggestion of a scar on her left cheek. She smiled coyly and held out a soft white hand. Peter shook it, nodding cordially, and gazed at the pair of them in expectation of some further introduction. But none was offered, and the three of them simply smiled at each other for an awkward stretch, she looking pleasant and mildly anxious and Uncle George pulling gently at the lobe of an ear.

'Yvonne has to pick up her little girl from school, so I thought we could offer a lift.'

Peter smiled and shrugged, unsure if this was a question or a statement. 'Well, of course ... we'd love ... I mean ... whatever ...'

They strolled to the car and on Peter's suggestion she took the front seat. From the back he saw them turn to each other with brief smiles. Then, as his uncle fumbled with the handbrake, he saw her hand slide over his in a caress so swift and discreet as to be barely noticeable. Moments later he caught fragments of their mumbled conversation: 'dinner', 'Thursday', 'neighbour', 'every fortnight', 'that depends'. It was the shortest of journeys, which, given the difficulty of parking, they could more easily have made on foot. They emerged into uproar, as excited children, laden with coats, satchels and the products of an art lesson, streamed through the gates of a red-brick building into the arms of adoring parents.

Festival

Nola was pretty and had her mother's features, except that her skin was dark and her head covered in tight black curls. She skipped up to them, shook out a scroll of paper and they all smiled at a ragged splodge of black paint. It was Daddy, apparently, and after some murmurs of approval she flung her arms wide, seeking a hug. Yvonne snatched her up, kissed her lavishly and the group began to drift towards the car. Nola was not yet ready to go home, however, and begged to be taken for a ride on the swings. Yvonne seemed unsure, but after some hesitation she threw a look of inquiry at Uncle George, who responded with a smile and a shrug.

On the way, Nola walked beside Peter. She kept gazing up at him and he took her hand.

'So how old are you, Nola?'

'I'm six and a half and my teacher's Miss Kelsey.'

'And is she nice?'

'Yes, she wears lovely dresses.'

'And she's kind?'

'Yes, but sometimes she says "I'm very cross with you all"'

'Oh well.'

Some boys were playing football in the park and a handful of children were sliding down the chute. But the swings were unoccupied, and Nola ran up to one eagerly and climbed aboard. Peter sat down on the swing beside her and for a short while they propelled themselves to and fro with gentle motion, moving in parallel. Yvonne and Uncle George watched them from a distance, smiling fondly. But when Peter next glanced in their direction he noticed that they'd moved to the far edge of the playground, where they were standing gazing at each other and holding hands. He looked away, mildly

A Canterbury Tale

embarrassed. Their behaviour had an air of secrecy, neither furtive nor quite open, and he felt, as in the car, that he was seeing what he ought not to be seeing.

Nola, going higher with every swing, was starting to show off, so he frowned and wagged a finger. She laughed wickedly, but on seeing his disapproval made a reluctant attempt to restrain herself. He risked another glance at the adults and felt another wave of resentment. He was being used, wasn't he? And what was happening now? His uncle was passing Yvonne something. Was it money? He looked away again. Nola was now standing on the swing, gripping the chains to keep her balance. He told her to sit down. She gave another wanton laugh, jumped off and raced across the playground, where she began to mount the climbing frame.

Secrets, he thought. His, mine.

There was no time to visit the Abbey, of course. After mother and daughter had been dropped off, Uncle George glanced at his watch and shook his head; a sprint around the site would be very unsatisfactory and there was always another day. Peter was secretly glad; he'd seen and heard enough and was feeling rather ruffled. He was now convinced that this trip to Canterbury was a pretext. Indeed, it struck him as characteristic of his uncle, from what he knew of his behaviour, to have planned the whole day for his own convenience. It might have lessened his resentment if the man had confided in him, but to keep him in the dark and offer no explanation was inexcusable.

'Pretty child, but a bit wilful.' Uncle George shot through a set of red lights and narrowly missed a

Festival

pedestrian on a crossing. His handling of the car on the drive back seemed even more erratic than usual, due perhaps to the pressures of the afternoon. 'I call her Topsy.' Another blustering guffaw. 'What's the expression? Touch of the tar brush?'

Peter made no response. There were several minutes of silence. Uncle George kept tapping the steering wheel. 'The thing is, Peter, I married a very silly woman. I was young at the time and thought I was in love. I was in Canada, a young country, at the start of a new phase of my life. I wrote home to my childhood sweetheart. She came out to meet me and we began a life together. It was like a dream. And I can't remember when the dream ended. There was no moment, just a slow fading.'

They drew up behind a long line of cars at a junction; the homeward rush had begun.

'There were others before Yvonne, of course. I won't bore you with the whole list. Some of them were mercenary bitches, but some I loved dearly. And the latest one, the one I loved most, I left behind when we moved back. Broke my heart.'

They crept forward a few more yards and pulled up again, still some way short of the junction. There was another period of silence. Peter kept his eyes on the road and tried to look relaxed, but his ears were burning.

'I met Yvonne at the hairdresser's. I used to wait until Len was free, but he wasn't there that day. So when she called for the next customer, I went and sat in her chair. And I was captivated by her soft hands and gentle fragrance. Decent cut too. So now I just visit her at the flat, never at the shop.'

A Canterbury Tale

The queue started to move again, and this time they managed to reach the junction and turn left. But the traffic was still heavy, so no more was said until they pulled up outside Dolly's place.

'The truth is, Peter, she needs me. She does. She's all alone in this world and she's got that kiddie to bring up. And I do help her. I help her all I can. The father's a brute. A street musician from Trinidad. One of those boys with dreadlocks. But I've never met him. I'm only going on what she's told me.'

Peter, still gazing ahead, was silent.

'Bea knows nothing, of course. She wouldn't understand. She's never understood. So I'm relying on you to be … well, you know …'

Peter, inspecting his fingernails, made no immediate response. Then, turning to his uncle with the ghost of a smile, he gave the faintest of nods.

His uncle returned the nod and bibbed the horn, and shortly Aunt Bea came drifting down the garden path, clutching her bag of knitting and fumbling with the clasp of her cape. On reaching the car she waved to Dolly on the doorstep and climbed onto the back seat. Uncle George bibbed again, and they shot forward with a jerk.

'So what's the news?'

'Oh, she's not too good. Touch of the old trouble, but cheerful as ever. We drank pots of tea and had a good old chinwag. So what about you? What sort of day have you had?'

The men were silent for a moment. Then Uncle George piped up. 'Actually, we've had a fascinating little jaunt, haven't we, Peter?'

Festival

Peter turned to his aunt and nodded. She smiled sweetly.

'Ah well, I'm sure you've been good company for him, Peter. He needs someone to share his little jaunts with. It happens every time we come to Canterbury. He goes off on his own – often for hours – and sometimes I wonder what he gets up to.'

Uncle George made a strange throat-clearing noise. 'Now, don't miss the towers on the left, a medieval replacement of the Roman west gate – rebuilt around 1380 – primarily as an entrance for pilgrims visiting the shrine of Becket in the Cathedral …'

Moving On

The man at the next table was deep in a crossword. Luke, biting into a Danish, glanced at him and instantly snatched his eyes away. Then he sneaked another glance. Unmistakable, surely? The straight nose, the cleft chin, the jutting brow. Yes, it was Jason, without a doubt. But what had happened to that halo of blond hair? Gone. The lot. And in its place a shiny brown dome, flanked by jug-handle ears. The change was huge and shocking.

Luke kept his eyes lowered and hid his disquiet with a sip of coffee. It had been a long time. Seven years, to be exact. The day as clear as yesterday. Jason had come to his room and spoken rather formally. 'You're very young. Still a student. There are guys of your own age all around. Why fixate on me? I may have misled you. It was a great night and I'd like to see you again from time to time. But you must stop phoning me. You must move on.'

Luke had held on to his words for seven years.

Festival

He wondered what to do. He was too flustered to speak and decided to keep his head down. He fumbled in his bag for something to read, but could find nothing but a government guide to tax codes. He thumbed through it slowly, pretending to be engrossed. Perhaps the thing to do was to leave now, briskly and purposefully, before Jason had a chance to lift his eyes from his crossword.

He sneaked another glance. Oh hell! Jason was looking at him, though with a puzzled air of only half-recognition. Well, that was understandable; *he* had changed too. He was no longer a boy. He now wore a suit, worked in a law firm and lived in a smart parkside flat with a long-term lover.

Jason caught his glance and smiled. 'Small bird with Iberian head and weapon in the tail, seven letters,' he mused aloud, looking mildly embarrassed, as if he sensed that he ought to know Luke and was obliged to speak.

Luke, seeing that further pretence was silly, said, 'Oh, Jason, why ask me? You know I was never any good at that sort of thing.'

Jason stared, the smile frozen on his lips. 'Oh my God!' he gasped. 'Luke, I'm so sorry … It's startling … the change … I mean, what happened?'

Luke shrugged. 'Time, I guess. It happens to all of us. Look at you, for instance.'

Jason grinned and passed a hand over his pate. Then, picking up his newspaper, he moved to Luke's table and dropped onto a chair.

'Yeah, well, it's been … how long?'

'Seven years,' said Luke promptly.

'Seven years!' Jason whistled, studying Luke's face

as if staggered at this instant response. 'Well, well. And now, get a load of you. You're looking good. *Amazingly* good. So what have you been doing these past seven years?'

Trying to forget you, Luke wanted to say, but a self-protective wall prevented him. In any case, he was reluctant to plunge in with such a challenging reply. So he smiled and said, 'Ah well, growing up, I guess. Getting on with it.'

'You qualified, of course.'

Luke nodded. 'I'm with Wesley Mitchell now.'

'So a rising young professional.'

'No need to sneer.'

'Hey, I'm not sneering, I'm envious.'

'Oh really? Well, you *have* changed.'

Jason shrugged and fell silent. 'So are you seeing anyone?'

'I live with Patrick. He runs his own business. Financial services.'

'Wow. Financial services.'

'And you? How's the writing?'

'Ah, not good, not good.' Jason massaged his brow. 'I mean, let's face it, no one wants my plays. And I've written nothing – or nothing I like – for a very long time. The truth is I'm not a writer, Luke. I just thought I was.'

'You *are* a writer. I've seen your stuff and it's impressive.'

'Thanks, but …'

It was the first time Jason had confessed to failure, and he wondered if it was seeing Luke again that made him want to open up and admit all the setbacks of the intervening years. He could scarcely believe the change in the lad. The gawky, raw, tongue-tied student had

Festival

been replaced by an engaging young man with attractive looks and a pleasantly confident manner. The soft brown eyes had a frankness, a sympathetic appeal, that seemed to pull you in and break down any lingering reserve. Jason felt himself irresistibly drawn. It was perfectly ridiculous. He was going to fall in love again – and with the boy that he'd spurned seven years ago in an awkward meeting on the first floor of a student hostel.

He felt a stab of guilt. At the time, his response to Luke's attachment – a devotion he'd thought of as pestering, but which had amounted, he now realised, to an unstated declaration of love – had probably been heartless. But then, sometimes, as the saying goes, you have to be cruel to be kind. Still, it bothered him that he'd seen nothing of Luke since the meeting and had more or less put him to the back of his mind, giving little thought to the way the break-up might be troubling him. Was that because he knew he'd acted badly and couldn't bear to think about it? Had he banished Luke, buried him deep, to keep his conscience clear? Well, perhaps. But hell, he'd had problems of his own at the time. Besides struggling with his writing, he'd fallen out with some colleagues at work and become caught up in a tense affair with a married man. So there *were* excuses, and though he might have slightly mishandled the situation, he couldn't quite blame himself.

'So what are you doing, if not writing?'

Jason smiled. 'Still bartending. But not at Chez Louis, of course. As you know, I change my job every six months. It's the only way to keep sane.'

Luke shook his head. 'That's sad, Jason. You're wasting yourself. Are you living with anyone?'

Moving On

Jason chuckled. 'I was living with a guy called Nathan for three years. But then it all fell apart.' He scratched his cheek. 'It was my fault. I started an affair with a fellow barman. It was a casual fling, nothing serious. I just wanted to upset Nathan. I thought we were too settled and needed shaking up.'

'So you shook things up and the sky fell in.'

'Yeah. I blame my self-destructive streak. I didn't allow for his insecurity, did I? Eventually, in revenge, he started an affair of his own, and I came home one night to find him snogging a cute Caribbean lad on the sofa. It was now my turn to get mad and I started jabbing his lover in the shoulder. There was a fight and the police came.' Jason looked away to hide the welling in his eyes. 'Nathan and I broke up a few weeks later.'

He fell silent and stared ahead, chewing the side of his thumb. Luke studied his face. A greatly changed face. More lined and mature, more richly marked with experience. The callow arrogance of youth had gone. And yet ... it was still the same old Jason. The Jason that he'd loved and wanted so desperately, had thought about day and night. The Jason that he'd called one evening after far too many beers and kept on the phone for almost an hour while burbling on shamelessly, brimming with confession and teetering on the brink of self-embarrassment. The Jason that for the past seven years had never been far from his thoughts, that he had never stopped loving, that even now called up a strange fluttering thrill in the centre of his chest.

Jason snapped out of his musing and turned to Luke with a weak smile. 'So now, what about you? Tell me more. Is life good? Who's this Patrick?'

Luke shrugged. 'Life? Well, it's okay. And Patrick?

Festival

He's a sweet guy. We met in the Musée d'Orsay. I love all that impressionist stuff, as you know. I sat down in front of a Renoir and he came and sat beside me. Apparently he'd been dogging me all day, following me from room to room. We chatted, gazed at each other, and after a while he took my hand. Simple as that.'

Jason was staring hard at him, stroking his chin. 'Hmm … and you're happy?'

Luke lowered his eyes. Then he lifted them with a straight look. 'Hey, I'm comfortable, I enjoy my work and I live with a man who worships me.'

'That's not what I asked.'

Luke wriggled. 'Happy? Oh Jason, for Christ's sake, how do *I* know?'

They fell silent, and Luke, frowning slightly, turned his sightless gaze on some people passing in the street; Jason's question had unsettled him. Was he happy? It was not something he'd asked himself recently, or perhaps ever. He'd been too busy getting on with it, to recall his earlier remark. And he resented the sudden, careless intrusion. What right had Jason to come barging back into his life, probing, prying, stirring up discontent. If there was lack, if he was less fulfilled than he might be, then the cause was sitting right here in front of him, thoughtlessly – or deliberately? – relighting the flame on which he'd already burned his fingers. And happiness? What was that, anyway? It was a by-product, a condition seen in retrospect, not something to go for. If you had it, you didn't know you had it, and only not having it made you think about it at all.

Still, the question bugged him. Was he happy? Well, sometimes. But in general? Hm, probably not. Oh God, Patrick was a sweet guy, he'd not lied about that. Mild,

Moving On

loving, considerate, but a bit dull. A workaholic, nervously obsessed with share prices, percentages, sheets of figures, clients. No, there was no denying it, not a bundle of fun. And as for the charge between them – well, what could you say? The buzz when they looked at each other, the feeling when they touched, was so low that it scarcely registered on the scale.

Jason broke into his thoughts. 'Luke, I'm sorry if I hurt you that night and truly sorry we split in that way. I didn't mean to be unkind, please understand that. I didn't mean to crush you, I simply handled it badly. I can be – well, you know – a bit clumsy ...'

'You spoke down to me, Jason. Like my father.'

'Yes, I know. But there was the difference in our ages. You were *very* young at the time and I had a lot on my mind. I was involved with another guy, actually.'

'None of which stopped you tumbling me into bed.'

'Jesus, Luke! ... I've said I'm sorry.'

They lapsed into tight silence. Jason felt a mood of depression descending on his head like a rain-cloud. It was one of those fits that in recent times he'd experienced with increasing frequency The worst of these had come just after the break-up with Nathan, which had coincided, cruelly, with the rejection of his script by the ironically named Serendipity Theatre Company. The greyness that had enveloped him then, the frozen monochrome of the room where he was living, the turning of the key in the lock, the little mound of pills in his palm, the hammering on the door, the bursting in of two policemen in the company of his distraught landlady, were memories that haunted him still. His friends, Tony and Bruce, had rescued him, taking him in for a while and talking through his distress

Festival

until some degree of equilibrium had returned. But his confidence had gone and would he ever get it back? Recently he'd bravely begun a new script, but the going was hard and sometimes he wondered if he had the talent or the will to finish it.

He glanced at Luke, who was studying his fingernails with a look of wounded abstraction, and wondered what was going through his head. He felt another stab of guilt for having treated him so badly. He'd given precious little heed to the pain he'd caused him at the time and then dismissed him from his thoughts. So what sort of brute was he? He was learning something about himself and it was a hard lesson. But perhaps it was not too late to make amends. Did Luke still have the same feelings for him? He thought perhaps he did. It was the way Luke looked at him, his sympathetic manner, his expression of concern. And his feelings for Luke? Well, they had certainly changed. He'd blossomed into such a fine, self-assured young man. And now this chance meeting – it was as if fate had brought them together. There was Patrick, of course, but that was no great obstacle. Patrick was not a passion; he was merely comfortable; it was plain as daylight. On the other hand, the mutual attraction that he now sensed between himself and Luke looked full of promise. Yes, they needed each other, he felt sure of it.

He reached across the table and took Luke's hand. Luke looked up with a wry smile. 'You're right, I did speak down to you. And I repeat, I'm sorry, though I can't recall exactly what I said.'

'Okay, I'll tell you. You said: "I may have misled you. It was a great night and I'd like to see you again. But you must stop phoning me. You must move on."'

Moving On

Jason stared, rigid with astonishment. 'Christ, Luke, that's creepy! It's seven years, for God's sake.'

'I know ... I *told* you how long it was.'

'So you *haven't* moved on.'

Luke flinched and glanced away. Not true. Putting Jason behind him had been an uphill struggle, but he'd come through and made a life for himself. That first week, when he'd lain in bed all day, staring with tense horror at the bottle of pills on the bedside cabinet, had been the worst. But on emerging from his room, he'd been relieved and strangely comforted to find the student life around him going on just as before. Gradually he'd begun to socialise and attend lectures, and in the following term he'd run through perhaps a dozen or more lovers before slowing down. True, the image of Jason had never quite faded. True, he always scanned the papers for any report of a new play. True, he sometimes conjured up Jason when making love to someone else. But year on year the pain had lessened until its rawness had eventually healed. And his new protective skin he sometimes called 'Life with Patrick'.

'It's been hard, Jason. At times, very hard. Do you recall what *I* said that night?'

Jason shrugged. 'Eh ...'

Luke sniggered, flinching with irritation. 'Anyway, I meant it.'

'So what are you saying? That you have the same feelings for me now, seven years later?'

Luke swallowed the dregs of his coffee and looked away. He could feel Jason's eyes burning into him.

'Luke, what can I say? I'm amazed, truly. If I'd known, if I'd only known. I've caused you a lot of pain, I can see that. Can you forgive me?'

Festival

Luke turned again to his fingernails.

Jason shifted. 'Look, I know you're living with this bloke, but perhaps we could meet from time to time? Maybe here, or somewhere else? I'd really like to see you again. I can't believe the change in you. You're looking so ... so *good*.'

Luke smiled wryly and raised an eyebrow. 'And not too young?'

'Oh Luke, please, that's not fair. I'm truly sorry. How many times do I have to say it? The fact is, as you may have gathered, I've had a fit of the glooms for a while now, and right at this moment I'm at a low point. I've no one to talk to, no one to love, and that's why I say I'd like to see you again ... You say – or don't deny – that you have the same feelings for me, and I sense – oh I don't know – that you're not happy. Is that fair? So maybe we need ... can help each other? ... It's not too late, is it, to bring each other a little comfort? To make up for the bad times?'

Luke stared hard at the face before him. At the straight nose, cleft chin and jutting brow, now astoundingly transfigured by the shiny brown dome and jug-handle ears. Stared hard at the face that he'd held in his mind's eye since that painful night, the face that he'd ached to see again. Yes, the tug was still there, and if he stared hard enough he could feel something twisting in the space behind his ribcage.

The lightning strikes just once. Isn't that what they say? And isn't that the dread point? It strikes just once, and never again. It blasts you with galvanic fury and leaves you scorched and wounded for life. Jason had asked if he was happy, and he thought that if happiness was possible the time to seize it had passed. What had been his chances of finding happiness with Jason in any case? And were they any greater now than then? He thought, too, that it was probably a mistake to become involved with a frustrated writer, sensing that he might end up as a cross between a muse and a nurse.

Besides, there was Patrick to think about. No small consideration. Patrick, who was probably at home at this moment, swivelling on the chair in his snug little office, perhaps speaking on the telephone or lifting sheets of data from his printer. Kindly, unsuspecting Patrick. To start seeing Jason now, even on the sly, would be not only wrong but probably fatal. It would put everything in jeopardy. There could be no half measures with Jason – he'd devour you whole, and the likeliest outcome was that it would all end in misery. No, if the tug was still there, it had to be fought.

Reaching across the table, he took Jason's hand. 'Hey, Jason, I'm sorry you've hit a bad patch. And you're right ... my feelings for you ...' He wriggled in confusion, clutching his brow. 'Look, I won't deny them, they're as strong as ever ... But as for happiness, I don't know ... I doubt that we can help each other now, it's too late.'

Jason spread his hands, twisting in anguished disbelief. 'Luke, don't be absurd, it's never too late.' He leaned forward with a look of desperate urgency. 'Look, I'm not asking to run away with you – just to see you from time to time. You can allow that, surely? It would be good for both of us, wouldn't it? Well, good for me, I know that.' He fell back with a snort. 'Christ, Luke, are you going to *tear* it out of me? I *need* you, for God's sake.'

Luke leapt up, though a sudden weakness in the legs

Festival

made him clutch the table to steady himself. His heart was pumping and his eyes had started to prick. His head was a chamber of echoes. *Why fixate on me? You must move on.*

'No, it wouldn't be good for us, Jason. Can't you see that? It's too late. We must put a stop to this now, before it takes a grip.'

But Jason was scarcely listening; he was too busy scrawling something on a scrap of notepaper. 'Look, here's my number, Luke. Don't cut me out of your life, I beg you. Please phone me, *please* …'

Luke, recoiling slightly, made no move to take what was thrust at him. 'Oh, Jason, isn't that what you once asked me not to do?'

Hesitating for a moment, as if sensing a need to say something more, he blinked at the wavering image of his former lover, at the face wide with pleading concern that was swimming before his eyes. Then, with a look of sorrowful regret, knowing that if he stayed a moment longer his resolve would give – that he'd take the number and stow it in his wallet, where it would burn a hole in its clamour for attention – he dashed a hand across his face, turned and hurried into the street.

Jason sat staring through the window for the next forty minutes, watching the sun drop behind the buildings opposite. The street darkened, the lights of evening came on. And when he glanced round, he saw that the place was almost empty, the two other remaining customers preparing to leave. He shivered slightly and pulled up the zip on his jacket. No, he couldn't face going home just now. Not to the dog howling in the next garden, the tread of footsteps overhead, the barren drabness of his room. He'd eat out tonight. Somewhere warm, busy, brightly lit. Perhaps look in at Chez Louis and share a laugh with some of his old mates. Yeah, good plan. He felt slightly cheered. But then a cough at his elbow made him turn. The waitress was smiling. She asked after Luke. He made some excuse, fumbled in his pockets and paid for both of them. Then, with a brave grin, his newspaper tucked under his arm, he strolled out, screwing up the scrap of notepaper and tossing it fiercely into the bin at the entrance.

Festival

A shaft of sunlight broke through a gap in the blind. Tom raised his head from his pillow and glanced about. The place, he thought, resembled a barracks. Men lay all around, sprawled on camp beds, many only half-covered by a blanket and naked to the waist or even lower. Indeed Howard, snoring on his back in the next bed, was almost indecent, his blanket having slipped to the floor, his underpants bulging immodestly. Tom feasted his eyes, then turned away, afraid to be caught leering. He was deeply drawn to Howard, who in his view was hypnotically gorgeous, the best looker in the company.

He rose, dressed and drifted down the corridor to the vast kitchen. Penny and Prue were there, chatting at the sink. They smiled as he came in. The other person in the room, Duncan, was sitting at the old pine table writing with fierce concentration in a thick spiral-bound notebook. He looked up.

Festival

'Morning, Tom. Good to see you, we need to talk. But fetch some breakfast first.'

Tom smiled, took a bowl from the stack and opened the pantry door. The choice of cereals was bewildering. There were eighteen people in the company – actors, technicians, organisers, not to mention hangers-on – and hence many mouths to feed and tastes to cater for. You had to admire Duncan and Penny, whose venture this was. The fulfilment of a dream, apparently.

He shook some cornflakes into a bowl and sat down.

'I've been thinking,' said Duncan. 'That moment when you read the letter. It'd be better if you moved downstage right, so as not to block Penny's entrance.'

'Okay, Duncan. Another late change, but I'll note it on the script.'

'No scripts allowed, Tom. Just keep it in your head. We open tonight, remember.'

'Well, well, you *do* surprise me.'

Duncan grinned and patted Tom's cheek. 'Relax, Tom. We'll try it out this morning before the final run-through.'

Bags of charm, thought Tom, gazing at the boyish face. He liked and respected Duncan – what was his research? Synge? Lorca? – though he was often amused by his driven manner, particularly the way he stalked about on set in baggy jeans and sloppy sweater, his wiry frame twitching, his mobile hands flailing. Still, it was good that he took his role so seriously: being producer, director and manager was no small task, even with the able support of his partner Penny. Were they married? No one seemed to know. Anyway, her soft face and mass of silky brown hair were the perfect complement to her earnest, inquiring manner. A reliable actress too.

Festival

Where had she trained? RADA? Central School? Anyway, her part in the production seemed to come second to playing mother to the whole team.

'When do you want us, Duncan?'

'Ten o'clock on stage. We'll work on the letter scene. Then the final run-through at eleven.'

Tom nodded. There was time for a stroll. So after washing up, he fetched his jacket from the dormitory, the room still vibrant with snores, glanced briefly at Howard, now lying prone, his pants stretched tight over his shapely arse, and stalked out into the sunlit street. But within a few yards the dark outline of the Castle, high on the Rock, brought him to a standstill. It always did. Even now, after three days, he still couldn't quite believe that he was here. He gazed around. Tall buildings everywhere. Dark granite blocks, just as he'd been told.

Someone was running up behind him and he turned.

'Tom!' It was Prue, struggling into a cardigan. 'Where you off?'

'Eh, nowhere special. Just taking a stroll. What about you?'

'Grassmarket. There's a shop there sells everything. I need safety pins, drawing pins and a teapot.'

'A teapot?'

'You know, for the opening scene.'

'But I thought we had one.'

'You haven't heard? Gordon dropped it.'

Prue, the front-of-house manager and general dogsbody, was an amiable chatterbox. She tended to hang around Tom quite a lot and he supposed she had a crush on him. On one memorable occasion she'd doubled up at some feeble joke he'd made as if tickled

Festival

to the point of collapse. She had a toothy smile, a faint northern accent and a habit of constantly flicking her hair out of her eyes. She was always fretting, always on the go, though it was never quite clear where her 'go' went. All her efforts seemed to sink under a welter of fuss. Duncan was always in dispute with her.

'Are we ready, Prue?'

'God, I hope so – Mum, Dad and Auntie Dot are here.'

'How are sales?'

'Hm, not bad. But we need to keep leafletting. Aim for a full house, I say.'

It was too early for the touts, but posters were everywhere and flyers from last night littered the pavement. *Hamlet: A Play for Our Times ... Komedy Klipz will split your sides ... Mary Queen of Scots Revisited ... Carry On, Brezhnev: the new review from Snarling Dog ... Oedipus: A Musical on Roller Skates.*

In Cowgate, a scrap of paper gusted down the road and attached itself to Tom's foot. He peeled it off. 'Oh my God, it's one of ours.'

'What?' blurted Prue. 'Oh, that's *not* on! Tossed aside before we've even opened.'

'Hey, calm down – it's only one and we've handed out hundreds.'

'It's still a damned cheek!'

In Grassmarket she disappeared into a hardware shop and emerged five minutes later holding a bright blue teapot and looking delighted.

'Excellent,' pronounced Tom.

'Gordon should pay for this. He broke the last one.' She squirmed indignantly. 'How d'you get on with him, by the way? A bit arrogant?'

Festival

'Oh yeah – and touchy as hell. But I guess we should make allowances. It's *his* bloody play, after all.'

She turned weak with laughter. 'Oh Tom, you're a caution.'

He walked off briskly. 'Hey, come on, we've got a rehearsal at ten.'

They were amazed to find the hall set out with lines of chairs when they arrived and turned to each other with raised eyebrows. It was a sobering reminder that tonight they would play to a real audience. Penny and Gordon were sitting in the front row and Duncan was pacing up and down, glancing at his watch. He liked punctuality and the company as a whole was rather lax. There was a tendency to drift in ten or fifteen minutes late with a look of having just slid out of bed.

'Any sign of the others?' he asked.

'Hints of movement,' Tom offered.

Duncan sighed.

The next to arrive was Howard, bleary-eyed, his hair ruffled, his jacket buttoned up wrongly. Duncan greeted him with a frown that made him blush. Tom's heart went out to him. He had a soft spot for Howard, a warmth that was only partly due to his looks. He was clearly a sensitive soul, vulnerable to criticism, and Tom was often tempted to put an arm round him.

'Sorry, Duncan. We stayed up late with some bottles of beer.'

'Really? The night before opening.' Duncan threw up his hands. 'Anyway, there's enough of us to make a start, so let's begin. I want to go from Tom's line, "I just don't get it. What are you saying?"'

Tom, Howard and Penny trooped on stage and sat

Festival

around the table. Gordon, rising wearily, followed them and sank into the armchair. He had the lead part in his own play and, at thirty-something, was a little older than the others, though even with make-up it was difficult to make him look convincing as the father of Tom and Howard, a problem he shared with Penny, in her role as the mother. Still, they were strong actors with some professional experience, which partly made up for their lack of wrinkles.

No sooner had they settled than Prue dashed on stage and placed the blue teapot on the table. Gordon, clearly exasperated, threw a despairing look at Duncan and then turned to Prue.

'Is that essential, Prue? We're trying to get on here.'

'Just doing my job, Gordon. Supplying a few props – or rather replacements.'

'Oh, for Christ's sake – it was a bloody accident.'

'No more props, Prue,' called Duncan. 'And can we get on, please.'

Three more members of the company arrived. Mike, the gangling engineer who handled the sound and lighting; Dora, the talkative drama student in charge of costumes and make-up; and André, the breezy stage hand who wallowed in his minor acting role. They sat down in the middle of the third row and tossed their coats aside with a clatter. Duncan hissed 'Shush!' and there was a flutter of suppressed giggling.

The scene began and went tolerably well to the point where the sons were left alone on stage and Howard reached into his back pocket.

'Hold it,' called Duncan. 'Howard, when you pass the letter to Tom, be less casual. It's not a shopping list. It contains information vital to the family.'

Festival

Howard blushed, and Tom, feeling his discomfort, threw a look of reassurance that failed to catch his eye.

'That moment is actually the first climax of the play,' Gordon called from the wings.

'Who's directing here?' muttered Prue, watching from the front row, and Duncan turned and stared hard at her, shaking his head.

'Now, Tom,' he continued, 'when you read the letter, move downstage right, as I suggested. That allows you, Penny, to enter in full view, so as to convey the mother's look of shock.'

They played the scene three times, Duncan responding to their third attempt with a shrug that might have signalled satisfaction or resignation, it was hard to tell. 'Short break for coffee,' he announced, 'then back here for the final run-through.'

Mike immediately glanced at André, flashed a packet of fags and the pair shot outside. The others, however, drifted into the dressing-room where, on a coffee-stained table, a litter of plastic cups and filthy spoons were strewn around a battered kettle with an alarmingly frayed lead.

Duncan approached Tom. 'That move seems much tidier. What d'you think?'

'Yeah, I agree.'

'One thing. Pause a bit longer over the letter and try to show the power of its impact through your frozen posture.'

Tom nodded and Duncan, flashing him a distracted smile, bounced off for a quick word with Gordon. More people were drifting in. Tess and Maeve, who helped with front-of-house duties; Angus, Gordon's brother, who worked alongside Mike in some mysterious

Festival

capacity; Miranda, who would turn up later in the play as the wayward daughter; and finally, Jinny, the prompt. There was also a newcomer: a shy young man in scuffed jeans and a leather jacket, who followed Miranda around like a dog. They wandered from person to person and eventually arrived in front of Tom.

'Tom, I don't think you've met my boyfriend Scott. He's going to stay until the end of the run and sleep in the men's dorm, so I was hoping you'd show him the ropes.' She giggled. 'You know, tuck him up at night.'

Tom blushed. 'No problem,' he murmured.

Scott smiled sumptuously and Tom, staring at his ample lips and gleaming teeth, wondered how he'd contain himself, what with Howard in the next bed and now this added distraction. He tried to find some way to continue the conversation, but suddenly the pair had moved on and Penny was nudging his elbow.

'First-night nerves, Tom?'

'Yeah, I guess so.'

'Me too, but think of them as a necessary spur.'

'I'll try.'

Duncan clapped his hands and cleared his throat, but his call to attention failed to quell the hubbub. He tried again, this time with more success, though Prue and Gordon, locked in some intense dispute, could not be brought to heel. Penny whispered in Tom's ear: 'Don't tell me they're still going on about that bloody teapot.'

Duncan held his tongue until silence fell. 'Hello, everyone. So this is it, our final run-through. But it's there, we've got a play. So keep focused, give it all you can and the audience will love it.'

'Duncan,' Gordon piped up, 'that spat between the boys on page sixteen.'

Festival

'I thought we'd sorted that.'

'I'm not sure that we have.'

'Well, it stands, sorted or otherwise. So take your positions, everyone, please. We begin in three minutes.'

There was a drift back to the auditorium, the noise settled down and Duncan gave the signal to begin. The play began with Penny walking onto an empty stage, and the first spot of bother came immediately, in what seemed a portent of disaster, when the clasp on her skirt broke and she was forced to walk about holding it up. But she went gamely on until Prue came to the rescue with a safety pin.

Then came another upset. Howard, still looking mildly dissipated from the previous night, threw Gordon a wrong cue, with the result that the dialogue shot forward to a later point in the script. Tom glanced at Jinny, who, as prompt, was frantically searching for a seamless way to backtrack. She eventually prompted Gordon, who fixed her with an evil eye, clearly furious at the suggestion that he was unfamiliar with his own play. Tom glanced at Howard, now pink with confusion, flashed him a smile and played calmly on, inwardly amused at the blazing row that he knew would follow.

Fortunately further mishaps were minor and Duncan wrapped up this final session with words of praise and encouragement. 'Well done, everyone! The creases will iron out during the week and the presence of an audience should rouse you to new heights. Now go and enjoy some fresh air, and make sure you're back here in good time.'

Robbie's, the self-service restaurant across the street, was a great favourite with the company. Catering to the

Festival

student population and attracting visitors and performers at Festival time, it provided cheap and filling meals in a cheery plastic setting. Tom, as ever, went for fried haggis, chips and beans, and joined Penny, Prue and Howard at a table by the window.

'Countdown,' said Penny. 'I'm so excited.'

'Yeah, good luck, everyone,' said Tom. 'It's going to be great.'

'But is his lordship happy?' muttered Prue, lifting an eyebrow and glancing across the room at Gordon, who was eating furiously while engaged in a head-to-head with Duncan.

'Too late, just bash on.'

'Be positive, all of you,' said Penny. 'And Prue, stop obsessing about Gordon.'

Prue shrugged and flicked her hair from her eyes.

'Here they come,' said Howard.

Mike, Dora and André, who tended to hang out together, tipped through the door and, spotting the group at Tom's table, stopped for a word on their way to the counter.

'*Courage, mes amis,*' declared André.

Pretentious prat, thought Tom, you're not even French.

'I'm having second thoughts about that shirt, Tom,' said Dora. 'It's a bit dazzling on stage. I'll find you another.'

'I'm not changing now,' Tom insisted.

'No more changes, Dora,' said Penny with a smile.

'Suit yourself,' said Dora. 'Just trying to be helpful.' She wiggled her fingers and the trio passed on.

'After tonight,' said Howard, 'we'll have a little more free time, won't we?'

Festival

'Yes, and I'm looking forward to catching a matinée or a late-night show,' said Penny.

'That Dracula spoof got a glowing review in the Scotsman.'

'And McKellen, I hear, is brilliant as Edward II.'

Howard, dunking his chips in mayonnaise, was tucking into his meal with gusto and Tom, gazing at him, wondered why he found him so captivating. Was it the dusky complexion, the hint of growth on the chin, the slender frame, the soft eyes, the shy manner, or simply the whole package? More to the point, was there a faint chance that the attraction was mutual? Howard had no visible girlfriend, showed no particular interest in women and tended to attach himself to Tom whenever there was a spare moment. Tom wondered how to handle the situation. Should he declare himself? A rebuff would be mortifying. In any case, there was never a time when he had Howard to himself, though he fantasised about such moments.

Duncan rose and stopped at their table on his way out. 'Everyone happy?'

'Very excited,' said Penny.

'I need to get back and speak to Tess and Maeve. We've not decided who's on the door tonight.'

'Are we really free this afternoon, Duncan?'

'Absolutely. Take a well-earned break, all of you.'

He flashed a benign smile round the table and left.

'Well, there's no rest for me,' said Prue, flicking her hair. 'I'll be leafletting and flyposting.'

'Relax, Prue,' smiled Howard. 'We'll lend a hand, won't we, Tom?'

Tom, taken aback, was a bit resentful. He'd been looking forward to a stroll down the Royal Mile. But

Festival

then the thought of spending the afternoon with Howard quickly won him over.

'Of course, glad to help. Tell us the plan, Prue.'

'Oh well, thanks, guys. I thought about starting in New Town and then returning to Princes Street.'

'Okay, so where should we meet?'

But before she could answer, Gordon, whose approach had gone unnoticed, suddenly appeared at their table, looking drawn and grave.

'Howard and Prue, I need to apologise. I was very rude this morning, please forgive me. I know I've been testy lately, but it's *my* play, after all, and I'm understandably anxious for my darling. It's the agony of the artist. It's going to be fine, though, I just know it. So I want to thank all of you for your efforts and wish you the very best of luck tonight.'

The table stared and, without waiting for a response, he turned and walked out.

There were some moments of silence before the group broke into splutters.

'Oh my God, what the hell's got into him?'

'Christ, it's the conversion of Saint Paul.'

They met at two o'clock outside the hostel and as they walked past Waverley Station the sun became oppressively hot. Prue, lugging a ton of leaflets and rolled-up posters in an enormous satchel, kept sighing and mopping her brow with a grubby hanky. Princes Street was seething and there was the usual throng around the Scott Memorial. They watched a juggling monocyclist for a few minutes and caught the closing moments of a limbo dance. A clown was stumping around on tall stilts shouting through a megaphone.

Festival

Prue, expiring, leaned against a set of railings: 'Phew, let's lighten the load.'

She dropped her satchel, produced a wad of leaflets, handed some to Tom and Howard and they spread out.

There were some eager takers, some reluctant accepters and many adamant refusers.

'I've been thrust at a dozen times in the past hundred yards,' blurted a red-faced man, raising a flat palm and marching resolutely on.

A teenage boy took one, stared at it and wandered towards a litter bin.

'Don't you dare!' Prue erupted. 'Take that with you or return it!'

The boy shrugged and stuffed it into his back pocket.

They shed half the load, and then, at Prue's suggestion, crossed the street into New Town. She thought George Street looked promising, so they stood in a stream of shoppers and disposed of another bundle before she came up with a bright idea.

'Let's see if these shops will take a poster.'

The first one they tried was a drapery, where an immaculate lady with a clipped *Airdinburgh* accent studied the poster closely.

'What *kaind* of play is it?'

'A family play,' said Prue.

'Well, I hope it's a *naice* one. You know last year we had the *nehked* fringe.'

'Oh, it's nothing like that.'

There were two more acceptances, but several shops refused on the grounds that they had no more space and the owner of a snack bar was depressingly grouchy. 'I'm not against the Festival, good for business, but it's getting too big. Turns the place upside down. And no

Festival

offense to you young people, but some of the types that come in here.'

This felt like the moment to stop. They were almost out of leaflets and Prue had an arrangement to meet Mum, Dad and Auntie Dot at a hotel in Queen Street.

'Why don't you come?' she suggested. 'How d'you fancy tea and cake in a swanky lounge?'

Tom had been hoping for an hour alone with Howard, a brief interlude in which to test his theory that his feelings were returned. He'd imagined taking a stroll with him in Princes Street Gardens before steering him into a bar. But it seemed it was not to be: Howard was nodding and grinning at Prue's proposal. So, with some hesitation, Tom swallowed his disappointment and forced his face into a smile of consent.

The Lanark was a solid, four-square building with walls of honey-coloured stone. Prue marched in, the boys at her heels, and spoke to the receptionist. Her family, it seemed, were waiting in the lounge. So they crossed the lobby and trouped into a bright room with high windows and plush red furniture. Prue spotted them instantly and went to greet them. They exclaimed and rose to embrace her. Her father, a tall blazered man with a neat military moustache, his greying hair brushed back over a thinning scalp, was brisk and sprightly, but her mother, a large woman in a floral dress, had difficulty getting to her feet, and Auntie, who was wrinkled and frail, stayed in her seat.

'This is Tom and Howard,' said Prue.

'Charles,' said Dad, crushing them in a painful grip. 'Nice to meet you.'

'Myrtle,' said Mum, dangling a plump hand.

Auntie clutched them bonily and looked confused.

Festival

'Dorothy,' she mumbled, as if not quite sure.

They all sat down.

'Nice place,' said Tom, glancing round.

'Oh, splendid,' said Dad. 'Comfortable, central, everything shipshape. We came yesterday and quickly settled in, thanks to Prue who met us at the station.'

Mum beamed at the boys. 'Are you in the play?'

'Yes,' they said together.

'They're awfully good,' said Prue.

Auntie peered at them through thick lenses attached to a loop round her neck and fumbled with her hearing aid.

'Who *are* they?' she asked.

'This is Tom and Howard,' said Prue, speaking slowly and distinctly. 'They're in the play.'

'Which one is the boyfriend?'

'Oh Auntie, *please* – I don't have one.'

'Well, it's about time.'

A young woman in a blue uniform appeared, trundling a trolley with a squeaky wheel. Smiling shyly, she told them to use the bell if they required anything more and left.

'You will stay for tea, won't you?' said Dad, turning to the boys.

Tom looked at Howard, who nodded assent. 'That would be lovely.'

'I'll do it,' said Prue, glancing at Mum, who was again struggling to rise. She poured tea from a large white pot and handed out slices of cherry cake.

'Tell me about the play,' said Auntie. 'I'm not sure I'll hear it.'

'You're in the front row, Auntie.'

'Toe? Whose toe?'

Festival

'Front *row*, dear. You're in the front row.'

'Oh well, I'm not sure that will help.'

Dad, swiftly changing topic, said, 'How are sales?'

'Not bad,' said Prue, 'but I'm hoping for a full house. D'you think the hotel would display some leaflets?'

'Well, there's no harm in asking.'

Mum asked Tom about his role in the play. Had he done much acting? It took nerves to face an audience. She couldn't do it, she'd fall apart.

'The waiting's hard,' he said, 'but on stage you just get on with it.'

'What about sleeping arrangements?' Dad asked.

'Bit of a campsite, but somehow we rub along.'

Suddenly three young people in troubadour costume came bursting through the door and all heads turned. They stood in line and broke into French song. Then they bowed, handed out leaflets and disappeared. Everyone studied the flyer. *Les Compagnons de Chanson. Courtly love in medieval Provence. Parliament Square, 8pm.*

'Too bad,' said Prue 'We're otherwise engaged.'

'More tea, anyone?' said Dad.

'I think we should be getting along,' said Tom. 'Curtain up at eight.'

'You go,' said Prue. 'I'll stay for a bit.'

The boys shook hands with the family.

'Enjoy the play,' said Tom to Auntie, kissing her.

'If I hear it,' she grumbled. Then, drawing him close, she lowered her voice: 'And listen – see if you can find that girl a nice young man.'

On South Bridge, Tom halted in front of a bar. 'A wee dram, Howard? To launch the play? We've got time.'

Festival

'Hm, dunno. What if Duncan spots us? I'm in the doghouse already.'

'Duncan's fretting elsewhere, and a tipple will fuel your performance.'

Howard looked doubtful. He spread his hands. 'Okay, just the one.'

They pushed through the revolving door. The place was packed and they struggled to the bar through a rumble of Scots voices.

'My treat,' said Tom, flashing a tenner. '*I* dragged you in.'

They took their drinks to an empty snug, clinked glasses, then savoured the golden liquid, grinning at the burn in their throats.

'Duncan and Penny are wonderful, aren't they?'

'Fantastic.'

'And you're a fellow student?'

'Yeah, but I don't see them much.'

'So what's your specialism?'

'Marlowe.'

Marlowe, mused Tom. Hm, tobacco and boys. Promising.

He gazed at Howard, captivated again by the lean face, the shadowed jaw, the strands of dark hair, the soft eyes, the shy smile. But none of these, he again decided, was the main draw. It was the entire package, the whole person.

'Well, that's timely – isn't Edward II playing at the Assembly Rooms?'

'That's right. With McKellen. I just hope he tones it down.'

'Tones it down?'

'Oh, you know – the camp.'

Festival

They grinned at each other again, spluttered and dissolved into giggles. It was a bonding – a moment of pure magnetism, of thrilling intimacy. Desire flared up in Tom like a torch. It's now or never, he thought ... and leaning forward in a heedless rush, he pressed his lips to Howard's astonished mouth. He felt a surge of blood and instantly pulled away. Howard coloured up too and they drew apart.

For a while they sat in silence, avoiding each other's eye.

'Sorry,' Tom mumbled.

Howard stared into his glass. An age passed.

'Tom ... I don't know ... I'm not sure ...'

'You don't have to say anything ... I mean ... just leave it ...'

They finished their drinks.

'Time we got back?'

They trailed to the hostel without a word, and in the dormitory Howard began searching for something in his bag.

Tom, grabbing a towel, went for a shower.

The poster for the play, displayed on a stand outside Saint Andrew's Church Hall, was colourful and dramatic. Tom paused to reassess it on his way in. '*Brightness Falls,*' he read. 'A play by Gordon Betmead. A family at war. Guilt, anger, truth laid bare. Tonight at eight and every night this week.' Hm, he mused, bold, eye-catching. He nodded approval and entered the lobby. Tess and Maeve were sitting behind a desk with a cash box, a stack of programmes and a book of cloakroom tickets.

'Hi, Tom. So this is it. Curtain up. Excited?'

Festival

'Terrified. Is everyone here?'

'Pretty well ... except Howard.'

He felt a tremor of alarm. 'Oh well, I guess he'll be along shortly.'

A large board, displaying photos of the actors, stood in the lobby. He strode over to take a look. They were studio portraits, the results quite pleasing. He was glad that he'd chosen to wear his blue chain-stitch for the shoot and regretted that his parents would miss the performance. His dad, a self-employed builder, claimed he couldn't spare the time: 'It's fine for you. All that leave. Teachers don't know they're born. Some of us have to work.' His mum had been keen to come, but was nervous of travelling alone.

He passed through the auditorium to the dressing room. Duncan came towards him and clasped him in a hug. 'Best of luck, Tom. A bloke from the Scotsman is coming tonight, but don't give it a moment's thought. Just focus on the play. It'll be fine.'

Penny, dressed for the play, was sitting in a corner, hands clasped in her lap. Tom sat down beside her. She turned and smiled. 'Hi, Tom. I'm composing myself. You know, with deep breaths. It's the only way. A Scotch, in my view, does *not* improve performance.'

Tom gulped. 'Oh, absolutely.' He glanced around. 'Any sign of Howard?'

'No, I hope he's okay.'

'Oh, I'm sure he's fine.'

Gordon, also dressed for the play, was sitting in another corner staring ahead with a glazed look. Tom, throwing him a smile, got a blank reply.

Dora, chatting incessantly, was applying make-up to André, the pair as giggly as ever. Tom started to dress

Festival

for the play in a dither. He thought he should go and look for Howard, but he could hardly go in his stage costume, and anyway he needed to sit and compose himself like the others. So he finished dressing and had just taken a seat when Prue appeared from behind a side curtain. Her face was white and she sat down beside him, flapping a hand in front of her face.

'Oh, Tom, I've just had the fright of my life.'

'Why, whatever's happened?'

'Well, I was checking the props – you know, in that wooden trunk at the back of the stage – when a mouse jumped out.'

'A mouse? Good grief! I thought you'd seen a dead body at least.'

'I don't like mice, Tom – they give me the willies.'

'Oh, for God's sake, Prue, they're completely harmless. It's just a daft phobia.'

'I don't care *what* it is – I don't like them.'

'Ah, come on, let's go and find it. You can hold it and tickle its tummy.'

'Oh, Tom, *please.*'

Duncan appeared beside them. 'Everything okay, Prue?' He studied her closely.

She frowned. 'Well …'

'Actually, she's a bit shaken,' said Tom. 'She saw a mouse.'

'A mouse? Well, that's the least of my concerns. Has anyone seen Howard?'

Tom swallowed hard. 'He was with me an hour ago. We'd been leafletting with Prue. I went for a shower and haven't seen him since.'

Duncan shook his head and shuddered. 'Well, if he's not here soon, we'd better start looking for a stand-in.'

Festival

'A stand-in? Do we have one?'

Duncan chuckled grimly. 'Well, there's always the bloody mouse, I suppose.'

He strode off. Then Maeve flew in from the lobby. She made straight for Prue in a flap. 'Oh, Prue, can you come, please. There are problems at the desk.'

'Like what?'

'Well, the man from the Scotsman is here asking if we can reserve him a seat at the end of a row.'

'So that he can slip away after ten minutes? Is that his plan?'

'Oh God, I don't know, do I?'

'Okay, so what else?'

'Well, then there's a man asking if his mother will have to pay if she sits beside him in a wheelchair.'

'Of course she will. It's not a bloody charity show, is it?'

'That's what I said, but he's still arguing. There's also a weird couple asking about strong language in the play.'

'Okay, let's go.'

Prue disappeared with Maeve. Tom folded his arms and closed his eyes. He needed to compose himself. But how? He was squirming with guilt. Surely he was to blame for Howard's absence. He'd thrown the poor bloke into confusion. He'd coaxed him into a bar, pressed him to an unwanted Scotch and then made a clumsy pass. What a damned stupid thing to do! It was unforgivable. Especially just before a performance. He clenched his fists, filled his chest with air and, trying to focus on his opening lines, fell into a trance.

Minutes later he came out of it to find himself gazing across the room at Howard, who was changing into his

Festival

costume beside a row of wall-pegs. Oh, the relief! It flooded over him, and as he watched him loosen his belt, slip his shirt over his head and modestly slide out of his jeans, he thought he'd never looked so beautiful. Indeed, the sight was so captivating that for a while he simply drank it in, his joy gushing over into a kind of love. Then he sprang up, crossed the room and stood over him as he tied a shoelace.

'Howard, are you okay?'

Howard looked up with a smile. 'I'm fine.'

'Howard, I'm so sorry ... honestly ... I don't know what ...'

'There's no need, Tom, I'm fine. I just ... well, you know ... didn't realise.'

Duncan appeared beside them. 'Are you *trying* to alarm us, Howard? I mean, what the hell's going on? Sabotage?'

'Please don't blame Howard,' Tom cut in. 'It's my fault.'

Duncan looked exasperated. 'Okay, Tom – so would you care to explain?'

'Oh God, I dunno. It's like ... well ... a long story.'

Duncan threw up his hands. 'In that case, save it. We don't have time. About fifteen minutes to be exact!'

He turned and stalked off.

Howard smiled sheepishly. 'Thanks, Tom.'

Dora appeared. 'Touch of make-up, you two.'

'Do we have time?'

'Of course – you're not on at the start.'

'Okay, if you say so.'

She led them to a stool before a mirror and Tom went first. She took a sponge, ran it over his face, brushed his cheeks and applied a liner to his lips and brows.

Festival

'Oh God, I look like Ivor Novello.'

'Stop fretting! You'll look perfectly natural on stage.' She patted his head. 'Now you, Howard.'

A low rumble of voices came from the auditorium. Tom climbed into the wings. Penny was there, walking up and down. Tom took her hand and squeezed it. She flashed him a fleeting smile. He peered around the curtain. The place was filling up to a surge of noise and bustle. He spotted Prue helping her family to their seats in the front row. Auntie, clutching her handbag, was fumbling with her hearing aid, and Prue, fussing around her, was trying to get her to settle.

Someone poked Tom in the side. It was Howard. Tom put a finger to his lips and pointed to the faces in the front row. Howard peered over his shoulder and grinned. Then he pressed his mouth to Tom's ear. 'Good luck,' he breathed, and Tom, flushing in the darkness, felt his heart flutter. If I've thrown you into confusion, he thought, you show no sign of keeping your distance.

Duncan arrived, closely followed by Gordon, Prue and Dora. 'On your marks, everyone. We're off.'

The lights dimmed, the audience fell silent, and Penny walked onto the empty stage after a signal from Prue. She had a few moments of hand-wringing before being joined by Gordon. Their confrontation, lasting about twenty minutes, was so well rehearsed that Tom and Howard, waiting in the wings for their cue, found themselves listening to lines they could recite in their sleep.

Tom recalled his remark that the worst part acting was the waiting, and sure enough, he felt a kind of prickly sensation running all the way from his feet to his scalp. He supposed Howard must be feeling the same

Festival

and was tempted to take his hand, but instead stood perfectly still gazing ahead.

The performance went well until André, in his role as family solicitor, had trouble with the catch on his suitcase. He wrenched it, injured his thumb and faltered over his next lines. Fortunately Jinny came to his aid with some deft prompting. Then, shortly after this, Prue, hovering in the wings beside Tom, gave a tiny shriek. She clapped a hand to her mouth and pointed to the floor. 'Oh my God!' she gasped. 'It's back!' He followed her finger, spotted the mouse and made a grab. But it got away, scuttled across the stage and disappeared on the far side. A titter ran through the audience.

But there were no further disturbances, and after taking a bow they retired to the dressing room to congratulate themselves with hugs and kisses.

'Splendid!' declared Duncan, cracking open a bottle of champagne. 'Some ironing out to do, but we'll tackle that tomorrow.'

Tom, facing Howard with a shy grin, hesitated. Should he risk a hug? Would it throw him again? He was anxious not to compound his earlier blunder. To his amazement, however, he was spared any possible embarrassment when Howard stepped forward, wrapped him in a tight embrace and planted a faint kiss on the nape of his neck. Indeed, he was so surprised and thrilled that he felt a stab of resentment when they were interrupted by Prue, who turned up to say that her family were waiting in the auditorium and would love to have a word. They broke apart and followed her to the front row, where Mum and Dad pumped their hands and Auntie offered a cheek.

Festival

'Did you hear it, Auntie?' asked Tom.

'Hear it? I had to lower the volume. What a quarrelsome bunch! I'd knock their heads together. And that daughter's a sly little minx.'

'Well done,' said Dad. 'Strong performances from you boys, and also from the leading couple. You say he wrote the play, Prue?'

'Yeah ... the cocky pillock!'

'Language, Prue, please.'

She arranged to meet them the following day and with a final hug they departed. Back in the dressing room, Miranda, who was as fiery off stage as on, was in dispute with Dora about her costume.

'Look, I just don't feel good in it.'

'So why didn't you say before?'

'I did, if you recall.'

'So what's wrong with it?'

'It's drab! ... I mean, she's just back from Paris, the city of *chic*.'

Duncan clapped his hands. 'Don't forget to tidy up, everyone. There's a show playing here tonight in just twenty minutes and the players will be using this room, so please leave it as you'd wish to find it. Oh, and it's a snappy production, I'm told, so some of you might like to support them.'

Howard turned to Tom. 'Hey, I'm up for that. How about you?'

'Yeah, why not.'

They hung about and, finding that many of the others, including Duncan, Penny, Prue, Mike and Maeve, intended to go, they joined them in the queue for tickets. But there were only a few left, so they all sat together on the back row for what turned out to be a

Festival

fiercely topical review – an hour of sharp comment on Vietnam, Woodstock, the Troubles and much else, in which satire was mixed with poignancy. 'Where are the songs of yesteryear?' sang a plaintive young woman, with allusion to the Paris riots and the suppression of the Prague Spring.

At midnight they trailed back to the hostel in a straggle, discussing the show in a buzz of excitement, everyone fired up by it. But on arrival, there was a flurry of goodnights as the group, with flagging energy at the end of such a long day, dispersed to the dormitories.

'Actually, I'm hungry,' said Tom to Howard. 'Could do with a slice of toast and a mug of tea. How about you?'

Howard shrugged and smiled. 'Well, now you come to mention it.'

There was no one in the kitchen. They made tea in a big brown pot, slapped a couple of rounds in the toaster, plunged knives into a jar of marmalade and chomped away, facing each other across the table. Whoops of laughter sounded in the street. Tom, fluttering with fear of messing up again, felt a return of that now-or-never feeling.

'Howard ... about this afternoon ...'

'Forget it, Tom ...'

'I panicked when you were late ... thought you mightn't show ...'

'As I say, I didn't realise. I'm a bit slow. Sometimes I wonder if I realise anything. I mean, what do *I* know? You took me by surprise.'

'Yeah ... threw you into turmoil ... almost sank the play.'

Festival

'I was confused, Tom. Until that moment there was just you and me, and I'd never really put us together. I lay on the bed in the dormitory … wrestling with … well, you know … just everything.'

Tom put down his toast. 'Everything?'

'Feelings … feelings I'd been afraid to recognise … that you'd stirred in me … feelings that I see now have been there all along.'

They fell silent. More noisy revellers passed in the street. Tom fixed his eyes on Howard, scanning his face. 'So where are you now?'

'Oh God, not sure. Still coming to terms, I guess. Give me time.'

'Of course.'

Tom reached across the table and took Howard's hand. He squeezed it gently, then withdrew. There was a long pause. He finished his toast, poured more tea and groped for a way to proceed with delicacy.

'Howard … am I … I mean … have you ever …?'

'There's never been anyone, Tom.'

They sat for a long while, staring into their mugs, until interrupted by André, who drifted in, raised a hand in greeting and took a gulp from a carton in the fridge. Tom waited for him to leave, then took Howard's hand again.

'Hey, it's a beautiful night out there.'

'Fabulous.'

'Shall we go and take a look?'

Howard nodded and Tom, hauling him to his feet, led him down the passage to the back door. Outside, still holding onto each other, they climbed the metal staircase on the rear of the building and sat on the highest step gazing over the rooftops. The city, wrapped

Festival

in an orange glow, sent up a dull roar, and pale stars, lost in a fleet of ghostly clouds, drifted around a crescent moon.

'What a thrill, Howard! ... I mean, Edinburgh ... just being here at this time.'

'Amazing ... I'll never forget it.'

Tom felt an aching desire. Dare he ...? He recalled his blunder in the bar ... Still, the situation was different now ... Howard had admitted to feelings ... he just needed time ... The problem was they didn't *have* much time. A week? Delay could be as fatal as haste ... Still, for the moment ...

'We should get some sleep. Another day tomorrow.'

'It *is* tomorrow.'

'Great start, though.'

'Yeah, brilliant.'

In the passage they glimpsed Prue in the bathroom brushing her teeth. She spotted them in the mirror as they drifted past and called out.

'Hey, Tom, I meant to say, we need to catch that mouse, don't we?'

'Oh, for God's sake, Prue, not *now*. Give it a break, lovie.'

They entered the dormitory, which shook with snores, groped through pitch darkness to their beds and began to undress. Tom, sensing the raw nearness of Howard, felt an overpowering urge to embrace him again, but instead folded his shirt and jeans and slipped them under the bed. Then, squeezing Howard's arm, he whispered goodnight, climbed in and lay staring upward.

A great day with a feeble ending. He regretted holding back. His courage had failed. Howard was on

Festival

the brink; a nudge would do it. The desire was there; had been there all along. They needed each other; were meant for each other. Time was short; they were both aroused. He should have seized the moment; it might not come again ...

He twisted in torment, groaned softly.

Then a rustle beside the bed made him turn. A presence was hovering, sliding in beside him, drawing him close. He felt a waft of breath on his cheek, then lips pressed to his ear in the softest of whispers.

'Tom, go gently, please ... I don't know anything.'

Chance

Stephen consoled himself that it was early, that there was still time for the place to fill up. Yet even if it did, what was the use? It was unlikely to fill up with people he wanted to meet. So what was he doing here on the so-called English Riviera? Indeed, why was he touring the West Country in a worn-out Morris Minor that might not survive the trip? Why hadn't he taken a flight to Paris, Berlin or Amsterdam? Well, he knew why. It was on a whim – a fleeting rush of oh-to-be-in-England that had surged through him on the first day of his holiday, sparked by a glimpse of April sunlight on dazzling forsythia. But a few hours later, on the painful crawl out of London, his mood had sunk as low as the fuel gauge. Under sagging clouds, the wipers struggling heroically with the cascading windscreen, his enthusiasm for this trip had sluiced clean away.

Still, dry roads had appeared in Dorset, followed by patches of blue. Since when the sun had shone, with just

Festival

the occasional threat of a shower. So if he now had a sense of having chosen badly, it was not entirely the fault of the weather. Rather, it was down to lack of company. These coastal towns of south Devon were charming and pleasant to wander in, but full of families and married couples. In short, not his scene. He was already missing the adventure of abroad, the colour and excitement of cities, the thrill of the chase.

His thoughts turned to Bernardo. He saw him in the restaurant rolling pastry, travelling home on the tube, in the bedsit watching television, and wondered how he was coping. He felt a pang of sympathy, but had no regrets. It was better like this. In the long run they'd survive; they were made of strong stuff.

He glanced up. The people in the bar were mostly in pairs or groups. There was just one other person sitting alone, though his table was some distance away on the far side of the room. He had a half-empty glass in front of him, but in the dimness it was difficult to discern much about him except his slim figure and tousled hair. Smoke drifted up from his fingers and the end of his cigarette flared slightly whenever it rose to his lips.

Shortly, however, he drained his glass and moved to the bar. Seeing his chance, Stephen followed. They bought drinks, leaned on the rail and nodded to each other. The man, who looked in his late twenties, had a lean, angular face, a covering of dark stubble and a gold ring in his left ear.

'Fine stretch of coast, this,' he said.

'Delightful,' said Stephen. 'You from round here?'

'Nah, Bristol. Down on a job. I'm a chippy. Done now, travelling back tonight. How about you?'

'Oh, just kicking around, taking a spring break,

Chance

fleeing the clamour of London. It was a toss-up, go north or west. So I flicked a coin and guess which won.'

'What, on yer tod, are ya?'

'Yeah, that's the problem – I do a lot of talking to myself.'

'Well, bring your glass – my table's over here. It's Martin, by the way.'

He was deep-voiced, strong and compact, a hard nugget of energy, with a sudden laugh, sharp eyes and a quick apprehension of life. He spoke in a large, warm, generous way, with nothing mean or finicky about him, words shooting straight from his core without hesitation or fuss. Stephen, entranced, stumbled along in response, trying to match his vigour, but mesmerised into awkwardness. He felt excited, apprehensive, obscurely drawn, yet conscious of hidden dangers. What did he and this bloke know of each other beyond the male codes of friendship they displayed, the social customs they performed? What lay beneath the camaraderie? When would they strike a hard patch?

Stephen never lied about himself. Until recently he'd spoken openly of his love for Bernardo. But that was over. He had no ties now, and didn't want to suggest that he had. Nor did he want to be too direct for fear of rejection. He decided to parry any probing and keep his companion guessing. He was likely to gain more under cover. With a mask, they might reveal themselves.

The probing never came, however. Instead, they veered off the highway onto a side road. 'I'm looking into my family history. Ever looked into yours?'

'No,' grinned Stephen sheepishly, as if ashamed of his neglect. 'Well, not deeply – you never know what you might turn up.'

Festival

'My father was Polish. He fought the Germans in 1939 at the fall of Warsaw. He then went underground and escaped to France. I've been reading his diary. He went through hell. Never really recovered. He was always slightly screwy. After the war he settled in Gloucestershire and worked on the land. He met my mother at a dance in Stroud.'

Stephen nodded, his eyes fixed on Martin. 'Mm, diaries are fascinating. We should all keep one.'

They got onto books. Martin was not a natural reader, but some years earlier he'd picked up a tattered copy of *Animal Farm* at a market stall in Taunton and had devoured it in a single sitting. Since then, he'd always had something on the boil. He was now several chapters into a spy thriller. Stephen confessed to liking all kinds of stuff, but was currently working his way through the novels of Paul Bowles, a name that clearly meant nothing to Martin. Still, in general, they accorded more in their reading than in their listening. Martin loved rock, Stephen swooned to soul and the soupier bits of Rachmaninov.

They bought each other drinks, and returned to the fall of Warsaw, the perils of occupied France and the value of keeping a diary. Stephen felt easy with Martin, though not entirely easy. He had decided to parry personal questions, but was bothered by their absence. Paradoxically, he wanted them to arrive, so that he could see them off. And what about his companion? The man was a mystery. Why, beyond mention of his Polish origins, had he said so little about himself?

'Last orders!'

They looked around in surprise. In their absorption they'd not noticed the approach of closing time. Martin declined the offer of another pint; he'd not intended to stay and had to drive back to Bristol. Stephen, now warm with conviviality and the stirrings of desire, felt a sense of let-down; the evening was going to end abruptly, in sudden farewell. He wondered whether to pass Martin his phone number. But would that be too obvious?

They drained their glasses in a single gulp, made for the door and hung back. Rain from a heavy shower was bouncing off the pavement.

'So where are you staying?'

'Oh, five minutes away. In a guesthouse on the seafront. I looked in here after a walk.'

'The van's round the corner – I'll drop you off.'

'Oh well, thanks – if it's no problem.'

Pulling their jackets over their heads, they sprinted through puddles. The van smelled of timber, sacking and oily rags. The passenger seat had a deep rip in it and the engine sounded clogged. Still, they shot out of the car park with alarming speed. So alarming that Stephen gasped and gripped the seat belt. But Martin's handling of the vehicle quickly restored confidence, and on the road he turned to Stephen with a grin. 'No need to whiten your knuckles – I know all the tricks of this old bus.'

Stephen chuckled and a few minutes later pointed to a three-storey building with a trim garden and bay windows. 'That's the place – the one with the Morris Minor in the drive.'

Martin drew up in the parking bay across the road, the nose of his van facing the winking lights and moored boats of the harbour. Strollers on the quay were struggling to control their umbrellas, tall-masted ships were rocking slightly, the moon was casting a wake of broken light across the choppy waves.

'So that's the plan? Seriously? Drive back to Bristol tonight?'

'The roads are much quieter at night. I'll be home in two hours.'

'Ah well, your choice. Anyway, take care. It's been good to meet you and thanks for the company.'

Smiling bravely, Stephen reached out to shake Martin's hand. But as he did so, he felt something brush the back of his neck. And only then did he realise that Martin's arm had been resting, possibly for some time, on the back of his seat, holding him round the shoulders in a loose embrace.

It was a double, after all. And if there were any rules about guests, he hadn't seen any. But as they crept up the stairs, he wondered what to say if they were spotted. Ah well, too late to ponder that now, but typical of him to plunge in. Would some plausible explanation arise? Or, imagining the worst that could happen, would they be both be evicted after an embarrassing fracas?

Fortunately they met no one.

In the room they stood facing each other, then fell into a light hug. The first kiss was tentative, but quickly turned into something more urgent. Stephen was keen to slow the action and let the sap rise, but it was difficult to restrain Martin, who seemed bursting with pent-up lust. He fumbled with the buttons of Stephen's shirt, slid his hands beneath his belt and drew him close, kneading his buttocks. He slobbered his ear, bit his lobe, nuzzled his neck. Then suddenly he broke away, flung his boots across the room and began to tear his clothes off.

Chance

Stephen let his jeans fall to the floor. Martin dropped to his knees and, bearing a rod before him like a flagpole, shuffled across the floor to bury his face in the hollow of Stephen's belly.

In bed there was some initial awkwardness. They were both nervous, unsure how to handle each other. Stephen tried to steady the headlong rush; he wanted to enjoy the Martin's strength, play with his chest hair, savour his reek, but the man was a dynamo of restless energy. Eventually they fell into step, found a pace, a style, a rhythm, and after changing roles a few times built to an explosive climax. Then they kissed, lay back exhausted, and minutes later Martin was snoring in convulsive spurts. Stephen lay awake, however. He thought how much he'd like to do this again, to wake up every morning with this smouldering hunk beside him.

Then, as if conjured by the thought, it *was* morning. Daylight suffused the rectangle of the window and dimly lit the furniture in the room. Stephen recalled where he was and glanced at the other side of the bed. Empty! He went to the window and peered through a crack in the curtains. The van was no longer in the parking bay. He stared in shock. It was a blow to the stomach. He felt suddenly weak and hollow, as if everything had dropped out of him. He returned to bed and lay gazing at the ceiling. To leave without saying goodbye? A heavy gloom descended on him. The holiday was over. It was all downhill now. To prolong the trip, doggedly seeking pleasure, was pointless. Any company he found was bound to disappoint. Better to go home and seek the solace of friends. He lay there for a long time, and when at last he rose he was almost too late for breakfast. In any case he didn't feel much like

Festival

eating. He took a mouthful of scrambled egg and then gave up, though he did manage to raise a weak smile for the concerned couple who kept beaming at him from the next table.

Settling back into work the following week was harder than ever. He was restless and distracted to a degree that drew comments from nearly everyone. The office seemed to him the most insufferable place on earth and Karen's prattle in the tearoom drove him almost insane. In the evenings he had no interest in going out and sat slumped before the television watching programmes that made his eyes droop. He wondered if he'd come out of it or spiral down into depression and illness.

On Thursday evening, in desperation, he called Bernardo.

'Hello, who's calling?' said a voice he didn't recognise.

'Eh … it's Stephen … Is that …?'

'Bernie? You want Bernie? Hold on.'

A long pause.

'Hi, Stephen.' Bernardo sounded breathless. 'So how was the trip?'

'The trip? … Oh, fine … Am I interrupting?'

'Well, I've got Khalid here, but it's not a problem.'

Stephen scratched his nose. 'Yeah, okay … I'll call later.'

He rang off and for ten minutes sat staring at the wall.

At the weekend he went shopping and called at the library. He scanned the shelves, found the section he was looking for and shrank at the daunting range of choice. He flicked through a couple of fat volumes, but thought they might rip a hole in his bag. Finally he settled for a slim paperback, called simply *A Brief History of Poland*. It was worlds away from the sort of thing he normally read, but he took it home and glanced through it that evening. Skipping the early chapters, he went straight to the twentieth century. The concise account of the German invasion of 1939 was dry but fascinating, and from the bare facts he tried to imagine the life of a Polish soldier at this time, facing the vastly superior forces of the invading army, then fleeing and hiding from the enemy in war-torn Europe.

At the same time, he began to take an interest in the little Polish delicatessen that he passed every day on his way to work. At first he did no more than peer through the window, but then one day he dropped in and lingered for a while, casting an eye over the shelves, inspecting the goods, sniffing the spices. A short, grey-haired man in a striped apron was slicing some cured meat at the counter and speaking to a customer in Polish. He smiled at Stephen and invited him to sample some pork pâté. Stephen accepted, nodded his approval and bought a jar. Then, a few days later, he looked in again, and before long he'd become a regular, trying out new things at every visit, filling his larder with jars of pickled gherkins, red cabbage and beetroot, and sometimes taking home a Polish pastry to have with his coffee. He loved the way the owner and his wife greeted him every time as an old friend, as almost a member of the family, inquiring about his life, listening with interest, remembering the stories he told them.

He presumed his memories of Martin would fade, but three months later they were stronger than ever.

Festival

Sometimes he thought he glimpsed him in the street, or found himself staring at someone in a shop or café, someone with a passing resemblance. I'm going off my head, he thought; I need a change, a complete change. I hate my home, my work, my pointlessness. I've got to abandon this life; it's tedious and futile, and only *he* can save me. If I could just phone him now and invite him out for a drink.

On his next visit to the library he went straight to the desk. The assistant smiled.

'Which area?' she asked.

'Bristol,' he said.

She brought a tome and he took it away to a table. There was a section listing carpenters and joiners. He studied the entries. There was one for Wozniac, Martin. He stared at it for a while, then wrote the number on a slip of paper. It was crazy, the wildest shot, but the find lifted his spirits, and as he trailed home, past tireless footballers in the park, buskers in shop doorways and news vendors yelling on street corners, he felt buoyed by an absurd flush of hope.

A few days later, on a Wednesday night, he lifted the receiver and dialled.

'Hello.'

The voice was distorted, but still unmistakable.

'Martin?'

'Yeah ... who's that?'

'It's Stephen.'

No response. And the silence was unnerving, dispiriting.

'Brixham? ... Sunnyside Guesthouse?'

Still no response. It was clearly *him*. So was he genuinely dumbfounded or just being canny?

Chance

'Martin, I've tried to forget you, but I can't ... Why did you leave like that? ... Martin, it hurts ...'

A shuffling noise. Then a brisk retort, dry and formal: 'Look, I'm busy at the moment, but what's the number? I'll call you back.'

When the call came three days later, Stephen was taking a shower. He heard the phone ring, tore out of the cubicle, grabbed a towel and ran dripping into the sitting room.

The voice, low, edgy, conspiratorial, started without introduction: 'Can't speak for long, but what are you doing this Friday? I'm coming to London.'

Stephen paused, then gave a bemused snigger. 'Friday? ... Hm ... I guess I'm off sick.'

They met for coffee at a place in Soho. It was frantically busy and noisy, the sharp clatter of crockery punctuated by alarming blasts from a pair of tireless espresso machines. A keen young barman was snatching up mugs from glaring customers who were still drinking, while a huddle of lively youngsters at a central table, looking as if they'd bunked off school, were babbling inanely to a chorus of whoops. Further off, at a table near the window, an elderly Japanese couple, shaking their heads in doleful confusion, were poring over a tourist map.

Martin was in his work gear and kept glancing about. He looked awkward and out of place. Reaching across the table, he squeezed Stephen's hand, then paused as if uncertain how to begin. 'Hey, it's good to see you again.'

Stephen raised an eyebrow and fixed him with a long hard look. 'If only by merest chance.'

Festival

Martin looked stung. 'The thing is, I'm not a free agent, am I?'

'Martin, I know nothing about you. What *is* this?'

Martin sat back and stared out of the window.

'Okay.' His fingers drummed the table and it was several minutes before he spoke. 'So I married Beth ten years ago, didn't I? When we were still kids. We'd known each other for ever, it seemed, so why not?' He paused and took a sip of coffee. 'We have kids of our own now. Jonathan, nine, Katie, six.'

'And you love her?'

'In my way.'

'And what about me? Why are you here?'

'I had to see you. I've thought about you a lot. Every day, in fact. I wish I could get you out of my mind, but I can't. It feels wrong, this. Very wrong. It's not fair to you or her. Sometimes I think I'll go mad.'

Stephen chuckled wryly. 'Oh well, that makes a pair of us.'

There was no one about as they climbed the stairs to Stephen's flat. Martin lifted a box of crackers from the coffee table, a box with a Polish label, and examined it with a smile. But they were too hungry for further talk and almost immediately they fell together in a crushing embrace and devoured each other with wet mouths. Martin pulled Stephen towards the bedroom, but Stephen steered him onto the sofa and lowered the blinds. The insistent afternoon sun, trying to spy on them, striped their bodies black and gold. They ended up sprawled on the sheepskin rug that Stephen had bought from a stall in Camden, their limbs entwined like carvings on a Hindu temple.

Chance

Martin reached for his watch. 'I must go ... or miss the six-fifteen.'

'You came by train?'

'I had to. I don't know London, do I? The van's in Bristol, parked in a side street.'

'What have you told Beth?'

'She thinks I'm at work.'

At Paddington, with just minutes to go before departure, the train was filling up. They hung about on the platform, not knowing what to say.

'So what next?' said Stephen.

'I'll call,' said Martin. 'Well, you know ... whenever I can.'

Stephen nodded and looked away. His bottom lip was trembling. Life was cruel. Hitherto he'd known nothing but casual affairs, and now, within sight of real happiness, it was about to be snatched from him. He'd fallen for someone seriously, only to be forced into a world of coded messages and secret meetings. The situation was hellish, and he wondered how long he could endure it. This thing was unlikely to end soon. It might last for years. Might never end. Still, he had to endure it, there was no alternative.

The guardsman blew his whistle. Martin kissed Stephen briefly on the cheek and leapt aboard. Stephen watched him settle into a seat and waved as the train slid away. Martin responded with a smile, though his face was anxious, his gaze turned inward. It's as hard for him as for me, Stephen thought. Is there no way out? Perhaps if the situation becomes intolerable, it will find its own solution. We'll stop seeing each other or he'll break away. I can't see how we could settle for

Festival

something in-between. But is there a chance, the smallest chance, that we'll come through it, all of us, to a new and better life?

But that, even if imaginable, was surely a long way off, and with dwindling hope he watched the train shrink to a spot on the line.

Balloon

Jake watched Ivan picking flakes of dry skin from the soles of his feet. The room was stuffy and fetid. Ivan, stripped to the waist, was squatting on a filthy mattress on the floor, his skinny white body hard, wiry and hairless. He glanced up and smiled, as if he sensed he was being studied. Jake, in sudden confusion, flicked his eyes back to the TV. The three contestants in the game show were being quizzed by a smarmy host with gleaming teeth and a dead cat on his head.

Apart from the mattress, the TV and a few sticks of furniture, the room was bare. There were patches of damp on the walls and a naked light bulb hung from the ceiling. It was temporary, according to Tony. He'd find them a better place soon. But that was more than a week ago. Besides, he'd not paid them yet. Oh, he'd slipped them a few tenners now and again, but that was hardly payment for a week's work. He'd pay them properly when the legal arrangements were sorted. Oh yeah? Tony was about as legal as the Great Train Robbery. A

Festival

crook, a wheeler, a scumbag. They'd known that from the start. But then, in this life you take what comes.

Two-thirty. The windows were grimy, but Jake could just make out that it was a fine afternoon, the sun blazing in a clear blue sky. Watching TV was no way to spend their day off. He lifted the last bottle of beer and threw Ivan a questioning look. Ivan nodded and Jake refilled the polystyrene cups. Ivan rarely spoke, and when he did he never said much. Was it just the language problem, or were Ukrainians naturally reserved? Still, he was a gentle, good-natured soul with a smile that made the back of your neck tingle. But his attraction was strongest at night. They had to share the mattress and an old grubby quilt, and when their bodies touched it was a painful struggle to resist the warmth of his limbs.

Jake sometimes thought that Ivan was the only reason to stay. It was a mug's game, this. Early morning starts, backbreaking hours in the field, and little sign of getting paid. He was sick, too, of the smell and taste of strawberries and had stopped gorging on them. In this fine summer weather it was tempting to return to the streets. To a blanket, an upturned hat and a tin whistle.

'Fancy a walk, Ivan?'

'Walk?'

'To the shop. We need more beer.'

'We need money, my friend.'

'We *have* money.'

Jake got up, lifted the corner of the carpet and raised a loose floorboard. He reached into the hole, groped around for what they called the kitty and pulled out a ragged tenner and some coins.

Ivan grinned and nodded.

Balloon

Halfway down the stairs they heard the bullying tones of Tony's voice. He was giving orders to Reg, the whiskery geezer who lived on the ground floor with his dog. Reg, who kept an eye on the place for Tony and seemed to work for him in other ways, was a nosey old blighter, mean and suspicious. Pretty sharp, too, in spite of his deafness, though Tony always treated him like an idiot.

As they approached, Tony turned. 'Hello, lads. Off on the town?'

'Fat chance. When are we going to get paid, Tony?'

'A bit short, boys? Need some cash?'

Tony, jaunty as ever, pulled a wad of notes from his pocket and ripped off a couple of tenners. Jake took them and waved them under Tony's nose. 'No, Tony, this isn't what we need. We want our wages.'

'I know that. Give me another day or two. I'm sorting it.'

'Yeah, you said that last time.'

'Look, lads, it's not easy when paperwork's not in order.' He gave Ivan a hard look. 'There's been a bloke round asking questions, so don't get pushy. You're in no position. You've got a roof, boys, and you'll get your money when things are sorted.'

He turned back to Reg. Jake gave a snort of disgust, and he and Ivan passed out into the street.

'What he say?' muttered Ivan as they strolled along.

'He says there's been a snooper. You know? A snooper?'

'Yeah, I know.' Ivan's face turned grave. 'It's true? A snooper?'

'Well, that's what he says ... if you believe it.'

Jake chuckled, but Ivan was clearly not amused.

Festival

They walked on in silence to the supermarket and grabbed a couple of cans. Then, still without speaking, they strolled down Blackfriars, over the bridge and along the Strand to Covent Garden. It was a walk they'd taken before, so the route was familiar and almost automatic. They liked the Garden; the bright bustle of the place was a welcome relief from the drabness of their room. They sat on the steps, watching and listening. People in smart clothes, dining at outside tables, were drinking from tall glasses, and a glamorous couple, posing like models in a fashion magazine, were drifting about in an open-top car. Further off, a large cheering crowd had gathered to watch the antics of a trick-cyclist. All about them they heard the carefree chatter of people with money.

Jake turned to Ivan, who was even more silent than usual. 'Hey, cheer up, mate.'

'Jake, I'm sorry ... I'm trouble ... trouble for you, trouble for me.'

'Ah, forget it. The real trouble is Tony.'

'Yeah, he's trouble. He's big trouble.'

Ivan shook his head. Jake put an arm round him and for a while they sat staring at the crowded scene. Then Ivan cleared his throat.

'Listen, Jake ... I go tomorrow ... move on.'

'What? Don't be a bloody fool. He owes you money.'

'You see how he look at me? He's trouble.'

They fell silent again, and a deep glumness settled on them. Jake, glancing at Ivan, saw in the set of his face that there was no point in trying to change his mind. Besides, perhaps he was right. Perhaps it was best to clear out. And as they trailed back to the room a sense

Balloon

of desolation stole over him. If Ivan went, surely he'd have to go too. There was no staying without Ivan. The room would become a shell, an emptiness, a place of eerie memories.

Back in the room they sat cross-legged on the mattress facing each other and Ivan pulled a half bottle of vodka from his bag. It was almost empty.

'Cheers,' he grinned, taking a nip and passing it to Jake. 'To us, my friend.'

'Well, well,' Jake chuckled, lifting the bottle to his lips. 'You slyboots.'

They gazed at each other with shy smiles and passed the bottle between them. Several minutes passed.

'So you mean it, Ivan? You mean to go? Really?'

'Tomorrow, my friend. Is not good here.'

'But where will you go?'

'Don't know. To Epping, maybe. To friends Viktor and Maria. They have van.' He glanced up with a wry smile. 'And you, Jake?'

'What will *I* do?' Jake shrugged and lowered his eyes. 'Miss you, I guess.'

There was another long pause. Jake scratched his ankle. He was squirming with confusion. He wanted to propose that they leave together. Reluctant as he was to let Tony rob them, he was ready to jump ship. But what did Ivan want? If he'd just offer some sign, some hint. But Ivan said nothing, so after a while Jake fetched his pack of cards; no point in wallowing in despondency. He dealt a couple of hands and they played their usual round of pontoon. Then they watched a game show on TV until they began to yawn.

'Time to turn in?'

Festival

'Yeah, an early start for me ... so perhaps we should say goodbye, Ivan.'

They clasped each other in a lingering hug. 'Hey, good luck, my friend. And take care. I hope we meet again.'

Jake could barely speak; the hug seemed to squeeze the life out of him.

The room was still very warm. They flung open the windows. In bed, Jake watched Ivan undress, entranced by the way the moonlight threw into relief the contours of his arms, the line of his neck, the curve of his spine. For a long while they lay on their backs, their arms outside the quilt, and it was clear to Jake that they were both wide awake. Ivan was often the first to drop off, signalled by a sharp snore, but tonight was different. Tonight he had a lot on his mind. Jake, too, was in turmoil. He stared at the drifting shadows on the wall. He didn't want to stay here, or return alone to the streets. He knew all too clearly what he wanted; and now, at this point of separation, he knew more than ever. But what did Ivan want?

Time was passing. Indeed, running out. And when at last Ivan rolled onto his side, his back towards Jake, the moment seemed critical. Jake considered the risks, and a sudden hot daring seized him. At worst he'd lose a friend, but that would happen anyway unless he took action. So, in a blind, headlong move, he snuggled up behind Ivan, slid an arm round his chest and sunk his nose into his neck. Ivan had a rich, mouldy smell like a bowl of decaying walnuts and his skin was soft and intoxicating. But to Jake's surprise he made no response, not the flicker of a muscle, though his breathing and heartbeats seemed to come a little faster;

Balloon

and for several minutes they lay quite motionless, save for the gentle nuzzle of Jake's nose against the lobe of Ivan's ear.

Despite some loss of heart, Jake decided to press on. He slid his hands down the sides of Ivan's body and drifted them over the bony humps of his hips. Still no response. This was discouraging, but there was no turning back. So he passed a hand over Ivan's chest and brought it to rest on the hollow of his belly, from where it was just a short hop to the discovery that he'd stiffened promisingly. But at the same moment Ivan shifted and turned on his back, and Jake's courage failed. He broke away and they lay, as formerly, side by side, staring at the ceiling. He'd done it again, broken the code; he was beyond the pale, alone and friendless. Something flared in his chest. He felt his face burning. He lay breathing hard, crawling with shame, lust and hurt.

Some minutes passed.

Then Ivan chuckled. 'What it say? That song?'

A brief pause.

Jake sniggered. 'That song?'

'Don't leave me this way, you know?'

'Yeah, I know. Don't leave me this way. That's what it says. What are *you* saying?'

Another low chuckle. 'What you think, for fuck sake?'

Daylight flooded the room. They'd snatched no more than a few hours of sleep. Stumbling to their feet, yawning and stretching, they began to stuff things into their bags. It was important to make an early start, to be gone before anyone noticed. Tony owed them, but there

Festival

was no knowing what that tricky bastard might do. Threaten them, call in the roughnecks? Best be on the road with the milk vans and street cleaners. The decision to leave together had been taken in the early hours, while the sweat was still warm on their bodies.

As they crept past Reg's door, they heard the dog yelp and bolted into the street. There was a loud knocking and they glanced round. Reg and the dog were staring at them through the window. The dog, its paws on the sill, was straining its thick black neck and Reg, a mug of tea in his hand, was shouting something they couldn't hear. The boys waved with casual insolence, but when Reg, his face twisted in fury, spilled his tea and the dog began to scrabble at the pane, they dashed off.

Another fine day. They bought some bacon rolls from a cheery bloke in a van and found an empty bench by the river. They gazed at the churning river-craft, the human traffic swarming over the bridges, the hot-air balloon rising majestically out of the tower blocks on the skyline; and as it lifted clear of the heat-haze, glinting like a jewel, they turned to each other with small thrills of delight, grinning like urchins on the banks of the Ganges.

'We could try my friend Pete,' said Jake. 'Bethnall Green.'

'Paperwork,' said Ivan wryly.

'Ah, he'll know. Plenty of fruit in Kent. No questions asked.'

Ivan shrugged and looked doubtful. But almost immediately his face lit up, as if to say 'glad of you, though'. That smile again, thought Jake. Knock you for six. Nothing like company. Good to be on the road with

Balloon

this guy, lounging in sunlight, catching the tang of the river breeze, letting your socks hang out on the blue morning air. Good to be shot of that crowd. Not much dosh. A couple of dog-eared notes and a fifty-kopeck piece. Still, now's the thing; the rest can take care of itself. Bread'll come from somewhere. Earn it; beg, borrow or steal it.

'I'm trouble, Jake. You could have work, my friend. Money.'

'Ah, but what's that song say? I've got you, babe.'

Ivan threw him a shy glance and chuckled.

A squirrel descended a tree, floated over the ground and, planting its paws on the bench, reached up to them, sniffing the air. Pushy little blighter, thought Jake. On the scrounge, just like us. Still, some of your bloody cheek is what we need, mate. He tore off a piece of his roll and tossed it at the twitching nose.

Tracking James

And after all she was not a prying mother. She'd always respected his privacy, his right to live his own life without interference. She'd never so much as passed comment, had she? Well, nothing beyond a mild hint here and there, a light nudge in the ribs, and surely any mother was entitled to that. How strange if she were to show *no* interest. He was her only child, for heaven's sake, and now that Gordon had gone to live with that woman, almost her only family. So why didn't he see that? Why didn't he call more often, lift the lid a little? Why must he always play the dark horse?

She hauled her shopping trolley up the steps and let herself in. The cat rose from its basket, arched its back and stretched a rear leg like a ballerina. She bent to pick up the post, the cat nudging her ankles, and noticed immediately the pulsing light beside the telephone. She snapped on the machine. 'Hi Mum. Why are you never there when I call? Anyway, just making contact. Got some news. Will try later.' She shook her head and smiled. Never there! So that's the excuse. Still, a move in the right direction. Yes, speak of the devil. She was inclined to call him back on the spot. But no, be patient. Let *him* make the effort.

'You remember Roddy? The guy I met at the sailing club?' She scratched her head. 'Anyway, he's going to move in ... share the flat with me.'

They were sitting in the kitchen, drinking coffee. He'd come round after work to tell her. Yes, actually made the trip across town to pay her a visit. He seemed very excited, as if announcing an engagement.

'Well, that's lovely, dear. A bit of companionship and someone to share the rent.' She hesitated and her brow creased a little. 'Enough room for both of you?'

He shrugged and smiled. 'A bit intimate ... but well, you know ...'

She could recall just three names: Nerys, Pippa, Betheny. None of them had lasted long, Nerys and Pippa no more than a few weeks. In fact, Betheny had been the only one that she'd properly met, having dined out with her on one occasion. But the girl was an absolute pain. Couldn't stand her. Spoke so fast you couldn't catch a word she said and every remark punctuated with shrieks of nervous laughter till you felt like cracking her on the head with a dinner plate. It had been a relief to hear that he'd dropped *her*. Still, that was an age ago and for the past few years no new name or girlish giggle had come along to tickle her ear or try her patience.

How would they cope in that small flat, two great hulking lads? Well, okay, James was scarcely hulking

Festival

at just five foot ten and slightly built, and she knew nothing about Roddy's corporeal dimensions. But they were yachtsmen, after all, and men of whatever size need space. They're naturally messy creatures. They don't use drawers and cupboards; they simply step over things, or even *on* them. They have no sense of delicacy or things in their place. They spread jam like tarmac on a road and leave lids off jars. She couldn't see how it could *possibly* work. The place would be a pigsty within a fortnight.

So she allowed rather more than a fortnight before deciding to drop in. Meanwhile, with no communication of any kind from James, her curiosity, already keen, grew avid from lack of news. Timing was crucial, she felt, so she planned her visit carefully. It had to look natural; there must be no sense that she was checking up. She therefore settled on a Saturday morning, when she could reasonably claim that she was just passing on a visit to the shops. The flat was on the third floor of a large house, and normally, on arrival, she buzzed James on his intercom. But on this occasion she dived in just behind his neighbour, the old lady from the ground floor, who was entering at the same time.

The door to the flat was opened by a tall young man with an exploding mop of spiky blond hair, whose dishevelled appearance – he was wearing nothing but a pair of jazzy boxer shorts that hung hazardously from his pelvis – suggested that he'd just tumbled out of bed. He scratched his skinny white belly, gave a squeak like a chipmunk, and they stared at each other for a few moments with looks of bemused inquiry.

'Oops,' she said. 'Have I made a mistake? I'm looking for James.'

Tracking James

But at the same moment James appeared, holding together the flaps of his dressing gown. 'Oh crumbs!' he gasped. 'What a turn-up!'

She smiled. 'Well, aren't you going to invite me in?'

The living room was a mess, as expected. Newspapers littered the floor and a couple of plates bearing the congealed remains of a meal wallowed shamelessly on the coffee table. James, quickly snatching things up, told her to take a seat. Then both men disappeared. She gazed around. It was months since she'd been here, but the place seemed no different except for a couple of additions: a mirror in a pine frame and a stylish magazine rack. Oh, and those two framed photographs standing side by side on the drinks cabinet. She got up to take a closer look. They were snaps of James and the man she'd met at the door, presumably Roddy. In one, they were seated in a boat, gazing at each other and laughing wildly. In the other, they were standing on a beach, grinning at the camera and clasping each other round the neck.

And it was only then, with what she took as the visual evidence before her, that the thought which had been growing in her mind for some time split from its pod, so to speak. She assumed that she was ignorant about this kind of thing, but in fact she knew a good deal from what she'd read. She'd picked up a lot, too, from Annabel, her hairdresser, whose husband had left her for a man he'd met on the common. 'It's strange, Marian,' Annabel had said while snipping away. 'Sometimes it's there right under your nose and you don't spot it.' Marian studied the face in the photograph and rehearsed the name in her head – Roddy – the name she assumed she'd now have to live with. But no, she

Festival

just couldn't make it sound right. She disliked these diminutives; they were weak and affected. Why not Rod? She could live with the name Rod; there was something dependable and solid about that.

The two men reappeared in jeans and T-shirts, and when James had made a pot of coffee they sprawled on the sofa.

'So far, it's been hunky-dory,' said James. 'We're both thoroughly satisfied with the arrangement, aren't we?' He and Roddy threw warm smiles at each other.

Marian watched their interaction keenly – with such fascination, in fact, that she spilled coffee into her saucer while lifting the cup to her lips. Every word, every look, every gesture seemed to confirm the idea that had now lodged itself in her head. And when, having absorbed the initial shock, she began to adjust to the new knowledge, she found herself quietly thrilled by it. James had been a mystery for so long: so cut off, so unknown, so untouchable. This tore down the hedge between them: the hedge that had seemed to grow higher year by year. This brought them together again. She scarcely listened as they chuntered on about their division of labour; her mind was elsewhere. She was already planning to invite them to her place for a Sunday roast or a candle-lit dinner.

After some talk about the sailing club, the neighbours and Roddy's line of work as a marketing manager for a chain of hotels, there was a pause. She glanced at her watch. 'Look, I must go,' she said. 'I'm sure you've got things to do and I've kept you long enough.'

'Not at all,' said James 'In fact, why not stay for a spot of lunch? A couple of friends are looking in.'

Tracking James

'Oh?' she said, her curiosity piqued again.

Who could this be? More lads from the club?

'Yes,' said Roddy. 'Caroline and Julia. They're great company. You'll like them.'

There was a tight little pause. She glanced from Roddy to James and back again.

'Oh well,' she said, her face a mass of confusion. 'If I won't be in the way.'

When the women arrived they burst in with noisy excitement like children from a playground. They tossed their shoulder bags aside and kissed the men on the lips with a richness that sounded almost lascivious. Caroline was lanky and had long blond hair that cascaded round a radiant pink face. Blooming with health, bouncing with energy, she threw off an air of wellbeing like a figure on a box of breakfast cereal. Julia, on the other hand, was short, dark and petite. She had an elfin face, sharp brown eyes and a permanently wry expression that seemed to say 'Come off it, ya wally, ya can't con me'.

'This is my mum,' said James.

They beamed. 'Hello, Mum.'

'Call me Marian,' she said.

And they *were* like lads from the sailing club. They had photographs on a smartphone to prove it. Snaps of themselves in a dinghy, ploughing through ruffled waters on a blustery day, clinging to the tiller in windcheaters zipped to the chin. Others showed them in a pub, lifting pints to their lips, surrounded and regaled by men in woolly hats and thick black sweaters. Marian peered at the screen on the device that Julia handed her, a bemused smile on her lips. To someone like herself,

Festival

raised in Cotswold gentility, these robust outdoor girls, with their beery pleasures, seemed vaguely improper, as if the world were turning topsy-turvy.

Lunch was a ramshackle business. The various parts – the quiche, the salad, the French sticks, the cheeses – were fine, but everything arrived in haphazard fashion and was badly presented. Napkins were tossed out in the middle of the meal and the dressing turned up in a jug with a chip on the rim. No one seemed the least bit put out, though. Wine – white, red and pink – was sloshed into bulbous glasses and knocked back voraciously, and the women contributed with some bottles of sparkly stuff and a sherry trifle from the local supermarket. The table rocked with the wildest laughter throughout the entire meal.

Marian studied the scene avidly. What was going on here? Caroline had a roving eye, but it always came back to James. Julia, however, seemed much more interested in Roddy. She had a glow in her cheeks, a gleam in her smile, whenever she turned to him. Yes, that was surely it; that was the picture. Marian had them paired off nicely. And the more she watched, the more convinced she became.

Towards the end of the meal James raised his glass. 'To the holiday.'

'Oh?' Marian glanced around with a smile 'So you're going on holiday?'

'Yes,' said Caroline. 'We're off to Dubrovnik … In just a few days, actually.'

'What? … The four of you?'

Marian took a gulp of wine and coloured slightly. Was that a silly question? She didn't know where it came from; it just popped out.

Tracking James

'Oh no ... Just me and Julia ... We always go away together.'

'I see.' Marian's mental picture lurched again, but she managed to hide her lack of composure. She hesitated for a few moments, and then: 'So do you also' – she simply had to clear this thing up – '*live* together?'

'Oh no!' shrieked Caroline, and everyone roared with laughter. 'We live with our husbands.'

Marian said very little after that and half an hour later excused herself, saying she had an appointment with a chiropodist. Halfway down Hurley Street she turned into Goodison's Bakery. It was fairly busy, but she took a seat and ordered a pot of tea. It was an old-fashioned place with check tablecloths, and its leisurely good manners always calmed her nerves. Life was a trying business; she couldn't get the hang of it. The visit had dragged her this way and that, upsetting all her notions. She couldn't decide whether James was nearer or much further off. Roddy seemed nice – well, nice enough – but quite as mysterious as James. And how did those two women fit into the picture? The whole thing was maddeningly opaque. She wanted to talk to someone about it. But who was there? She could call in on Annabel, but Annabel would be busy with customers. In any case what could she say? She had never dropped a hint to Annabel about any of her concerns, and now they looked like the half-baked notions of a muddleheaded woman. And could Annabel be trusted not to pass on her confidences as gossip?

When she got home she dropped into her easy chair. The cat leapt onto her lap, trod in a circle kneading her skirt and then curled up. She snapped on the radio. Someone was playing the piano: a slow, meditative

Festival

piece that sounded like Mozart. She closed her eyes. Annabel's words kept rattling round in her head: 'Sometimes it's there right under your nose and you don't spot it.' But did it matter if you didn't spot things? Sometimes you could get into trouble trying to spot things. Sometimes you could just try too hard. She decided that she *would* invite them to dinner. Yes, all four of them. And she would listen and watch and wait. She would hang around, serenely, for the thing – whatever it was – to reach up and paw her on the nose.

Late Call

Another bleak day in prospect. I've got a splitting head and this coffee tastes foul. Sunday mornings used to be friendly, I seem to recall, though that was an age ago. I guess I should lay off the drink, but meeting the lads on a Saturday night is now my only pleasure. I see she's pottering in the garden again, watering the dahlias with her little green can. Is it to make me feel bad about lying in, or because she likes to talk to them? A touch of both, if you ask me. I reckon they comfort her. They're her friends, her only company now. She's become a stranger to me and to everyone else.

Fair enough, she's got her grievances. I'm no angel, I know that. I played the jackass at school and left at sixteen. I worked in a timber yard for a couple of years, then dropped in at the Army Recruitment. They said it was a good career, with training, support, a chance to travel. They made it sound like fun, but the reality was something else. After the first week I lay in my bunk with sore feet and aching limbs wondering what the fuck I'd done. My training officer at Catterick was short and thick-set, with a bristly moustache and big meaty hands. He played everything by the rules, but there was a hard piercing look in his eye, a look that said 'I'm going to break you, sonny'. He did too, on many occasions, doling out penalties with a gloating smile. Keeping myself under control was an eye-watering struggle. Among ourselves we called him some choice names and boasted about reporting him, but none of us did. We'd have lost face. It just wasn't done.

After initial training I was sent to Aldershot, where I learned vehicle maintenance and gained a qualification. Then came a stint in Belfast. And frankly I date all my problems from that time. To be honest, I've never been quite right since and the less said the better. So we'll pass quickly over that and skip ahead to Julie. She was someone I'd been keen on at school and I used to look her up whenever I came home on leave. One Christmas, sitting on the sofa at her place, she turned to me with a nervous smile. Her parents had gone to bed and she'd been rather subdued all evening.

'Listen,' she said. 'I've got something to tell you. Something important.'

I stared at her and said nothing.

'Yeah,' she said. 'I suppose you've guessed.'

I scratched my neck and studied the floor.

'Are you quite sure?' I said. I felt slugged in the stomach.

'Of course,' she said.

I didn't speak for ages. Then I swallowed hard.

'So how d'you know it's mine?'

'Trust me,' she said. 'I know.'

Late Call

I was in a weird state at the time. I'd been through hell in Belfast and dreaded going back. I was living at home, having fits of craziness, shouting at the family, upsetting everyone. I didn't want a child. I wasn't ready for it. I mean, how could I be a father? I couldn't even handle myself. But I could see the consequences of not doing the right thing. My life, my family ties, my friendships would all fall apart. I'd be shunned; I'd be on the outside.

So I looked at Julie, smiled weakly, and took her hand. She smiled back and gripped me tight. We got married at the register office on the last weekend of my leave.

The following March I left Belfast and returned to Aldershot. The baby was born six months later. We called him Michael after Julie's father. I was present at the birth, and after the swabbing down I studied his features closely. He had Julie's nose and chin, but I couldn't see anything that was clearly mine. Later that day I took him in my arms and he wrapped his tiny fingers round my thumb. Hello you, I murmured, wondering how we'd get along. I had these strange mixed feelings: part bewilderment, part awe, part resentment.

Julie and I were now renting a flat, and every weekend I'd drive home at breakneck speed, burning the car up in my urge to flee the barracks. What I wanted when I burst in was a warm welcome, a passionate embrace, a sense of being the central figure in our little family. But Julie had no arms to enfold me; she was always cuddling Michael. She seemed rather distant, too. She'd give me a kiss, of course. But it was a wifely

Festival

kiss, a kiss that was nothing like the kisses she'd once given me. And I quickly saw that I was no longer the centre of her life. Nor was I the centre of the family. The centre was a pink blob, wrapped in crocheted knitwear. A blob that kept kicking and fisting the air.

It was the same in bed. Julie would lie with her back to me, I'd snuggle up behind her and after a while she'd turn to me with a sigh. Then Michael would start to cry and she'd go to comfort him. This was the new routine, and for weeks nothing changed, until one night, in desperation, I twisted her round, pulled her close, and forced myself on her. After which she never refused me. But it finished us; we never recovered. From then on she was always somewhere else, while I simply smouldered in a glower of shame.

She was the world's best mum, I'll give her that. Throughout his childhood she dressed him in perfectly pressed shirts and neat ankle socks. I couldn't bear it; I could see what she was doing to him. I used to ruffle his hair, roll him in the grass. She'd shoot furious looks at me when we came back from walks. What *he* was thinking I never quite knew. He never complained, but I sensed a vague hostility in the frown he sometimes wore. I was mad keen to bind him to me. I bought him treats, walked him in the park, took him to the zoo. I wanted a son, a real son, a son to biff a ball around with, but I could see he wasn't the type. I'd lost. He was hers, not mine.

Time passed, he grew to manhood, we drifted further apart, until in his teenage years he became a near stranger. He was a shy boy, but a fine scholar, unlike me. He played the violin, spoke French, wrote poetry.

Late Call

He was only sixteen, but I felt like a clod beside him, and that stung at times. I felt he looked down on my coarse hands, my rough voice, my blunt manner, and the sense of distance between us sometimes flared into resentment and cruelty. I'd turn bitterly sarcastic and feel a need to hurt and humiliate him. Sometimes I'd spar with him or challenge him to a bout of arm wrestling. Could this boy really be mine? I mean, how could I have fathered this paragon, this model student? Yet there were times when I felt envious and proud and ached to be closer. I was conflicted, a bundle of confusion.

One day, for a test, I invited him to come to the dog track with me. He looked doubtful.

'Dunno. I'm not sure if it's my thing.'

'What *is* your thing?' I said.

'Leave him alone,' said Julie. 'What a sleazy place to take him.'

But he shrugged and agreed to come. I introduced him to a few mates, showed him how to place a bet. We won a bit and lost a lot, and when it was all over I took him into the bar. He was under-age, but as tall as me and no one was likely to ask. We took our drinks to a table in the corner.

'So,' I said, 'have you enjoyed yourself today?'

He hesitated, nodded, smiled feebly.

'Good,' I said, nudging a pint towards him. 'Now get that down ya. Put some hairs on your chest, some lead in your pencil.'

I grinned, but he looked at me as if he hadn't a clue.

'Well, well,' I said. 'What a clean-living lad you are. You don't smoke, drink or swear. You don't date girls.' I paused. 'Have you ever, you know, *had* a lass?'

Festival

But again, this went nowhere. He stared at me with another deep frown, as if I'd just dropped a dog turd on the table.

I'd left the army by this time and had my own little garage. But the army was following me around. I was still having nightmares.

'What you need is a job,' I told him. 'A holiday job. Money's tight.'

I inquired at the brewery. I knew they took on temporary workers and it turned out there were vacancies. 'It's loading trucks. It'll do you good. Knock your corners off. Get yourself down there.'

But he wasn't keen and came home after his first day looking glum. 'I'll never stick that. They're a bunch of roughs. Some of them have been inside.'

'That's life,' I said. 'You need to mix with all sorts.'

He showed me his hands.

'They'll heal and be stronger for it,' I said. 'The hands of a musician need toughening.'

Julie, who was standing in the doorway, flounced off. I flew after her and hissed in her ear. 'He needs to learn. Life's not feather-bedded.'

But a week passed and every day he became glummer. He turned quite sullen, in fact. He'd lock himself in his room and appear only at supper.

'He's being bullied,' she said one evening. 'He's got bruises on his arm.'

I stormed up the stairs and she followed. He was working at his desk. 'Show me,' I said.

He got to his feet, rolled up his sleeves.

'Complain,' I growled. 'To the foreman, the management, whoever.'

Late Call

He snorted with contempt and turned away. 'Ah, what do *you* know? That would just make things worse.'

I grabbed his arms and slammed them up behind his back. 'In that case, fight, lad. Stand up for yourself. *I* had to. You don't know the bloody half of it.'

He winced and struggled. I let him go and turned to face Julie. She was staring at me with eyes of pure hatred.

It was a week later that the knock came. She was washing up in the kitchen, I was watching a cartoon on television. We were just about to go to bed. Michael had gone out earlier, saying he was going to visit his friend Luke. They were an odd couple, always hanging out together. Not that I inquired too deeply. Our only anxiety was the time. He'd never stayed out this late. Still, he had his own key.

Halfway up the stairs we were stopped by four heavy raps. And if I know anything now, I know this: there's nothing more dread than a late call. Not even a sniper's bullet. I can still hear those raps. They punctuate all my days and nights like hammer blows.

The two people on the step, a man and a woman, looked grave. And the mere sight of their uniforms seemed to bring the world to a standstill.

'Can we come in?' they said.

I've been over and over it. Replayed it so many times the grooves have worn to ruts. There are phases when I think the only sane response to life is what we call madness. I didn't dare look at Julie that night and she refused to look at me. We knew the final link between us had snapped. It was the beginning of what I call 'the

Festival

silence'. We simply sat on the sofa in a rage of pain, waves of incomprehension crashing over us.

The coroner described the death as accidental. Julie read the report, then tossed it aside.

'So how would *you* describe it?' I said.

'How would *you*?' she scoffed.

I spread my palms in protest. 'Look, he simply drank too much.'

'You think that explains anything? He hardly ever touched the stuff. Why would he suddenly swallow half a bottle of vodka, then wander into the road?'

'It was probably a dare,' I muttered. 'Boys incite each other to that kind of thing.'

We were staring at the floor, avoiding each other's eye. She gave a harsh little laugh. 'He was alone, you denying bastard. Walking the streets with a bottle of grief.'

I guess I should ditch this coffee. I still have a throbbing head. I see she's stopped watering and is now snipping. So let me predict how the day will go. She'll enter shortly and arrange some cuttings in a vase. Then she'll make a spot of lunch. Homemade soup, followed by apple flan. Not a word will pass between us as we eat, and this afternoon she'll visit her sister while I watch the sport. Tonight, she'll bury her nose in a book while I listen to Stevie Wonder through headphones. After an hour I'll dose off and at eleven she'll wake me with a nightcap. Then to bed – we sleep separately now – and the many terrors of the night.

Is that enough? You've got the picture.

I tried moving out two years ago. I found a place on the other side of town. I couldn't hack it, though. It's

Late Call

too late for me to move now: I'm too worn and wounded. I stuck it for three months, then begged her to take me back. I promised not to bother her. She shrugged. She said she didn't care whether I moved back or not. But I don't believe that. I reckon she needs me like I need her. I reckon we're bound together, she and I. Permanently yoked by our shared pain, shut up in this torture for the rest of our days.

I see the sky has cleared. The leaves of the beech tree are dancing in sunlight and a squirrel is flitting in the lower branches. The kids next door are playing patball in the garden. I sometimes raise a prayer for kids, godless creature though I am. Do they know how short life is, how breakable? At other times I look at people in the street and wonder about the shape of their lives. I mean, are we helpless? Can we change anything, end a cycle? Ah well, who knows? I guess we can only make the effort. So would she agree that it's a crime to waste such a lovely day? Should I ask her to take a stroll with me by the river?

Freewheelin'

So what in the name of the blessed Saint Patrick was *I* doing at a classical concert? Me, Gary Pickles, Led Zep fan? Well, I'll tell ya. Sheltering from the rain, that's what. I'm in Manchester, see, passing this posh building, all swanky pillars and brass fittings, when it starts to piss like a long-distance trucker after sixteen pints on a Friday night. So I leap up the steps and dive through the front door, and it's the interval, yeah? And all these nobs are standing around with drinks in their hand, saying ooh and aah, and did you *evah* hear anything so absolutely *divaine*? And while I'm standing there, shaking the rain from me jacket, this cool young chick with a tray of glasses comes right across the room toward me, flashing the world's juiciest smile. I thought, Christ, I'm dreaming. Either that, or I've gone to the other side.

She says, 'Red or white?'

'Ow much?' I says.

'Oh no,' she chuckles. 'It's all part of the ticket.'

Freewheelin'

'In that case, make it red,' I says.

She hangs about, and I take a sip or two while noting every curve of her slinky torso. She's wearing this tight black outfit clinging to a brace of firm jugs. Peachy brown, with a fair display of cleavage.

'So are you enjoying it?' she says.

'Oh, yeah,' I says. 'Divainely.'

And she smiles again. Like an angel.

'There goes the interval bell,' she says. 'The second half will begin soon. But you can take your glass in with you.'

So I was stuck, wasn't I? No sliding off. But in any case, with even half a chance of pulling this vision of delight, I was keen to stick around. And if I failed, at least I was in the dry.

I waited at the back of the hall till everyone was settled and then slipped into an empty seat. Shortly, a pint-sized geezer in a penguin suit came trotting onto the platform, all fluttery, pink and nervous, followed by this big old girl in a green smock, who strolled on beaming like royalty. They stood side by side, his bald head about level with her waist, and took a deep bow. The room went wild with applause. Then he sprang to the keyboard, plunged into some racket, and seconds later she opened her gob and let forth a blast that made the chandeliers rattle. This went on for ages. Christ knows what she was shrieking about. She'd got something on her mind, I could see that, but it was all Greek to me. I glanced around in desperate hope, but sadly there was no sign of the Angel.

Gloom!

I took another slosh of the wine and slid down in me seat.

Festival

During the applause after the first number, there was a little buzz in my right ear and I turned to find the guy in the next seat leaning in close. He had a touch of slap and his hair all swept up.

'Don't you just *adore* Rachmaninov?' he breathes.

'Love him to bits,' I says, struggling to sit up.

He points to the guy on the other side of him.

'I'm Teddy and this is Peter.'

Peter was tall, with silver hair, a neat little tache and the look of a military officer. I gave them both a nod and their eyes devoured me.

'Gary the Unwary,' I says. 'Pleased to meet ya.'

A hush fell, the bloke on the ivories struck up, and I looked around for an escape route. But all the doors was closed and guarded, so I'd got no choice but to stick it out to the finish, clapping each number and swapping smiles with this pair. I didn't even notice when the end came. I was sunk too deep in a catatonic trance.

Teddy touched my shoulder. 'Can we give you a lift? Where are you off?'

'Lewisham,' I says.

'Lewisham?' He stares in horror.

'Yeah, been deliverin'.'

'Oh really? Delivering what?'

'Oh, this and that.'

He gives me a funny look. 'But you can't set off for Lewisham now. It's a horribly wet night. And where will you sleep?'

'Back of the van.'

'Oh no!' He turns to Peter. 'We can't allow that, can we, Popsum?'

Fifteen minutes later I was gliding up a private drive in the back of a Daimler. We pulled up in front of a

Freewheelin'

classy front door with a porch, and Teddy led the way with his whopping mile-wide rainbow umbrella. Tristan, their Irish wolf hound, bounded to meet us in the hall. The sitting room was full of antiques and had three sofas. Teddy flopped back on a lounger and invited me to sit while we waited for Peter to park the car. He eyed me steadily. So steadily my cheek began to twitch.

'If you don't mind my saying so, Gary, you're very well put together.' I raised an eyebrow to the sound of feet being scraped in the hall. 'Oh, but there's Popsum.' He put a finger to his lips. 'So not a word.'

'About what?'

'Oh, you know ... our little thing.'

Peter came in smiling and stood around awkwardly. His manner was stiff and formal, but he ate me up with his eyes.

'I see you two are getting along famously.'

'Yes, of course we are. Oh, do sit down, Popsum.'

'Just take my coat off. Anyone for a nightcap?'

I nodded, thinking he meant a snort of brandy, but it seemed he had a mug of cocoa in mind. We shared a plate of custard creams. Christ knows what we talked about. Teddy's dance class and Peter's directorship mostly. Then Peter started to droop.

'Oh look, I'm going to turn in.'

Teddy gave me a sly wink. 'Okay, Popsum, up the wooden hill.'

Peter toddled off and Teddy sat smiling at me, eyes blazing in a blatant come-on. It was a tricky situation. Hold off or roll over? Either way I could be shown the door, and I didn't much fancy a search for the van in the teeming rain.

Festival

'Well now.' He pulls a bottle from his bag and removes the top. 'How about you? Ready for some livening up?'

He held it under his nose, breathed in deeply and passed me the bottle.

'Hm,' I says. 'Try anything once, me.'

I took a sniff and shot ten feet into the air. Then I floated to earth gently as we continued to smile at each other.

After a while he got up and joined me on the sofa, which is where the action really began. He was slim, cute, nicely perfumed, if not what I normally went for. Still, he had a seamless expertise that was very relaxing. He passed a hand through my hair and was unbuttoning my shirt when Tristan padded in and lay watching us, his head between his paws. I became jumpy, especially at the thought of playing to an audience, and when I felt a hand on my fly I panicked.

'Hey, what about Peter?'

'Oh, he's rattling the house with his snores. But we can go upstairs to your room if you'd rather.'

I said, 'Yes, I'd rather.'

The room he called *my* room had red wallpaper and this monster four-poster, all hung about with burgundy drapes and tassels. Tristan padded in behind us.

'Does *he* have to be here?'

'He won't let me out of his sight.'

Putting a finger to his lips, he turned the key in the lock.

The show lasted about an hour and passed through a series of contortions that stretched every muscle in my creaking chassis and left me aching with cramp. At the midway point I clapped him in a pair of studded leather

Freewheelin'

cuffs that he pulled from a box under the dresser. He said he liked to feel ravished and spread-eagled himself on the bed like a heroine in a Dracula movie. He also produced a long shaft of flexible pink rubber and shook it in front of my nose, but I fumbled with that and eventually flung it aside. I said I was afraid of doing some hurt. He said *that* was the point. Tristan sighed twice and whimpered just once.

When we was all done, he slipped from the bed. 'I must go. Peter and I sleep apart, but he likes to keep me under control.'

He snatched up his clothes and scuttled out bare-arsed. Minutes later I heard raised voices on the landing. I went to the window and noted a drainpipe with footholds. But within a short space of time the house had fallen silent, so I drifted back to bed.

I woke to knocking on the door. Daylight was fringing the curtains. I gave a strangled groan and Peter entered with a tray. He smiled and placed it beside me. 'Thought you might like some tea. Sorry about the disturbance last night.'

I waved that aside, and he sat on the edge of the bed.

'Gary, I hope you won't mind my speaking frankly.' I gulped. 'Teddy tells me that you made a pass at him last night. Now, don't look worried, I'm not here to complain. He and I are a freewheeling couple and what he does is his affair. But he's asked me to explain the coolness of his response. It's not that you're not desirable, Gary. No, not at all. It's simply that you're not his type. That's all, and we don't want you to feel rejected.' He patted my hand and gave a little cough. 'So I hope that makes things a little clearer. And now I'll leave you to enjoy your tea.'

Festival

He threw me a wonky smile and left. I had a lot of respect for Peter. He was a gentleman.

I supped the tea and gazed around. There was a jade statuette on the dressing table and I knew where I could pass that off. So I got up, locked the door and slipped it into me bag, along with a pearl-studded casket that also caught my eye. Bit of a risk, but that goes with the job. I felt like a turd, given the hospitality and all, but the boys could make a claim. I was sorry not to say goodbye, but then I had to be off and a nifty flit by the back route was the best way of avoiding detection, not to mention another grinding session with Hot Pants.

At the foot of the drainpipe I slipped and went sprawling on the gravel. There was a yelp and I saw Tristan's nose pressed to the window. I sprinted down the drive with a twisted ankle and scrambled over the gate like a squaddie on an assault course.

Back at base, Mick was a bit humpy. 'So where was you last night? I rang three times.'

'At a classical song recital.'

'Christ, what's got into you?'

'Culcher, mate.'

'Oh yeah, tell that to the staff sergeant. Anyway, get rid of that stuff?'

'No problem.'

I pulled out the envelope with the four hundred nicker. I didn't mention Teddy and Peter or the haul in me bag.

So business continued for a few more months and we eventually got nicked for doing a place in Forest Hill.

It's funny, though, how my thoughts often return to that night. Lying here in the cell, I dream constantly of the Angel, wondering what would have happened if I'd

Freewheelin'

told her the truth. Would we have made it into the sack? Would we have gone further and rode into the sunset? Who knows? But something else happened that night, though I'm not sure exactly what, or how to put this. Anyway, more and more I find myself looking – well, you know – sidelong at the blokes in here. So am I on the turn? Changing direction? Heading for a makeover? I don't think so. I mean, switch allegiance after a soggy night in Manchester? No chance. And certainly not where music's concerned. Nah, it's bollocks and brass knobs to Rachbleedinwotsinov.

Requital

This is a weird experience. A first for me. Never been to such a gathering. Suits, hats and rosettes everywhere. The place bustling with self-delighted busybodies. What did someone call them? The chattering classes? Yeah, love it. What a deadly barb. Still, no one is chattering to me. They know me for a disaffected intruder. It's the way I sit alone, surveying the hall with a jaundiced eye from the end of the back row.

I see from the programme that Simon is to speak at eleven. His subject? The Need for Integrity in Public Life. How predictable and juicily appropriate. I shall heed and relish every word. But I should have worn a different jacket. These sleeves are not wide enough to laugh up.

Let me ask you something. Have you ever shaken with emotion? I'm not sure that *I* ever had until last June. So the earthquake, when it came, took me by storm. It was the loss of control: the body acting independently. I thought, if I sit still – very still, listening to late Schubert – the tumult will pass. But here I am, three months later, in a rage of aftershocks that show no sign of letting up.

So how do I know Simon? Good question. How does an obscure insect like me come to know one of the exalted, you mean? Short answer: I met him at the Prince William in Haringey. No, not a queer bar. Simon, a clean-living Protestant, avoids such places. The pub is simply my local, and one that he occasionally dropped into on his way home from the gym.

Approaching the table where I was sitting alone, he startled me out of my musing.

'Mind if I join you?'

'Not at all. Be my guest.'

We sat smiling at each other. Then, craning forward, he peered closely at me.

'Long lashes.'

'Family trait,' I said. 'We're long everywhere.'

He didn't reveal much that night. Or indeed any night. But we'll come to that. Said he worked for the Government. Tricky as ever, of course. I thought he meant in Whitehall. Not for a moment did I suspect on the benches. He looked too young for an MP, let alone a junior minister.

'And you?'

'Me? ... I'm a model.'

Another tricky answer. But excusable at the time: we'd only just met.

An unlikely pickup. I doubt that his looks appeal to everyone. That dark bony face, that deep ridge beneath the nose, that steady gaze, framed by overlarge ears. But

Festival

I have odd taste in blokes. He bought me a drink, and we talked in a coded way about Berlin, which he'd just visited – I assumed on a pleasure trip, but suspect now on work-related matters. Then, in a lull, he leaned forward with a bold, confiding glint.

'So, Darren. This is your patch, you say? You're just around the corner.'

'Third floor up.'

'Then it's got to be your place. I'm way off on the other side of town.'

He was up at the crack of dawn, as if eager to be gone. I watched him hastily draw on his pants. He's unrestrained in bed, but hates to be seen naked. It's a mystery to me, because he's as fit as a whippet from all that squash. I called him back to bed, but he simply planted a farewell kiss on my cheek. He'd see me, same time next week, at the Prince William. He left no address, no phone number, no name beyond Simon.

And so our nine-month affair began. Is that long enough to fall for someone? It's long enough to spring new life. So yes, more than enough for me: I'm a romantic idiot, for all my cynical posing. He was there every week, same time, same place, and sometimes more frequently, by arrangement. Our routine scarcely changed: we'd drink, often till closing time, and then retire to the flat. Usually we went straight to bed, but sometimes we'd watch TV for a while, giggling at a chat show or making derisive remarks about some terrible movie. God knows what else we talked about. Food, I seem to recall. Books, music, news events. Favourite kinds of holiday, species of dog, brands of underwear. We sensed, though, that there were touchy subjects. We never inquired about work, education or background; never spoke about anything that might appear in a profile. It was a weird kind of taboo, and where did it come from? Did we simply read the signals? All I know is that an unspoken agreement took root that began as an intuition and became a kind of code.

Fine for a spell, but funny how imperceptibly life changes, how subtly affection grows, how slyly features and habits coil around the heart. Funny how a routine becomes a need. I didn't wake to my reliance on those visits until one night he didn't appear. Only then did I realise the extent of his insinuation. So when he turned up the following week, I tackled him with some heat.

'You come into my life and then vanish. I know nothing about you.'

'Hey, I'm sorry. I was called away.'

'So why can't I phone you? Give me a number.'

'I'd rather you didn't. I work in a sensitive area.'

I stared at him. Sensitive area? I struggled with the wildest speculation. Anyway, how did it affect the issue? Why couldn't I phone him? 'Well, if it comes to that,' I wanted to quip, '*I* work in a sensitive area – in fact, several.' But I let it pass. Instead I sulked for a couple of visits. Not too harshly, though, for fear of driving him away. I learned to live with the ache, the insecurity, the curiosity. It's just a fling, I told myself; it will end soon. The pain will fade; peace will return. But that was the head; the emotions had a different agenda. I found myself longing for each visit with almost obsessive craving. I'd count off the days mentally, and on the appointed night I'd sit alone in the bar, glancing anxiously at my watch, willing him to arrive, eyes glued to the door.

Festival

Oh, I know what you're thinking. You're wondering how I could become so attached to someone who was a near stranger. Fair enough, it's a puzzle to me too. But what's the mystery? We know that some people pass a lifetime in ignorance of those to whom they are devoted. The truth is, we know precious little about each other. Indeed, if we believe Freud, we know next to nothing about ourselves.

So we stumbled on. How much life was there in this frail arrangement? I lived for his visits, but came to dread them, expecting each to be the last. Then, as spring turned into summer – as parks burst into leaf, days pulled out and lovers strolled the Embankment – I longed for our meetings to emerge from the shadows and take a turn in the light of day.

'I love seeing you,' I said one night, hoping to extend the conversation beyond the casual.

He tapped my nose playfully. 'I love seeing *you*.'

'Couldn't we meet more often?'

'Not really. I'm just too busy.'

'Well, somewhere else then? Go for a meal some place?'

'Hm. Have to think about that.'

But before he'd done thinking, something happened. Just popped up brazenly, shortly after ten one night, before my bleary eyes. A news reporter on the green outside Parliament was interviewing someone called Stephen Eliot. Don't ask me what about; I wasn't listening; I was too busy staring – or rather, gaping – at the dark bony face, the deep ridge beneath the nose, the overlarge ears. But in a flash, before I could process the image, it was gone, and the reader had moved to a new topic. I gazed blankly at the screen for the next few minutes, rooted to the spot, the tip of my scalp tingling. Then I poured myself a slug of Scotch.

In one way it was a relief, for it cleared up much that had baffled me; and in the next hour, as I pondered our liaison, all sorts of fragments flew into place and ancient mysteries were resolved. I'd had my suspicions, of course, but I knew now why he always came late and left early, why we never ate out, why he couldn't risk being seen with me. In every other way, though, it was galling. For it clarified my status. I was his dark secret, his fall from grace, his weekly indiscretion.

We were due to meet the next night. Should I end this charade? I was torn, but decided to say nothing. It would bring matters to a head and probably lead to a break-up, an outcome I could scarcely bear to think about. But I overlooked the power of impulse, didn't I? The gap between what we decide and what we do. Most behaviour, they say, is involuntary.

He was cheerful when he arrived, full of the usual small talk. He commented that I seemed rather subdued. He rattled on. Something about the shrinking size of his favourite brunch bar.

'Busy day?' I blurted out after the second pint.

He peered at me quizzically.

'You never talk about work,' I said. 'Or *anything* much. What are you keeping from me?'

He scratched his cheek and looked away.

'I've explained,' he said. 'Haven't I?'

I didn't reply immediately; I was struggling to suppress my tongue. 'So tell me,' I said. 'Who *am* I? What do I mean to you? What *is* this thing we have?'

He stood up, drained his pint. 'Hey, look. I sense a change of atmosphere. Shall we skip tonight?'

Festival

And abruptly, with those few blunt words, it was over. As I knew even before he reached the door. I'd simply wanted too much, demanded more than my due, broken the code. Looking back now, I wonder what his thinking was, what he calculated. He knew, must have known, that I'd find him out. Indeed, from the odd way that I'd probed him that night, that I *had* found him out. But like me, he'd assumed a mere fling. We'd started something that had spun out of control. And it seemed to me that *I* was the loser. I mean, *he* simply feared for his reputation; *I* was guarding my sense of self-worth.

For the next few weeks I drank alone until the barman had a word in my ear. Then grief turned to rage. How dare he use me. Fling me aside for the sake of his grubby career. I determined to have it out; and in a fit, an attack of incandescent spleen, I sat down at the breakfast table, hunched myself over a notepad, and wrote to him at the House of Commons. A long, rambling, incoherent letter. Well, not so much a letter as a scorching harangue. I wrote in a frenzied scrawl for two whole hours and tore up several attempts. I began 'Dear Stephen'. Nothing came back, of course. So I thought about dropping into his constituency office, but assumed I'd be turned away. I was cut off, barred, beyond the pale.

Then, as my rage grew, I noticed the approach of the conference season.

Which is when I joined the Party.

So here I am again in this seaside town. It feels odd to be back. My last visit was four years ago. I remember it well. I came with my friend Spike for a binge weekend in August. It was all strolling, sunbathing and drinking.

Requital

I little imagined then the conditions under which I'd return. Last night when I arrived the place felt so different I scarcely recognised it.

I was resolute but nervous, so I fortified myself by leaping into a cab. Cabs are a confidence booster, I find. The Grand Hotel was full, of course, but luckily I caught a late cancellation at the Devonshire. A ruinous expense, but I'm determined to play this out in style. No one's going to write me off as a guttersnipe.

I made some inquiries and discovered that Simon – as I still call him – was attending a fringe meeting. So I turned up early and took a seat in the front row. He was on stage with several others, and I was told that the woman beside him was Anne, his fiancée. Glamorous, immaculately coiffured, smiling graciously in all directions, she was clearly an asset to a rising politician.

He didn't spot me right off, but when he did, his face froze to a grey sculpted block. I smiled and winked, but he turned sharply away. The topic for discussion was party finance. I yawned shamelessly throughout, and at the finish got up and approached him as he was leaving the stage. But he slid a protective arm around Anne and swept past me without a glance.

Today, in the main conference hall, where I'm sitting in conspicuous isolation, the line-up of speakers is reportedly impressive. Don't ask *me*, though; I don't have a political bone in my body. Still, it will be fascinating to hear what Mr Pecksniff has to say, what platitudinous homily he'll serve up. Oily hypocrisy, especially when aired in public, makes for great entertainment, don't you think?

So now the hour approaches, the high noon of our encounter. To be straight with you, I came here with no

Festival

clear strategy. I just wanted to be seen; to foil the attempt to rub me out. But overnight it became plain. And I tremble just thinking about it. I'll be despised, abhorred, reviled. They'll call me every name under the sun. And let me say, before the devout start to bleat, that I was raised as a Catholic, so I know all about mortal sin. But then I'm queer and haven't been to church for a decade, so I'm damned anyway. And even if I believed in all that, I couldn't save myself. The force within is too great. I'm already consumed by fire. What more can they do to me?

I won't make a move until Simon has spoken, though nothing he says will assuage my fury. On the contrary, his speech is likely to incite me more. And when it's over, I'll leave some time for the applause to fade and then approach that hungry group of journalists over there. I'll choose one carefully – one with a sharp, scandal-sniffing nose – and draw him to one side. And I'll say, 'I've got a story for you. Would you be interested?'

Pennine Winter

The house that stood alone at the top of the village had a forlorn, neglected look. The roof had holes where mossy tiles had slipped, the railing round the small front garden was half hidden in a tangle of briars, and the grimy windows, hung with ragged curtains, had the dull gaze of sad eyes. There were very few visitors. The milkman delivered daily, the postman occasionally, and Edna Mayes from the Chapel could sometimes be seen standing on the front step, Bible in hand, though no one had ever seen her step inside. The children of the village normally kept away, though the older boys would sometimes steal into the garden at night to peer at the person they called the bogeyman, and then run yelling down the path.

The man who lived there was a perfect match for the house. His trousers were baggy, his sweater full of holes, his shoes shabby and down-at-heel – and that was on a good day, since he often failed to change out of his work clothes, which were filthy with dust from the local

Festival

quarry. Labouring at the pits for five days a week, he was a lone figure, austere and mostly shunned by his workmates. He was a few weeks short of his twenty-eighth birthday, though the lank unkempt hair that hung around his straggly black beard made him look much older. It was only his lithe springy frame that betrayed his youth.

Where had he come from? No one knew. He had an Irish accent that sometimes puzzled his listeners. Arriving in the village seven years earlier, he'd bought the house through Spendlow and Curtis, the agents acting for the owner. But within a short space of time what had been a handsome property had become a disgrace. The village was scandalised. And it wasn't just the neglect. Other rumours abounded. It was said that the house was full of books. What kind of books? Strange, disreputable, dangerous books, as like as not. Which, in a way, was true. Many of the books were works of philosophy, addressing thorny, intractable questions to which the man applied himself every evening in search of an answer.

With little interest in food, he cooked himself the plainest of meals simply for sustenance, usually a grilled chop or a piece of fish with boiled vegetables. But at weekends he ate at the Saddler's Arms, sitting alone at a table with a book propped in front of him. The house was draughty, but on cold nights he stoked the fire and blew through the vent with a pair of bellows that stood beside the grate. He kept his bike and a stack of fuel in a rickety shed at the bottom of the garden. And that's where he was headed one night in early January, torch in one hand, a metal bucket in the other.

He stumbled around dustbins and discarded junk,

and on entering the shed his face broke through a clammy spider's web. He cursed and began to shovel. But it was not until he bent to lift a log from the pile that he heard the scuttling noise. His heart skipped a beat. He spun round and flashed the torch. The beam landed on a face. A lean, wide-eyed, urchin face, with a topknot of black hair. The boy was lying on the floor, wrapped in old sacks. The two of them stared at each other.

'I'll be gone by morning.'

The man frowned and eyed him closely. 'Make sure you are,' he muttered, then finished his task and trudged off.

But in bed he lay thinking. He shared his home with mice and spiders. Why turn the waif out? He passed a mildly troubled night and by morning had softened. He trudged back to the shed.

'Just off,' the boy said, leaping up.

'Ah, never mind that. There's some porridge on the hob if you're hungry.'

The boy nodded warily.

In the kitchen, he ate like a wolf, but said little, giving the sketchiest account of himself. His parents lived apart, his family were quarrelsome, he'd had enough. He was not going back, he was sixteen, it was *his* life.

'Not easy, though. What will you do?'

The boy shrugged, gazed around with a grin, and gave the man a bold look. 'Well, this place could do with a lick of paint and I'm good with my hands.'

The man considered the risks. There was nothing in the house worth taking. In any case he was not attached to property. He stroked his chin and took some while to respond.

Festival

'Okay. Make a start on the garden. You'll find some tools in the shed, some food in the larder. I'm off. Here's a bunch of keys. Be sure to lock up if you go out. It's Finn, by the way. What'll I call you?'

'Jamie.'

Finn peddled home fast that evening, avid with curiosity. What would he find? From the front the place looked no different. But when he pushed his bike to the rear, he was amazed. The jungle of long grass and weeds had been hacked down and stuffed into sacks. The soil had been dug and raked over.

'Well, well,' he breathed. 'Not bad.'

Jamie was in the kitchen, stirring something on the hob. 'Soup?'

Finn peered into the pan.

'Leek and potato,' said the boy. 'With a splash of brown sauce.'

That night he moved into the back room, his arms loaded with sheets and blankets. Finn said goodnight and retired to his own room. He heard Jamie making his bed and smiled to himself. What a funny little scrap! But sparky, energetic, determined. Would he stay? And how would they get along? Spiders and mice keep to their corner, but could he share his home with this intruder?

When he came down in the morning, Jamie was in the kitchen making porridge.

'Tea? ... I know you like it strong.'

'Thanks,' muttered Finn, 'but I'll make my own.'

'Okay, suit yourself. But what shall I do today?'

Finn shrugged. 'Dunno. Surprise me.'

Pennine Winter

The boy grinned. 'Don't worry, I will.'

Not an idle claim. Finn returned that evening to a house transformed. The floors had been swept, the stairs and ledges dusted. Corners and cupboards had been tidied, and clutter stowed away in boxes. The bathroom mirror and the cracked washbasin positively gleamed.

'I hope I can find things,' growled Finn.

'Just ask ... I've made a list.'

Over the following weeks more changes occurred. The windows got cleaned and new curtains hung, the frames got puttied and painted, the railing was rescued from the choking grip of briars. A man was called in to sweep the chimney, another to unblock the drains, another to fix the roof. Jamie painted his room sky-blue and hung it with posters. He and Finn discussed terms, staked out their boundaries and agreed on a small wage to supplement the board and lodging.

The villagers were torn. Delighted by the changes but offended by the presence of the boy, they hardly knew how to react. Some threatened to report the matter, others said it was no one's business. Gossip in the village shop sometimes flared into civil war.

Praise for his management made the boy grow bolder. One day he tugged at Finn's beard. 'And for my next trick.'

'Oh no,' growled Finn. 'Forget that. You're not messing with me.'

But the next day the boy crept up on him with a razor and a jug of hot water.

'You heard me,' said Finn, jerking away as the boy started to lather his face.

'Hold still or I'll lop yer ears off.'

Finn snorted like a bull. But though nettled and

Festival

resistant, he was curious and persuadable, and the job took just ten minutes. Then, when it was over, the boy wiped the soap from Finn's face with a towel.

'There. What a lovely mug. Why hide it?'

Finn studied himself in the mirror with a frown, stroking his chin.

'Yeah, okay,' he scoffed. 'Anything else in mind?'

'Well, the hair,' the boy grinned, snapping a pair of scissors. 'Nothing major. Just a foot off the end.'

Finn continued to read in the evenings, and the boy, at a loss, played solitaire with a pack of cards he found in a drawer or loped about the house looking bored. Then one evening he began to explore the bookshelves, lifting down anything that took his fancy. They often sat reading at opposite ends of the hearth, occasionally raising their heads to make a remark or nod to each other with a smile. Sometimes Finn brought home bottles of beer and they played chess or backgammon at the kitchen table. Once, they ventured into the Saddler's Arms, but the looks they got were frosty and the landlady refused to serve a minor.

Jamie took care of the cooking from the start. He had an aptitude for it and a faint disdain for Finn's indifference. He experimented with sauces and tried his hand at pasta and curry. He bought jars of spice and started to build a collection of cookbooks. Once he even ventured as far as a pudding: an apricot tart served with cream. Then, on Finn's birthday, he produced his masterpiece: a walnut and cherry cake topped with white icing that drew a rare nod of approval.

During the day he busied himself with house repairs and maintenance. Every room needed renovating, but he started on the kitchen, painting the walls white, blocking up holes in the woodwork, tiling the area around the sink.

'You should advertise,' said Finn. 'Plenty of call for odd-jobbers round here.'

'Hm. Plenty to do in the house.'

'Okay, but don't feel trapped. Get out occasionally.'

'I do. When I've had enough, I go for a walk in the village or out on the moor.'

One evening, as they sat reading, Finn put his book down and glanced across at Jamie. He thought there was now a glow in his cheeks, if still too little flesh on his bones. Jamie lifted his head.

'Something bugging you?'

'I was thinking about your family. You never speak about them.'

'I told you, we had a row.'

'Any brothers and sisters?'

'Two brothers. We don't get on.'

Finn smiled. 'So what brought you *here*? To the village?'

'I thought I'd go to Nan in Sheffield. Never got there, did I?'

Finn nodded and lapsed into silence. It was strange, he thought, how little they knew about each other. They were two of a type. Reserved, clam-like, reluctant to talk about themselves.

'Don't you miss your friends back home?'

'Never had any. I like it on my own. There was Chiz at school. We hung out for a while, but then he moved away. Anyway, this is home now.'

Finn thought again how alike they were. He too was

Festival

a loner; he too had quarrelled with family. He recalled the bitter disputes he'd had with his parents back in Ireland, inflicting wounds that had still not healed. He'd thought that study would settle the mind, calm the spirit, but not so. His tutors at university were not philosophers; they were professionals, full of easy wisdom, glib answers. He had no regrets about dropping out. Like Jamie, he'd seen no choice.

A few days later, complaining of a headache and heavy limbs, Finn went to bed early. He spent the next day in bed, unable to rouse himself or eat. Jamie saw to his needs, checked him out regularly and brought him water. But the following morning he felt better and stumbled to the bathroom. He ran a deep bath, lowered himself in and luxuriated in the heat, wondering if he'd have the strength to get out.

A rap came to the door. 'Need help?'

'Well, maybe.'

Jamie came in with a clean towel. Finn was soaking in a mass of bubbles.

'Hey, sit up. I'll scrub yer back.'

Jamie knelt beside him, worked up a lather and applied a hard bristle brush. It was wonderfully invigorating. Finn tingled with pleasure, and after some minutes Jamie, chuckling at his groans of delight, began to massage his shoulders. But getting out *was* a struggle. Jamie slid hands under his shoulders and helped him to his feet. Then he towelled him down as he stood dripping on the mat, passing discreetly over his thighs, buttocks, genitals. Finn, feeling movement in his groin, shifted nervously.

'That's lovely, Jamie. Thanks.'

Pennine Winter

'You're looking good. All pink and glowing.'

They smiled at each other, and Finn saw the glint in the boy's eye, the admiring look he was sure he'd seen before.

The harsh winter dragged on. The ground turned rock hard, icicles hung from the water butt, filigree patterns appeared on the inside of the bedroom windows. Then came a night so cold they wrapped themselves in blankets as they huddled in front of the fire. In bed, Finn heard yelps from the next room as the boy drew the frozen sheets over him. Turning on his side, away from the sound, he stared deep into the darkness. He longed to go to the boy and enfold him; ached to comfort him, smother him in affection, bring joy to his young limbs. But he was afraid. Afraid to disturb the fragile home that had grown so mysteriously from nothing; from a casual brush with a runaway caught in the beam of a torch.

Three days later, on a Sunday morning, the snow came. It fell in flakes as wide as buttons and grew tall by the hour, burying the garden and clogging the sills. It dimmed the world for half a day and then vanished, leaving behind a glittering waste of smooth, rolling contours. They dug a path to the gate, but the road outside was impassable. They were marooned. They laughed, pelted each other with snow and built a fat snowman. They used pebbles for eyes, a parsnip for a nose, an inverted plant pot for a hat. And while Jamie stood gazing at their creation with silent amusement, Finn came up behind him, slid an arm round his waist and kissed the top of his head. Jamie grasped his arm and leaned back, and they held on for several minutes in a trance-like embrace.

Festival

Back in the house, Finn rubbed the boy's hands and they hugged each other for warmth. They ate biscuits and drank chocolate, holding the hot mugs to their tingling cheeks. Later, they threw logs on the fire, spread their feet on the hearth, and dozed in the heat. Aware that their guard had dropped, that a change had come over them, a change they hardly dared acknowledge, they eyed each other in a quiver of expectation, and at bedtime climbed the stairs together, their hands brushing as they drew apart.

Then, sometime in the dead of night, Jamie came to Finn's room. For several nights Finn had willed him to come, and thought in his dreamlike state that he'd come in answer. He saw the figure framed in the doorway and stretched out a hand. And when the boy climbed shivering into his bed and laid his head on his chest, he buried his nose in his hair and cradled him, as if he were a lost child that had miraculously come home. The feel of the trembling body next to his skin was like the release of a great pent-up flood. For warmth, they kneaded each other and entwined their legs, rubbing their feet together.

In the following days time stood still. It was Wednesday before the roads were clear enough to reach the village and for Finn to return to work. Meanwhile, with food in the larder, fuel in the shed, they relaxed into their newfound knowledge, aware of nothing but themselves. At first they were shy, hesitant, oddly conscious of their bodies. But caution and clumsiness soon slid away, and by the second day they'd become thoroughly easy, intimate, even bold in their nakedness. The boy's favourite trick was to drag a finger down the ridge of

Pennine Winter

Finn's back, from the nape of his neck to the tip of his spine. All this was new to Finn and each fresh venture took him by surprise, lifting him to a plane from which he took hours to descend.

The snow froze hard and clung on for weeks. Then one morning, as they lay in bed, holding each other in a loose embrace, there was a crack overhead, followed by the clatter of what sounded like a flock of birds landing on the roof. They looked up. Shadows flickered on the curtains as rubble of some kind fell past the window. They rose and peered out. Plants and shrubs in the garden, bent, battered and leafless, were emerging between patches of snow like prisoners from an underground cell. Spurred and elated, they dressed and went for a walk. The stream that ran in front of the house was a torrent, scooping the bends, flowing in humps over rocks, dragging the pebbles on the bed; while up on the hill the blue air was as chill, fresh and heady as a glass of white wine.

They sat on a bench and gazed across the valley. Finn took the boy's hand and tried to see the future. Whatever happens, he thought, you've changed me. I can never go back to what I was. If you leave, I'll sell up, books and all, and travel the world.

Jamie gripped Finn's hand, his eyes fixed on the horizon. If you tire of me, what then? I won't go back, that's for sure. I know who I am now, and owe that to you. Anyway, we're good for a while. We've only just begun. And actually you'll never get away, you're in my power. I cropped your hair, remember.

Wimbledon to Wood Green

Oh, hullo. Is that Stew? It's Rog. Yeah, that's right, Rog. Rog Molesworth. Bit of a shock, eh? This voice from the spirit world? No, honestly, it's not a hoax call. Yeah, I know it's been a long time, mate. Too long. And it's all *my* fault, sorry. I meant to stay in touch, but well, you know how it is – you put things off, life takes a funny turn, you hit a bad patch. Oh look, I won't bore you with the details. Anyway, I tried ringing Chaucer Road recently, but they said you'd moved years ago. Well, what did I expect? Then last week I ran into Chip Hines. He'd just knocked off. He's working in Smithfield, apparently. Some building site in the area. Anyway, he fishes out his little black book. He says, 'Stewart Penrose? That bugger? I saw him in the Greyhound, Walthamstow, just a few weeks ago.' And he stabs a finger at an entry in the book. 'As far as I know,' he says, 'that's still it.' So I write the number down on the back of my hand.

Yeah, I *heard* you got married. Chip told me. Nice

girl, he said. Rose or Rosemary or something? Oh, *Rosina*, I'm so sorry. I don't know why I misheard. I guess I was a bit flustered at the time. It was meeting Chip so unexpectedly and he does tend to speak – well, you know, in that mangled rush of his. So your wife is? Really? From Bologna? How nice. I love Bologna. Well, no, I've never been. It's just that, well, it's a lovely name and I think I may have seen – though I'm not quite sure about this – some photographs or paintings of it or something? At least … gosh, I'm wittering, aren't I?

Well, nothing much, mate. I've not been too good, to be honest. Thing is, I lost my job at McBride's shortly after you left. Yeah, that's right, lost. No, it wasn't redundancy or anything like that. To be frank, I don't like talking about it. It was all down to – well, let's call it an incident. You remember Gary Buck? Big, fat-nosed Gary Buck? Yeah, of course you do. Well, Gary got it into his head that I was always looking at him. Yeah, can you believe it? I mean, *looking* at him? Since when was it a crime to look at someone? In any case, it wasn't true. I hardly ever looked at him. I was always trying *not* to look at him. Christ, if you wanted to look at someone, the last person you'd want to look at is Gary Buck. I mean, a sixteen-stone Neanderthal with greasy hair and spots?

Anyway, eventually he went to management and complained about me. Not only was I looking at him, I was also making passes, apparently, by peeking at his schlong in the urinals. Ha, what a joke! The truth is, I never went near the urinals when he was there – he always stood in the middle and with his bulk it was hard to squeeze in. Anyway, Tony Shaw interviewed me and

Festival

played it by the book. He said sexual harassment was a difficult thing to establish, but he had to take the complaint seriously and issue a warning. Well, that was fair enough, but it wasn't the end of the matter, of course. Word went round – you know what the place is like – and soon everyone was whispering and sniggering. Then Gary made a second complaint. And when I heard the news I went wild. We were queuing in the canteen at the time and he was just a few yards ahead of me. So I flew at him from behind, gripped him by the neck and punched his head repeatedly, like a maniac.

You're right, Stew. It's not like me. Not like me at all. We don't know ourselves, do we? We're an enigma mostly – we just learn a little more when we're pushed. What's that? Disaster? You can say that again. It was hell at the time and it's been hell ever since. They told me not to apply for a reference. I couldn't find work, didn't even *want* work. For months I couldn't even bring myself to look for it. The one relief was that he didn't press charges, though don't ask me why, otherwise I'd have a record.

Eventually? Oh sure, eventually. Bits and pieces, temping work, you know. But nothing much. And nothing at all at the moment. As I say, I've not been too good. I get a bit sunk at times. Well, totally sunk, to be frank. But fortunately I've got this very understanding doctor. He knows just what I need. Well, his signature, I guess, for the most part.

No, I left Albert Road years ago. I've had umpteen addresses since then. The thing is, I don't seem to be able to settle. The last place I stayed, the landlord and his wife lived on the premises. They were fine, but their teenage son took a dislike to me. He may have thought

Wimbledon to Wood Green

I was always looking at him. Perhaps I was. He was certainly easier on the eye than Gary Buck. Anyway, we shared this kitchen and one day at breakfast he said, 'I don't know why I sit here every morning staring at your creepy mug.' So I said, 'That's funny, I was just having the same thought. And yes, it's a mystery. But relax, there's a simple solution – I'll eat alone in future.' I have this knack, Stew, you may recall, of making people turn on me. What *is* this knack? You probably know, but you've never dropped a hint, have you? You've never let on.

That lot? Rarely see them. Bradford's a long way off, thank God. I sometimes stay with Tom in Glossop, but that's about the size of it where family's concerned. Tom's the best of the bunch, though we've nothing in common and his prissy little wife Lynn, with her ruched curtains, her china cabinet and doilies, drives me to nose bleeds. As for their kids, words fail me. They're monsters, terrorists. They fight on the landing, tumble down the stairs and lie on the hall floor screaming. They slummock through the house looking bored and pinch the back of your neck as they pass. They trail in mud from the garden and never think to clear it up. Lynn runs around after them with a vacuum cleaner and a damp rag.

Remember Brighton? Of course I do. How could I forget? It was a great day, every precious minute of it. The ice cream on the pier, the paddle in the sea, the open-top bus ride. You in your loud shorts, me in my panama. The thronged cafés, the kids building castles, the gulls strutting the promenade, the red sundown. And yes, I *do* go back; I go back often. And always alone, of course. I tread the same route, revisit everything. And

Festival

when the time comes to eat I always go *there*. You know, *that* place. And honestly, it's a miracle. I mean, how many years since we ate there? And not a thing has changed. Even the waiter who served us – that little old guy with his hair parted in the middle? – he's still there. In fact he knows me well now and always greets me with the warmest smile. He says, 'Alone again, sir? Where's your friend?' And I say, 'Ah, who knows?' And he says, 'Same table, sir?' and I say, 'Yes, please.' And I order the same meal every time. Oh, sometimes he tries to lead me astray, to tempt me from the one true path. He says, 'There's a very nice special, sir,' and points to something on the menu. But I always wave the suggestion aside and he nods politely with 'Just as you wish, sir'. And when I come to pay I always tip him generously. I'm rather stingy in that department usually, but I make an exception for *him*. He's essential to the visit, after all. A vital link, an institution. He's kin. He's family.

The old crowd? Nah, scarcely catch a whiff. Meeting Chip was just a chance thing. I guess after – well, you know what – and then losing my job I couldn't face people and turned in on myself. Oh, sometimes I have a brainstorm and decide to join something. I took up weightlifting at the gym a while back, but almost immediately I sprained my back and was laid up for weeks. So I switched to Spanish at the language school, but eventually came to grief on the present subjunctive. Then I decided that I needed to be more creative and joined a life-drawing class. And all went well until I got rather too chummy with Dale, a member of the class who sometimes posed as a life model. And I'm not sure I know what happened there. I just know that we seemed

Wimbledon to Wood Green

to get on splendidly at first, meeting for coffee in town, going for a swim at the pool, taking in a film now and again. Then one day, right out of the blue, he said, 'Look, I'd be very glad if you'd stop pestering me.' Yeah, don't ask, I haven't a clue. I've reviewed all my actions, ransacked my memory, tried every which way to make out what he meant. Was it a case of *looking* again? Anyway, I went right back into myself, snapped on the telly and sat in front of it yanking cans from a six-pack. And that's where I've been ever since. That's where I am now, in fact, in front of the telly. Oh sure, I know *that* – but then, drugs have their uses.

Actually, speaking of the old crowd, I did see Kenny and Ange a while back. Yeah, just walked smack into them in Portobello Road. And what a pair, eh? They never change, do they? They're still in that top flat in Stepney and still not married. He punched me on the shoulder, she pinched my cheek. 'Good to see ya,' they said. So we reminisced and they asked after you. 'How's Stew?' they said. 'Dunno,' I said. 'I lost touch.' 'What?' said Kenny, holding up a pair of crossed fingers. 'And you were like *that*.' 'Yeah,' said Ange. 'So close, we thought you must have a crush on each other.' And they laughed, and *I* laughed, and we all three laughed and laughed. And when I got home that day I flung myself on the sofa and buried my head in a cushion and lay there for hours and hours.

Hey, mate, sorry to offload. You don't want to hear all this, do you? I guess I'm beginning to sound like Dorothy after the tenth shot of gin. No, not Garland, the other one – Parker? Oh, never mind. Anyway, Stew, I just want to say one more thing before I go. It's about that other incident. You know, *that* one. And what I

Festival

want to say is this. I'm sorry, I'm truly sorry. It was embarrassing, it was maudlin, it was self-indulgent. I get like that, as you know, when I've had too many. Which may be what I've just had. I mean, I've got a little Scotch right here in my hand and it's not the first. But then I needed a few before I could make this call. Anyway, I repeat, it *was* embarrassing and I shouldn't have said it. But what I want you to know is this. You're the only person I've ever said that to. I've never said *that* to anyone else, not ever. Nor, I think, will I ever say it to anyone again.

Stew, are you still there? ... Stew? ...

Ah well, whatever the case, I guess it's time for me to go now. So, if you're still listening, it only remains to say that I hope you and Rosina will be very happy. Very, very happy. Honestly, I mean that ... I mean that from the bottom of my heart. And I won't call again, I promise. Give my regards to Chip when you see him. He'll have all the details in his little black book, but please, I beg you not to bother. It's best if ... Oh Christ, I'm wittering again – something's started to interfere with my speech patterns. Look, I'm going to ring off now and then drift into the bedroom and lie down. And after a while I'll roll into a foetus and keep perfectly still till dawn. Then I'll get up, move to the window, pull the cord and the blind will fly up ... and I'll feed the cat, make myself breakfast, phone the surgery and then ... Stew? ... Stew, for the last time, are you still there?

Weekend

The back bar of the Crown was heaving. As always, it seemed to George, but then he only ever came on a Saturday night. He loved the back bar. There you could let your hair down. The front bar was mixed, more respectable, much less fun. Besides, the back bar had Gerry, also known as Geraldine, the dazzling head barman who flapped around in a pink frilly blouse, tons of makeup and a wristful of bangles. Too much for some of course, but a magnet to George, who adored all that campery. There was nothing standoffish about Gerry, who was always warm and matey, even to customers as heavy, bald and unglamorous as George. Seated on a bar stool, swapping banter with Gerry, George lost much of his shyness and became almost voluble. Gerry was a tonic and George his devoted admirer.

The problem for George was that he so rarely had a chance to pay a visit. He sometimes dropped in for the night under pretence of being elsewhere, but his best chance was when Barbara was away. Just now she was

Festival

staying with her sister in Leeds, who was depressed and in need of company. George had been married to Barbara for almost twenty years. They'd met at a New Year's party, where the hostess, who prided herself on the deft handling of shy people, had pushed them together. It had been a dull companionable marriage, punctuated by the odd passionate outburst, long periods of silence and frequent mysterious headaches. George had carried on labouring at the jam factory where he'd worked since leaving school and Barbara had accepted whatever temping work had come her way. They were comfortably settled in a bungalow a few miles out of town. The rooms were spotless, the hedges trim. They were on nodding terms with the neighbours and spent a fortnight every year at a guesthouse in Bournemouth. There were no children.

George eyed the man on the next stool. He was perhaps in his mid-twenties, but his crown of curly blond hair and boyish face gave him the air of a student. He was facing the bar, hunched over a glass of beer, and kept glancing around. He was wearing jeans, a check shirt and a pair of suede boots. On one such glance he noticed George's smile and smiled back.

'Hi,' said George. 'I've had my eye on you.'

'You have?' The man looked alarmed.

'Don't panic, I'm not Special Branch or anything.'

They chuckled, there was a pause, and then George's hand shot out.

'It's George, by the way.'

'Nice to meet you, George. I'm Hal.'

'Oh really? Is that an alias or something?'

'A nickname. My dad's a fan of Shakespeare.'

'Hm, you've lost me.'

Weekend

'Well, don't let it bother you. Is there some entertainment in here tonight?'

George winked. 'You mean like a boy stripper?'

'I mean' – Hal sounded aloof – 'like live music.'

'Eh, don't think so, but if it's entertainment you need, there's plenty of that at my place. So drink up and let me buy you another.'

'I don't want another. I've had far too many already.'

'Ah, relax. It's all good lubrication.'

'Well, if you insist. And your place? Where's that?'

The car was parked in Broad Street. It was a hatchback of some kind, but that was all Hal noticed. He was feeling heady, out of control, and not at all sure he should be doing this. George was a heavy, middle-aged man, a grizzly bear with hair sprouting from his ears. In short, not exactly his type. But to decline the invitation would mean going home alone, and that would be disappointing. He was eager for contact, rampantly horny and up for adventure.

George drove steadily, with silent concentration, and soon they were out of town, coasting along dark country roads. Hal, unsure of where they were, glanced about, hoping to spot a familiar landmark.

'Not far now,' said George.

They passed isolated houses, an abandoned petrol station, rows of cottages. Then a figure loomed out of the darkness: a hitchhiker with raised thumb. A slim figure, Hal noticed, in jeans and a bomber jacket. George drove on.

'Can't we offer a lift?'

'No point, we're nearly there.'

'But he mightn't be going far.'

Festival

George shrugged and pulled over, mounting the curb. They sat and waited, and shortly the figure came pounding up. George lowered the window.

'We can drop you at the next village.'

'That's fine. I'm going to the airbase. I'll walk the rest.'

He had an angular face and a shapely head covered in tight black curls. In his early twenties, Hal guessed. His complexion was dark and he looked Arabic, but he spoke perfect English in an American accent. Without hesitation he opened the rear door and slid onto the back seat. George drove off.

Hal turned. 'So you live at the airbase?'

'I'm stationed there. Work on the switchboard. Nothing fancy.'

'And you walk everywhere?'

The man chuckled. 'I'm saving to buy some transport. I mean I like to get into town now and again. Tonight I went to see this very sad movie about Billy Holiday.'

'Any good?'

'Brilliant.' The man paused. 'So what about you guys?'

George laughed nervously.

'We just met,' said Hal.

'Oh really? I took you for father and son.'

They were now in the village. George drew into a lay-by. 'This okay?'

'How far to the base?' said Hal. 'Can't we drop this guy off?'

George shrugged. 'Well, yeah … I guess.'

'Or perhaps you'd like to come in for a drink?' said Hal, twisting round.

Weekend

'For a drink?' The hitcher raised an eyebrow. 'Hm, sounds good.'

George stared stonily through the windscreen.

The bungalow was in disarray, as George knew. Though well trained, he lacked Barbara's standards and tended to lapse into carelessness when she was away. In the sitting room he snapped on the table lamp, not wishing to expose the mess to the glare of the main light, and invited the visitors to sit. They made themselves comfortable at opposite ends of the sofa and George settled into his armchair.

'Nice place,' said Hal, glancing round.

'Yeah,' nodded the hitcher. 'It's Ollie, by the way.'

The others introduced themselves, and then George got up and crossed the room. 'Now what'll you boys have?' He peered into his cabinet. 'There's a spot of everything, and a full bottle of Scotch.'

'Scotch for me,' said Ollie.

'And for me,' said Hal. 'Though I *should* lay off.'

'Ah, relax,' said George. 'It's all good lubrication.'

He poured three large measures and handed a couple to the guests. They clinked glasses and grinned at each other. There was a stretch of awkward silence.

'So you just met,' said Ollie.

'In a bar,' said Hal, whose face was flushed. He seemed emboldened by drink and on the point of blurting everything. George eyed him in alarm. But Ollie seemed cool and simply nodded with a faint smile.

'And you?' George broke in. 'Where are you from?'

'New Jersey. I came over last year. Had a hankering to see Europe. And it's been sort of fun, but I'm not sure how long I'll stay.'

Festival

'I'm in hospital management,' said Hal. 'And it's *not* fun, believe me.'

George was reluctant to talk about himself. No one wanted to hear about a bald, middle-aged bloke who worked in a jam factory. He answered all questions briefly, hoping attention would quickly shift to one of the others. He was happy to listen; he'd been a listener all his life. In particular he was anxious to avoid any questions about Barbara, whose studio portrait stood on the sideboard. But none came, and he assumed that the boys, who must have noticed it, were simply being discreet.

The talk went on, and George refilled the glasses. The evening was hardly going to plan, but what did he expect? His evenings rarely went to plan. So why not change tack? Why not be generous? It was clear to him now that the lads were more interested in each other than they were in him. They could share the bed in the spare room. There was no chance now of driving to the airbase; too much drink had been taken. Ollie could of course walk if he wanted to, but it would be cruel to turf him out at this hour. And if he had no interest in Hal's advances, he could always knee him in the groin. He looked fully able to take care of himself.

Settling back in his chair, George viewed the situation with resignation. It was a disappointment, this turn of events, but not a calamity. In any case, being used to setbacks, he'd developed a stoic frame of mind. He had a great fancy for Hal. He liked men to have flesh on their bones and Hal was square and chunky. He failed to see the appeal of Ollie, who seemed to be nothing but sharp edges. But which of them he fancied was now beside the point; he wasn't going to get either.

Weekend

Still, he couldn't entirely regret the evening; it gave him a secret thrill, this adventure. He felt excited by the thought of the two men thrashing about in the spare bed, and even more excited by the thought of joining them, however remote that possibility.

Hal woke in the dead of night and wondered where he was. Then he recalled. But he had no memory of going to bed. George and Ollie must have carried him, and somehow they'd managed to remove most of his clothes. He was wearing nothing but underpants and socks. He winced at the sharp throbbing in his head. Then he stretched and turned and felt something move in the bed beside him. Putting out a hand, he touched something warm and damp and recoiled as if from a hot wire.

'Hello,' said a voice. 'Welcome back.'
'Jesus,' said Hal. 'What happened?'
'You crashed ... remember?'
'No, not a thing. Oh Christ, my head.'

They lay on their backs for a while, still and silent, arms pinned to their sides like figures on a medieval tomb. Hal turned over the events of the night and wondered what to do next.

Then Ollie broke the silence. 'Well, here we are.'
'Yeah, here we are.'
'Shouldn't you be next door with George?'
'I guess. But as you say ... here we are.'

More silence. Then Ollie turned and tweaked one of Hal's nipples. 'Well, well, there's no point in being here if we don't *do* something, is there?'

Hal turned and stared at him with wide eyes.

'Hey, don't look at *me*,' said Ollie. 'I don't bloody

Festival

know, do I? I've never done this kind of thing. I'm relying on you.'

George, lying awake in the next room, surrendered to the vivid images of his heated imagination. It was amazing how excited he could make himself by merely picturing the activity that might be happening in the spare bed. Even more exciting was the thought of being in the middle of it. He'd left the hall light on and his door slightly ajar. He could hear a low blur of voices.

How sad, he thought. To be lying here, picturing and listening. That desire should come to this. Was a little warmth, comfort and love too much to ask? He'd been born too early, that was the problem. The younger generation had it all: looks, freedom, confidence. Courage, too. It was fear and lack of imagination that had made him settle for a life with Barbara.

A head peered around the door.

'George,' Hal whispered.

George sat up and Hal sneaked in. Light from the hall showed that he was naked. George stretched out an arm. 'Hey, come to bed.'

Hal took his hand and knelt beside him. 'Not now, George. I'm a bit caught up at the moment ... Sorry, give me an hour or so, eh?'

George smiled. 'Is he nice?'

'He's okay. A bit raw. Needs training. Know what I mean?'

They chuckled softly.

George woke at just after ten, feeling slightly hung over. Still, that was nothing new. Hal, as expected, had not reappeared. But George, though disappointed, was not

Weekend

bitter or resentful. He quite understood. In Hal's position, he too would have opted for a night with Ollie. True, Ollie was not exactly his type. Nor, it seemed, was he much good in bed. But in the end there was no getting away from it: Ollie, for all his shortcomings, was the better catch.

And it *was* an adventure, after all. He was enjoying the secret thrill of having the boys around, of breaking the barren codes of the bungalow and defiling its sterile air. He pictured the scene next door: the exhausted bodies, the sweaty limbs, the stained, twisted sheets. He reached down and brought himself off with a loud moan. A moan that he thought must have been heard in the next room, if not in the next street.

In the kitchen, waiting for the kettle to boil, he thought that he'd treat the boys to a lavish breakfast. Bacon and eggs perhaps, followed by toast and marmalade. He made a pot of coffee and knocked discreetly on their door. There was no reply. So he tried again. This time he caught low mutterings, then a weak summons: 'Come in.' He entered cheerily, carrying two steaming mugs on a small round tray. The guests were sitting up in bed, looking dazed and dishevelled. They were clutching the duvet as if they'd just hauled it off the floor to hide their nakedness.

Half an hour later they emerged fully dressed and fell back on the sofa, looking drained. Hal sat with his head in his hands.

'Now, what for breakfast?' said George. 'Something cooked?'

Hal groaned. 'Ah, not for me, George.'

'Nor for me,' said Ollie. 'But perhaps another coffee. Preferably black.'

Festival

'Is that all?' George looked disappointed. 'Ah well, coming up.'

Back in the kitchen, rinsing grains from the pot, he heard them talking.

'The name of that bar,' said Ollie. 'Tell me again. I might look in sometime.'

Otherwise the talk was sparse. George tried to lighten the mood, but without success. Forty minutes later he dropped Ollie off at the base and then took Hal into town. Hal asked to be dropped in Southside Walk. The two of them were silent on the drive, but when they pulled up at the drop-off point they turned to each other with a smile.

'So how was it?' said George, clapping him on the shoulder.

'Not too hot,' said Hal. 'Sorry, George, I've been a shit, haven't I? A total shit.'

George shrugged. 'Anyway, another time, perhaps.'

Barbara rang that evening. 'Ah, there you are. I called last night. Where were you?'

George coughed. He wondered whether to invent something, but then dismissed the idea. 'I went out,' he said.

'You went out? But you never go out.'

'I do when you're not here.'

'Do you? Well, I hope you went somewhere nice.'

'I went to a bar. Felt like a drink and a bit of company.'

'I see.' She sounded curious. 'A night on the town then.'

'Something like that,' said George.

She giggled and there was a pause. 'Anyway, I'm

Weekend

going to stay, George. Perhaps for a week or two. Kath's in a bad way and I can't leave her like this. I could kill Derek, the selfish toad!'

'That's fine, I'll manage,' said George.

'Good man. Have another night on the town.'

'Thanks,' he said. 'I will.'

When she rang off he wandered into the spare room and stood staring at the bed. He wondered what exactly had occurred last night and tried to conjure up the scene, hoping to excite himself again. What he saw, though, was a scrimmage of awkward fumbling. He inspected the sheet. Not a stain. He recalled the verdict – 'not too hot' – and smiled. Ah well, another time perhaps. There was still a chance. He was bound to run into Hal again. And still smiling, he stripped off the bedding, carried it to the kitchen and bundled it into the washing machine.

Roll-Top Desk, Bottom Left Drawer

Dear Tony, I'm writing to you – yes, after all these decades – with no certainty that my words will ever reach you. My hope is that someone will forward this letter or return it. I'll post it care of Ashton House. Will that find you? I still think of it as the family home, though your parents must surely have passed on by now. I remember their warm hospitality, their kindness, their eagerness to embrace me as your college friend. Which makes it all the more difficult to write what I feel I now must.

Someone at college – Mike Mackenzie? – described us as inseparable. I'm sure you remember those days as vividly as I do. Our adjacent rooms became a joint living space. We used to share provisions, call to each other through the wall and sit up half the night, discussing Marx, Freud and Camus over mugs of glutinous coffee. You even rigged up a speaker to my room as if to seal the intimacy, and woke me every morning to some radiant music evoking dawn. Yes, ravishing Ravel. The love theme from that piece still enthrals me and floods my entire memory of that time.

Roll-Top Desk, Bottom Left Drawer

Your elusive charm was quite unaffected, never winsome, and indeed a bit rough at the edges. You were a natural scruff. I loved the way you flaunted your ruffled mop, frayed collars and baggy-arsed jeans as if to defy the grace of your long, loose-limbed body. I loved the dark mole on the side of your neck, the suggestion of a scar over your right eye. I loved your habit of drying your tired socks on the radiator, of frowning whenever I said something stupid, of casually passing me a joint with yellow-stained fingers.

Did you know your effect on me? Sense my desire? I think you did, though you never played on it or showed any awareness of it. Indeed, your discretion gave the game away, for you sometimes spoke of girls you had known but never pressed *me* on the subject.

I was thrilled to be invited to your home for the vacation. Amazed to be so privileged. I groomed myself for the visit, pressed my shirt, scrubbed my nails, and on meeting your parents felt that I was more than a friend, that I was being presented as someone uniquely special.

That first day we climbed the hill behind the town. It was late June, the trees in luxuriant leaf, the fields a quilt of green and gold. You pointed out the landmarks: the hump of Medlock Rise, the church at Wethersham, the chimney at Stanton Mill. 'You can see three counties from here,' you declared with pride.

We walked down to the reservoir and hung in amazement over the mighty roar of the sluice. Then somewhere on the far side we sprawled on a bench and you pressed a passing hiker to take a photo of us, your arm around my shoulder. We liked it so much, we framed it. Stood it dead-centre on a shelf at college.

Festival

I forget when you took me to see Pippa. But it was soon – perhaps the day after my arrival? Anyway, we walked the handful of streets to her house and she came to the door in a bathrobe, her nut-brown hair hanging lank over her shoulders, her face pink and glowing. You leaned forward, kissed her, and she invited us in.

'I know who you are,' she said. 'You're Rob.'

'Oh?' I chuckled. 'What makes you so sure?'

'Intuition,' she said, tapping her nose. 'Tony never stops talking about you.'

'Oops,' I said.

Her eyes were sharp and ironic. I wondered what you'd told her. She'd just returned from Italy and confessed to being very excited about the new job she was about to start in advertising. So, as a treat, we took her to the local coffee house, where I saw – how could I miss? – the powerful magnetism between you, the spell she cast over you. Whatever her flaws – the short chin, the over-wide mouth – she was undoubtedly pretty.

I should say that in other circumstances she and I would probably have hit it off blazingly. She was vivacious, easy-going, full of fun. It was just that there was this rock, this stumbling-block, between us. Namely, you. An absurd situation, of course, because objectively I could see that she was the one – your soulmate, the key to your happiness, the perfect counterweight to your occasional over-seriousness.

But objectively? How naive to factor *that* into matters of the heart.

I've had years, decades, a near lifetime, to trace the steps that led to my action. So I'll start – but where does anything begin? – with the day she came to your house

Roll-Top Desk, Bottom Left Drawer

for tea. We were alone, the three of us, your parents out visiting friends, and on my return from a trip to the bathroom I heard you talking in low voices. So I stood at the door and listened.

'He's a bit of an oddity. Doesn't he have anyone?'

'He has *me*,' you said.

'Well, watch out, you might never get away,' she quipped.

And you both giggled.

I froze in mortification. Hurt blazed up in me and my face burned. In fact, several minutes passed before I felt composed enough to slink back into the room and take my place on the sofa, now in the cutting knowledge that I was a mild embarrassment, a kind of private joke.

Then, a few weeks into the new term, she came to visit us at college, and I recall the way she cast an eye over everything with a wry smile. I see her drifting around the rooms, inspecting the little white jug we bought at the antiques fair, lifting the carved wooden biscuit barrel, twirling the Spanish figurine. I hear her snort of laughter on spotting that framed photo of us lounging on the bench by the reservoir, your arm around my shoulder.

'Oh well, what a cosy little domestic set-up you have here,' she said.

Later we hired a punt and poled upstream with a loaf, some cheese and a bottle of champagne. And as I drove us forward and gazed at you two lying in the prow, she nestling in the crook of your arm, it seemed to me that her glittering eyes were gazing back at me with mingled triumph and condescension.

'Ah, this is heavenly,' she purred. 'But can't we find someone for Rob.'

Festival

'Leave the lad alone,' you said. 'He's got his hands full steering this punt.'

I didn't see her again until our graduation. She came for the ceremony, of course, and this time the glitter was not only in her eyes but on her finger. I was prepared for it – you had dropped a hint or two – but it was still a shock when she flashed her hand in front of my face.

'Congratulations,' I said. 'So when's the event?'

'Oh, nothing's fixed. But when it happens, we want you to be best man.'

'Me?' I said.

'Yes, *you*.' She pinched my arm. 'There are others we could ask, but I said that I wanted it to be you.'

She beamed, leaned forward, and kissed me on the cheek. And her piercing smile was like a final sword-thrust, a coup de grâce. I recoiled slightly and tried to return the smile, but I'm pretty sure I managed only a grimace.

'Oh well,' I said. 'That's very nice. I'll let you know.'

My resolve began at that moment. But I'm the mildest of types, as you'd admit, so don't ask me where it came from. In the following weeks it seemed to grow inside me like a tumour – an emotional impulse, almost physical in force, over which I had no control. During those weeks I seemed to stand outside myself, watching my hand move towards an action that still shocks me – of which, before that moment and in all the years since, I would never have thought myself capable. It was not instant; the delivery took almost as long as the gestation. I'm not a natural writer; I've struggled with this letter for days, and the one I wrote then took quite as long. But with this difference: there was no signature, or

Roll-Top Desk, Bottom Left Drawer

heading, or opening address. Also, I typed it – in a vain attempt, I suppose – did she know my hand? – to preserve the anonymity.

I've kept a copy, but I won't quote from it. I can scarcely bear to read it. It's an eruption of spleen, a pack of insinuations and lies. It seems, when I can bring myself to review it, almost deranged – like the invective of someone I don't recognise. Yet, for all my disavowal, this is undeniably *me* – a darker self, from the many of which we're made, that I'm now forced to acknowledge.

I remember the moment of posting, the hesitation at the slit, the long drop to the bottom of the box. Then months of dread, of ominous quiet. You and I were out in the big bad world by now and widely separated, you working in the City, me teaching in Leeds. We spoke a few times on the phone, but you made no mention of Pippa and I was afraid to ask. It was Christmas before we met again. The King's Head in Fulham. But it was hard to recapture the old magic. You were glum, unhappy at work, uncertain about the future. I sensed you slipping away, supped my beer mournfully, felt the loss of the bond we'd once shared. And to complete my frustration, there was still no mention of Pippa. Not the slightest hint of what I was most avid to hear.

Eventually, in desperation, I nerved myself to grasp the nettle: 'Hey, cheer up. Think about the wedding.'

'The wedding!' you scoffed. 'What wedding? She's called it off.'

I stared at you in a swirl of confusion. 'Called it off? But why?'

You shrugged. 'Well, how do I know? She's never said.'

Festival

I felt a rush to my cheeks, a flurry of excitement mixed with an evil churning in the stomach. I was dumb for a while as I searched for an appropriate response. Then I reached across the table and took your hand.

'Hey, I'm sorry to hear that,' I said.

And the rank hypocrisy, the sham sentiment, still stings to this day.

We lost touch for six months. Then came a letter. You were working in Singapore, had married a Malaysian – 'the sweetest girl on earth' – and were very happy. I'm not sure that I can say what my feelings were. Pain, relief, remorse were there, all mixed up with grief at the thought that I might never see you again.

In resignation I sank myself into the old routine. Work absorbed me, covered for the absence of any personal involvement. Oh, I wasn't celibate, don't get me wrong. I went through multiple hook-ups, many a hopeful fling. There was Frank, Martin, Winston, Big Jim, Little Pete. It's just that none went beyond a month, and most ended on a casual farewell after the morning mug of black coffee.

I wrote to you several times, but nothing came back. I assumed you had changed address and were now beyond reach. I ached with a sense of hollowness that over time simply faded to a condition of life, like a cleft palette or a club foot. It was five years before I heard from you again, by which time I was living in London, so your phone call came as a great surprise. You had traced me through the alumni. You were back in Britain. Could we meet? What about the King's Head in Fulham?

The proposal filled me with excitement and dread. I feared the effects of time and long separation, and my

Roll-Top Desk, Bottom Left Drawer

misgivings were fully realised. It was a painful reunion. You had changed. You were harder, more cynical, more than usually careless of your appearance. Your stomach was a paunch, you were running to flab, there were ragged tufts on your chin. The scruffiness that had once beguiled me had lost its appeal. You drank too much, became sloppily offhand, tersely bitter.

'How's married life?' I asked.

'Oh, that. It's finished. We had a couple of years. Wouldn't do it again.'

'So you're living alone?'

'Yup. Fancy free and loving it.'

We fell silent and stared into our beer. I thought of earlier times and nursed my guilt. You turned in on yourself. Then, after a while, we sat up and tried to steer the conversation around. We talked about our current work, remembered old friends, discussed the state of the world. But the old spark failed to ignite, and near the end the talk drifted, faltered, became maudlin.

'Pippa,' you said. 'You remember Pippa?'

I nodded. A surge ripped through me and a tic started up in my face. I lowered my gaze.

'She was the one,' you said. 'Yeah, I think it would have worked with Pippa.'

I looked up, struggled to meet your eye, shrugged. 'Well, maybe. Who knows?'

I pointed to your glass. 'Same again?'

And that, as you know, was the last time I saw you. I guess it's easier to maintain a friendship when the going's good, and I have a suspicion that it hasn't worked out for either of us. So I won't bore you with the sad saga of the past forty years, save to say, if you'll forgive the bald statement, that I am now dying. I'm told

Festival

that I have about six months to live. Six months to gather up the pieces, shed the burden of this tired old body, cast off the accumulated sins of seventy years. So Tony, if this letter ever reaches you, please understand that I'm not looking for pardon. I merely ask that you show compassion for a penitent old man, whose action all that time ago still appals and mystifies him.

It will come as no consolation, or mitigation of my offence, if I say that for me – to echo your own words – *you* were the one. There's never been anyone else. And I can only wonder at the forces that drive us. It is, of course, the eternal tragedy: the need to kill the rival, hurt the beloved. My action has certainly blighted my own life and probably the lives of at least two other people. So I'll end this letter with the words that resounded throughout my childhood, were rejected in later life, and have now returned to haunt me: *Agnus Dei, qui tollis peccata mundi, dona nobis pacem.*

Yours in sorrow,
Rob

Solicitor's note: this letter, found among Professor Kingsley's papers after his death, appears to have been posted but returned to sender.

Revenant

Forty-nine! ... Oh God! Birthdays are cruel, aren't they? Well, after a certain age, and especially if you live alone. I heaved out of bed, viewed my sagging figure in the mirror, and drifted into the lounge scratching my navel. A clutch of envelopes dropped through the box. I lifted them from the mat.Cards from Dermot, Carol, Mike. Cheerful, jokey cards that failed to cheer or amuse me. I tossed them aside, sat down to a breakfast of grapefruit and ryebread, and mulled over the way things had turned out. Then I fetched my phone, searched for the address I'd found the previous evening, and punched in the number. Time for a pick-me-up. Time to seize fate by the throat.

'When would suit?' someone asked. 'Ten-thirty, two-thirty or four-thirty?'

'Oh, make it ten-thirty,' I said, and then sat around for an hour, feeling buoyed by my decision.

But when the doorbell rang I was suddenly nervous. He was tall, six foot two at least, and sheathed in tight

Festival

black Lycra shorts. Early twenties, I guessed, though the dark stubble on his face disguised his youth. His arms and thighs bulged like melons, and his black sleeveless vest made a raised feature of his nipple-rings.

He said, 'Henry?'

'Yes,' I said. 'And you're ...?'

'Jock,' he said. 'Jock Wilde.'

I waved him in, staring at the plank under his arm with puzzlement.

'Portable massage table,' he grinned.

'Oh yes,' I said. 'Of course ... Sorry, I'm new to all of this.'

'First time?'

'Yes,' I chuckled. 'So I'm entirely in your hands ... so to speak.'

He glanced round and saw the cards. 'Special day?'

'Birthday,' I said.

'Oh well,' he winked, rubbing his palms together. 'Then let's make it *extra* special.'

'Mmm.' I gazed at him wondrously. 'So shall we start with a drink? What can I get you?'

'I never touch alcohol at work and I'm cutting down on caffeine. D'you have hibiscus?'

'Er ... don't think so ... What about passion fruit?'

'Perfect,' he said.

I made the drinks while he set up the table. Then we took a few sips and smiled at each other.

'Now strip,' he said.

'Strip?' I said. 'What? All the way?'

'As far as you like.'

I stripped to my shorts.

'Now get on the table, lie on your stomach and relax.'

Revenant

I climbed aboard and he cracked his fingers. Standing to one side, he gripped my shoulders and rolled his palms into them, kneading the flesh and massaging the nape of my neck with his powerful thumbs. Then he chopped all the way down my spine and thumped my arse. It was immediate – a miracle! The weight, the accumulated pain of forty-nine years, lifted in an instant and floated out of my jaded body. I was reborn.

But just as he started on my thighs, the doorbell rang.

'Oh Christ,' I groaned.

I slipped off the table and peeped through the window. It was Mad Maude. She was holding a potted plant swathed in pink tissue. Unfortunately, she saw the curtain twitch and waved.

'It's a friend,' I said. 'Oh God, I'll have to speak to her. Could you hide in the bedroom? She's a fearful gossip.'

He grinned, nodded, picked up the table and disappeared. I pulled on a singlet and opened the door. Maude beamed.

'Another milestone!' she shrieked, thrusting the plant into my hands.

'Oh thanks,' I said, 'but you don't have to tell the whole street.'

'My dear, you're not even dressed,' she said, bursting in without invitation. She's a formidable whirlwind. 'I fear you're going to pot, love.'

I opened my mouth to protest, but she stormed straight on. 'Have you seen the reviews?'

I shook my head. I never read reviews. I get them from her – verbatim!

'Who *are* these bloody people? ... Listen to this,

Festival

from some snotty shit in the *Argus* – and I quote from memory – *Maude Bristow's extravagant set seems determined to upstage everything else in this production and takes garishness to a new level* ... God, I flung a mug of tea at the wall when I read that. I mean, what this prick doesn't understand – *clearly* – is that I'm trying to resist the grey minimalism that seems to infect every production these days. After all, this is *theatre*, isn't it – not Monday morning at the goddamned stock exchange ...'

'Maude,' I broke in, 'I'm a bit off colour.'

She stared at me. 'Oh sweetheart, why didn't you say?'

'I did try,' I said.

'And on your *birthday*,' she wailed. 'Look, go straight to bed. D'you need anything – pills, capsules, powders ...?'

'No, no, I've got all that.'

'In that case, I'll vamoose – pronto! These things are catching. Now take care. I'll phone tonight.'

She blew a kiss. I saw her out and watched her drive off. But before I closed the door, Jeremy came lolloping around the corner, waving a foil-wrapped parcel.

'*Bonne anniversaire!*' he sang out. 'Hello, just out of bed?'

'Oh God,' I muttered, hitching up my drooping shorts. 'Come in before I get arrested.'

He slid past me and flopped on the sofa before I could stop him. I tore off the foil with indecent haste.

'Now this book,' he said, 'is a corker. You'll love it. It's set in Berlin around the time of reunification. You have two families who've been living on opposite sides of the wall ...'

Revenant

I nodded in a daze, groping urgently for some way to get rid of him. Jeremy is an omni-reader who's devoured everything from Homer to Hollinghurst. Without some intervention, he'd detain me for hours. Would the same excuse work? Luckily, he soon provided the spur.

'Oh, and by the way,' he said, 'I've got my latest manuscript here. I was wondering if you'd just take a look ...'

'Jeremy,' I blurted, 'to be honest, I'm not feeling too well.'

He said, 'Oh, lovie, why haven't you stopped me?' (I let that one pass.) 'But say no more, I'm off this instant. I'll leave the manuscript and phone later. Just take a pill, lie down and get well soon.'

I saw him out and as soon as he'd gone I looked in on Jock, who was perched on the bed. 'Sorry,' I said. 'I've drawn the curtains. To hell with the doorbell. How long have we got?'

'Next client's at twelve-thirty in Fairfield Road.'

I flung off my singlet, got on the table, and he started again on my shoulders. It was sheer bliss. I soaked it up, sinking away into total submission.

'So how's business?' I burbled.

'Booming,' he said. 'There's always a call for hands-on therapy.'

'Hands-on therapy,' I mused.

'Yes,' he declared, 'and it's the perfect way to finance my studies.'

'I see ... so what are you studying?'

'Sociology.'

'Hmm,' I reflected. 'Strange pairing – massage and sociology.'

Festival

'The perfect complement,' he said. 'You learn a lot about people when they're under your thumb.'

'Is that so?' I said uneasily, as a thumb jiggled my spine.

'Anyway,' he continued, 'what about you? Brighton your hometown?'

'Nah, London. I moved here for the sea and the scene.'

'Like me,' he said. 'So what do you do?'

'Charge nurse,' I said. 'At the Royal Sussex. But when I lived in Finchley I worked at Guy's.'

He made no reply and went silent for several minutes. Then gradually – very gradually – his kneading slackened until it came to a complete standstill. I turned and looked at him.

He said, 'So let's get this straight. You lived in Finchley and worked at Guy's as a charge nurse, right?'

'Right.'

'And you're Henry? ... Henry Tudor?'

I nodded, eyeing him closely. My spine, already buzzing from the massage, had begun to tingle.

'Henry Tudor,' he said. 'Not a likely name, is it?'

I frowned and blushed, bristling slightly. 'No more unlikely than Jock Wilde,' I snorted. 'But then aliases – they're common, I guess – especially in your field.'

'Yes,' he declared. 'Among workers *and* clients.'

I sat up and we stared into each other's eyes, swallowing nervously. I could see the molecules dancing in his brain, feel the wires humming in my own.

'Okay,' he said, 'let's cut to the chase. Finchley. Which street?'

'Napier,' I gulped.

'Number?'

Revenant

'Twenty-seven,' I murmured shakily.

A stunned silence fell. Our eyes remained locked, his face paled under his rich tan, and the tingle in my spine flared to high alert. Then, with a look of dazed incredulity, he turned and wandered off.

'I think I need to sit down,' he said, dropping onto a chair.

I was feeling pretty wobbly myself, but I managed to slide off the table. I approached him cautiously and squeezed his arm. Then I fetched the kettle.

'More tea?' I said, topping his mug.

We sat opposite each other, sipping at intervals, feasting on the person before us who'd just gained a new – or rather, new-found – identity.

I said, 'So ... to be quite clear ... you're Ben ... right?'

He nodded. 'So what should I call *you*?'

'Brian,' I insisted.

A long silence followed. A long, busy silence in which the world turned somersault and came to rest upended. We smiled shyly at each other.

'Looks like we've got a lot of catching up to do,' I said.

'Indeed,' he gasped, raking fingers through his hair. 'Anyway ... you begin.'

I stared at my feet. Begin? *Where* to begin? Life contains so much. And language? A cracked kettle on which we beat out tunes for bears to dance to. How to heave up everything, move the stars to tears? I took a deep breath and looked up.

'I loved your mother, Ben, but it wouldn't have worked. Nature asserts itself. I wasn't born to be a husband and a father, though God knows I tried.'

Festival

Another pause. He studied me closely. 'So what are you saying? You had lovers?'

'Yes, and I knew it was over when she heard me talking on the phone to Paul, a guy at the hospital. She was angry, bitter, distraught. You were a mere babe at the time.'

'And then?'

'In time she calmed down and we talked about it. But the hurt was still there. She told me to go. She'd manage. But we agreed that I'd send her money.'

'And not see each other?'

'Too upsetting, she thought. She wanted a clean break. She wrote, sent news, but wouldn't agree to meet. I was heartbroken, devastated, but I consented. It seemed for the best. Then she met Neil and we divorced.'

He got up, cracked his fingers, paced around. 'This is too much. I can't get my head round it. I grew up thinking Neil was my dad. You were just a shadow, the dimmest memory. She broke the news a few years ago, and since then I've been madly curious about you.'

'Ben, I'm sorry ... honestly ... so sorry I wasn't there for you.'

I rose to meet him. We stood facing each other. Then, moving forward, we folded in a long embrace. It was the strangest, most dizzying, most joyous moment of my life. The sheerest miracle: a transfiguration. I pulled back and gazed in wonder at this Jock Wilde – né Ben Gilmore – who moments before had been squeezing my thighs and thumping my arse. For the wheel had turned, the lost one was found, and what I held in my arms was my own flesh and blood.

We moved to the sofa, he took my hand, and we

gazed at the wall for a very long time, saying nothing. Then his head dropped onto my shoulder.

He said, 'How weird is this? ... Can you believe it?'

'Fate,' I said.

'I'm not sure,' he said. 'I mean ... why did I move here?'

'For the sea and the scene?' I offered with a grin.

He grinned back. 'Hey look, what are your plans? Can we spend the day together? We must, we absolutely must. I mean, come on, let's celebrate this day of all days ... your *birthday*, after all!'

'Have you forgotten Fairfield Road?'

'Fuck Fairfield Road.'

'And your partner?'

'Simon,' he said. 'He lectures at the university. He'd love to meet you, I just know he would. So shall I book a table for tonight? There's a great little bistro not far from the house ...'

And so he rattled on, bursting with excitement, filling in the gaps, tearing through his life history. And I've no idea how long we sat there. I was too amazed and happy to take note of time, or indeed anything he said. I simply fixed him in stupefied delight. We'd catch up later. There was endless opportunity. The rest of our lives, in fact.

My mobile buzzed at seven that evening as I was about to leave the house, and when I saw who it was my heart sank. But I had the perfect excuse to keep it short, so I snapped on.

'How *are* you? Not in bed?'

'I'm feeling great, Maude. Never better.'

'Oh really? Well, jolly good. Now listen, I'm writing

to the *Argus*. And it's pretty hot stuff. In fact I'm thinking of prosecuting.'

'Prosecuting?'

'For unfair reporting and defamation.'

'Oh, don't do that, lovie. You never know what you're getting into.'

'But you heard what that bastard wrote.'

'Just take it on the chin, Maudie. The man's an idiot. Doesn't know a backdrop from a cough drop. Your set is a masterpiece. It fills me with joy.'

'Oh … well … thank you, darling.'

'Now I must go. I'm off for the evening.'

'Oh really? … Well, you *have* improved … Off you go then … Have the loveliest time and toodle-oo.'

I ended the call, examined myself in the mirror, felt in my pockets for wallet and keys. But as I made for the door, the thing buzzed again. Oh God! Was she back? Too bad, let it buzz. But then I paused. Perhaps it was Ben with a change of plan. He'd failed to book a table, or discovered some prior engagement. But no, I knew who it was. It was surely Jeremy, with an inquiry about my health that was really an excuse to ask if I'd had time to look at his manuscript. A glance at the screen confirmed my hunch. So I snapped off. Then I checked the name of the restaurant, tucked the phone in my back pocket and, with a final inspection of my appearance, shot through the door in a glow of exaltation.

Coda

Charlie was dead. No doubt about that. Dead as a doornail. Or if you prefer, a coffin nail. I had to keep reminding myself, though, especially on waking. Sleep always threw me, wrapped me in forgetfulness. I had to reach out and feel the hollow in the bed before the cold, spreading upward from my feet, began to squeeze the heart. And I'd lie there, reluctant to get up. Me, the early riser, the tea maker, the catcher of the shipping forecast. Sometimes it was late morning before I drew the curtains. And rain or shine, it made no difference. I'd stare into the blank street and wonder what the point was.

It grieved me that I knew nothing about his condition. I don't even know when *he* learned about it. I guess he kept quiet to protect me. All the same I felt bitterly resentful. To my way of thinking two guys who've been together for twenty-three years should have no secrets from each other. At least, that's how I felt at the time. I've softened since. Even so, it still

Festival

hurts. Think of the difference it would have made if I'd known. We might have made trips to some of those places we'd long talked about seeing. We might have avoided some of those senseless little rows that blew up from time to time. We might have turned those last years – months, weeks, what were they? – into a glad celebration of his life.

'Listen to me,' said Rosie. 'Get out more. Meet other people.'

'Thanks, but I'm not interested in other people.'

'In that case, take cyanide. People are essential. They're the works, for fuck's sake.'

She's brutal, Rosie – and always annoyingly right. But where to start? I couldn't face bars. I've never liked bars, and the thought of being perched on a stool trying to engage some other lonely weirdo in conversation filled me with horror. No, I like to meet people in a more active situation, so I thought about joining an evening class and scanned some leaflets I found in the library. Nothing jumped at me, though. Then my mind flew to the Tiptree Players, an amateur group whose performances we'd sometimes attended. Their productions were often dire, but I love bad acting. I get more pleasure from bad acting than from slick professionalism. Besides, I had a secret fondness for this lot. They seemed nice – which is a vapid word, I know, but I can't think of a better one. I felt they were not too serious about themselves and knew how to have fun.

Let's be clear, though – I had no wish to act. The fact is I'm shy; I've a terror of the footlights. No, I just wanted to be part of the team. What I had in mind was lending a hand backstage, being ready with a prop or a

Coda

change of costume, that kind of thing. Nothing high profile. But then, what was it the poet wrote? They also serve who only stir the tea?

'Welcome,' said Liz, the director, when I turned up one evening. 'I'm delighted you want to join us. And as you can see, rehearsals are underway for our next production, *Jane Eyre*, so it's all hands to the pump because there's a lot of business with candlesticks and we finish with a house in flames.'

'Oh splendid!' I said. 'No snoozing then.'

'Absolutely not!' she shrieked.

The stage manager, Gilbert, was short and bald, with a bushy grey moustache and a Captain Mainwaring sense of self-importance. He gathered a little group around him and handed out photocopied sheets of diagrams, everything drawn up military-style. The crew consisted of two chatty women, whose frequent interruptions were a clear annoyance to him, a fat man in a boiler suit, and sitting next to me, a skinny lad with straggly blond hair who looked like a rebellious schoolboy.

I turned to him during the coffee break. 'It's Owen, by the way.'

'Vince,' he said.

'Your first time?'

'Yeah.'

'Same here. You look a bit dazed, like me.'

'Ah well, we're the rookies,' he grinned.

There was little chance to talk after that, but at the end of the evening he and I left together. 'Want a lift?' I said. 'Where d'you live?'

'Glover Street,' he said. 'D'you know it?'

'Yeah,' I said. 'That's near me. Hop in.'

Festival

In the car we said nothing for a while, but a few minutes into the journey I broke the silence. 'Fancy a drink? I've got some beer in the fridge. Or there's a spot of whisky, brandy, gin.'

He smiled wryly, shrugged. 'Perhaps a beer,' he said.

In the house he lolled back on the sofa, and when I returned from the kitchen with two chilled cans I found him leafing through a coffee-table book that he'd pulled from a shelf. It was a book of soft erotica: men lazing around a pool, or naked on horseback, or lying winsomely in a bale of hay, that kind of thing. I placed the cans on the coffee table, settled back in my armchair, and after a while he snapped the book shut and fixed me with a steely gaze.

'Hm, fascinating ... So are you queer?'

Now I'm not easily thrown, but the bluntness of that was a sock in the jaw. That's it then, I thought: the end of a potentially beautiful friendship. He's going to storm off and never speak to me again. My first attempt to meet other people and I've botched it big time. But at the back of my mind was an even more worrying thought: might he turn nasty? True, he didn't look like a thug, but you couldn't go by that. Perhaps I was about to hit the local front page: *Man beaten up in his own home*.

Still, if our friendship was to have any future, there was no point in lying. In any case I've never been one to deny who I am. So I took a deep breath.

'Yeah,' I chuckled. 'Queer as a nine-leaf clover.'

'Thought so. Better take me pants off then.'

'There's no need for *that*,' I said. 'I invited you in for a beer.'

'I thought you fancied blokes.'

Coda

'I do. But just at the moment I fancy a beer.'

He broke into a grin and we fell silent, gazing shyly at the floor and lifting the cans to our lips. The silence was mellow, relaxed, not in the least awkward. And so, quite naturally, I began to talk about Charlie: his love of good wine, his wicked sense of humour, his infuriating habit of dropping clothes everywhere – and of course the shock of his sudden collapse. Vince listened, sometimes wrinkling his brow, sometimes nodding, sometimes scratching his ear. Then, during a lull, he started to talk about himself. He'd been raised in an orphanage, but now lived in a hostel for young people. He worked in a warehouse and drove a forklift truck. He'd hated school and had left at the earliest opportunity. But he made an exception for the drama lessons. They were fun, and in the right part he was the perfect little show-off.

'So you want to act?'

'Maybe ... or work in the theatre.'

'Well, you've made a start.'

'Yeah ... and one day I'll run away and join the circus.'

We discussed the Tiptree Players, picking the whole company apart and having a good chortle over Captain Mainwaring.

Then we turned to the play.

'So what's it about?' he said, leafing through the script.

'Oh, it's a long story,' I said, reaching for the shelf and handing him a copy of the novel. 'But this is where to begin.'

He took it with a frown and scanned the first paragraph.

Festival

'She's an orphan, by the way. Could be just up your street.'

'I'll give it a go,' he said, slipping the book into his bag.

Rehearsals were weekly to begin with, but increased as the opening night drew near. At first Vince and I, who tended to stick together, simply sat and watched, but on each attendance we were given more to do – prompting, managing props, helping actors with their lines – and from time to time Gilbert would call us aside and instruct us on the scene changes. Bits and pieces of a set began to appear – a classical pillar, a gothic window, a tree with gnarled roots and branches – though it remained a mystery where they'd appeared *from*. The actress playing Bertha was great fun and always joined Vince and me for a chat. 'I love doing *mad*,' she said. 'I've done Anne Catherick and I'd love to have a crack at Blanche Dubois or Miss Havisham.'

Vince almost always came back to my place afterward, and usually he rolled a joint that we passed between us. Some nights we talked for hours. He told me a lot about the orphanage, the kids he'd known there, the people who'd run the place. There'd been a lot of bullying and one of the staff he'd hated intensely – a big bloke with an air of quiet menace. Indeed, he came close to saying that the man had abused him, though in what way exactly I was left to guess. Shyly he admitted to self-harm and showed me the scars on his wrists.

Life was better now; he had his own room at the hostel and more freedom. But the place was far from perfect, and some of the people he lived were sheer aggravation. Karen, for instance, who was always

Coda

losing things and accusing the others of theft. Then there was Sean, the dealer, who was always in trouble with the law, and Spike, the headcase, who played punk at full volume and left taps running.

So that night in bed I got to thinking. Why not offer Vince the spare room? If he moved in, it would benefit both of us. *He* needed somewhere decent to live, *I* needed company. It was selfish of me to occupy all this unused space. I mulled it over and when we next met I casually floated the idea. He looked at me sceptically, then nodded.

'Anyway, the offer's there,' I said. 'Think about it.'

Three days later, on a Friday night, the doorbell rang at around ten-thirty. I answered and found Vince sitting on the step. He was slumped forward, his back towards me, his head in his hands.

'Hello,' I said. 'What's up?'

'Everything,' he said.

In the kitchen he sat down and blurted out all his troubles, twitching nervously and running his fingers through his hair. It was the hostel. The place had been raided the previous night, causing Sean and Spike, who were always arguing anyway, to fall out dramatically. They were now using their fists. Moreover, Karen, when agitated, was apt to stand at the top of the stairs and scream. The tension in the place was constant and unbearable.

I listened in silence, and when he stopped I got up and pulled a couple of cans from the fridge. 'I reckon this calls for a beer.'

He nodded.

I knew what *I* was thinking, but was he thinking the

Festival

same? So I waited, hoping to hear something more. Nothing came, though. So eventually I spoke for the two of us. 'Look, why not stay for the night? You can take over the spare room and we can talk about this in the morning.'

He readily accepted, and the next day at breakfast we discussed the situation. Did he want to move in for a trial period? Yes, he said, he'd really like that. So we came to an agreement about the rent, and that evening he went back to the hostel and fetched his belongings.

It was awkward at first, this new way of living, and we were unsure how to handle it. We were cautious, overly polite, wary of stepping on each other's toes. I was always conscious of how strange it must be for him, living with a man three times his age. I told him to use the place as his own, but he tended at first to stay in his room. Some nights I heard him slip out and come home after I'd gone to bed. On other occasions he'd join me for a late-night drink. He had no interest in television and most evenings lay on his bed listening to music through earphones. He frequently rose late, skipped breakfast and flew out of the front door while still hauling on his jacket.

Meanwhile the play was taking shape, though with much concern about whether it was taking the shape it should be taking. We were just three weeks off opening night and rehearsing several times a week. Gilbert was instructing us like a drill-sergeant and growing evermore pompous with every practice session. As for Bertha, she was now so scary that we backed off whenever she came near. And Vince? He was in his element. He loved the rehearsals, I could see that. He'd

Coda

been initially shy, but now, a few weeks down the line, he'd shed his reserve and was chatting freely to everyone.

The person whose company he most enjoyed, however, was clearly Anna, the young woman playing Helen Burns. She was slight, raven-haired and vivacious, and in conversation with Vince she'd throw back her head and give a deep-throated laugh. I watched Vince when he was with her, and it was clear that he was utterly entranced by her. But I noticed that he never spoke about her. We discussed almost everyone involved in the production, and I waited for her name to arise but it never did. I've often thought about this. Was he simply shy of showing his feelings, or was there a kind of tact behind his reticence?

I'd assumed from the start, of course, that Vince liked girls. True, he never mentioned girls, but if he fancied blokes there'd been plenty of opportunity to tell me. Looking back, I can see that what developed between us, in those hours of shared intimacy, was a kind of conspiracy of silence: a silence in which I could hatch fantasies. And of course I knew, in some deep part of me, that they *were* fantasies: I was far too old for Vince, even if he did fancy blokes. But then we all tend to indulge ourselves, don't we? And it's amazing how strong fantasies can be.

Anyway, he started slipping out of the house more frequently in the evenings and returning after I'd gone to bed. I used to lie awake at night, listening for him, and usually I'd hear him come in, though sometimes he'd return after I'd fallen asleep. On one occasion I woke in the dead of night to the tread of feet on the stairs. I had no idea where he was going, but clearly he was seeing someone, and I was sure it was Anna. And with no evidence to support that conviction I'd lie there, flinching and twisting in a fit of resentment. I'd been the first on the scene, after all, with my cans of lager, my sympathetic ear, my offer of a room. Anna was a latecomer, an upstart. And yes, I know that sounds ridiculous, but then I *am* ridiculous. Sometimes I feel that all the conditions of my life have conspired to make me ridiculous.

I said nothing, however. Nor did he drop even a hint about where he went at night. And when we met in the mornings we carefully skirted the subject, talking instead about all manner of things, in voices that were unnaturally bright and cheerful. We strove in fact to keep things normal, but it was clear that we knew that a shift had occurred in our relationship.

The final rehearsal was manic. We knew it would be, but when Liz, the director, arrived an hour late, hobbling on crutches, the tension, already high, rose to fever pitch. 'Sorry, darlings,' she trilled. 'A slight mishap on the stairs. But I'm here now, and the show goes on.'

Gilbert stormed around like a general in the midst of battle. He kept waving his clipboard and barking orders as if we were troops about to go over the top. The performance went reasonably well until a fight broke out between two of the actors about who was to blame for a muddle in the lines. Then Mr Rochester crashed through a door rather too hard and cracked Mrs Fairfax on the nose. At this point Liz rose unsteadily on her crutches and bawled everyone out. We were all as slack as hell, apparently, and had better pull our socks up. The

Coda

actress playing Bertha – I forget her real name – sidled up to me during the break. 'I normally have to work myself up for my first appearance,' she muttered, 'but tonight I'm thoroughly worked up already.'

I glanced across the room. Vince was chatting to Anna, and from time to time they'd rock with laughter. She was leaning with her back to the proscenium and he was pressed close to her. I kept snatching my eyes away and then looking back. This is how things were now. He was spending more and more time with *her*.

Suddenly I needed fresh air; the place felt hot and stuffy. So I went outside. A bloke was standing at the front entrance, smoking a cigarette. I'd not seen him at rehearsals before, but his face was vaguely familiar. He was someone from the past, from a long way back. But what was his name and where had we met? It had been nagging me all evening. We smiled at each other.

'Hi,' I said. 'Could you spare me one of those? Sorry, I've left mine at home.'

'No problem.'

He offered me one and lit it for me. I took a deep draught. Apart from the spliffs I'd shared with Vince, it was my first lungful in years.

'I know you,' he said. 'You're Owen.'

I stared at him. He was about my age, but well preserved. He had a lean, shapely face, a tuft of greying hair and a mole on his left cheek. And then it came to me. My mind flew back twenty years and I saw this guy snogging me on the stairs at one of Eddie Brownlow's parties. It was an event that got me into trouble with Charlie. I was struck dumb for a moment and went on staring at him, feeling thoroughly discomposed. But he quickly jumped in to cover my embarrassment.

Festival

'It's Nick,' he said.
'Of course,' I said, and we shook hands.
'Still together, are you? You and him?'
'No,' I said. 'We're not.'

But I was too overcome to say any more. It was the wrong moment; my feelings were all astir. So after a few quick draws I stubbed the cigarette out. 'Oh look, it's a long story and I need to get back. Some other time, eh?'

'Of course.' He touched me on the arm and I hurried off.

Opening night was thrillingly shambolic. There was a problem with the curtain, Richard Mason missed his first cue, and Mrs Fairfax, to everyone's dismay, insisted on wearing a plaster over her wounded nose. Moreover, in spite of all the drilling we'd had, a number of scene changes went wrong, and Gilbert stood in the wings near to apoplexy. To add to the chaos, Bertha was so terrifying that a child in the audience started to cry and an elderly lady had to be helped from the room. Still, we got through it, and it was perhaps no surprise when Liz called us all together at the end and cracked open several bottles of champagne.

'Brilliant, darlings!' she sang out. 'You were all quite wonderful.'

Nick was there, of course, and indeed every night that week, though in the bustle there was no chance to speak to him more than briefly. Also, for reasons that I can't quite explain, I tended to avoid him. Was he a reminder of an episode that I wanted to forget, or was I just too preoccupied with Vince to welcome this strange intrusion from the past? I don't know. It was probably a

Coda

bit of both. I was in a muddle, I know that. All keyed up and struggling with confused feelings.

On the last night of the run there was a party at Liz's place. It should have been fun, but I got trapped in the kitchen with a couple of tiresome sound engineers. I scarcely caught sight of Vince, who was clinging to Anna at the centre of a lively scene in the sitting room. After an hour I glanced at my watch and decided to go. I looked around for Liz. She was in the study, holding a plate of sausage rolls, her crutches propped against the wall. Nick was standing beside her.

'Do you two know each other?' she said.

'Yes, we do,' I said. 'Hi, Nick.'

'Well, stick around. You're not going, surely? The night is young.'

'I've got visitors for lunch,' I said.

'Liar,' she grinned.

At home I went straight to bed and slept soundly until eleven. What woke me was the sound of voices in the hall. So I got up and peered out. Vince was closing the front door. He was in his underpants. Then he came up the stairs and disappeared into his room. He showed no sign of having seen me. I pulled on my dressing gown and crossed the landing. The bathroom was reeking of perfume and some strands of black hair were clinging to the sink. I got dressed and went downstairs. I made myself some breakfast and switched on the radio. Shortly after this, Vince appeared. He smiled at me, and I tried to smile back, but my lips were trembling.

'Vince,' I said. 'We need to talk.'

His face fell, and he looked me straight in the eye, as if he knew what was coming.

'Oh really? What about?'

Festival

'Perhaps I should have mentioned it before, but I don't allow visitors.'

There was a long period of silence. I sat motionless, he stood stock still, and we went on staring at each other with strained faces.

'Yeah, you should've,' he said at last. 'Anyway, don't bother to explain. I think I know what all this is about.'

And with that, he made a smart turn and left.

Twenty minutes later I heard the front door crash, and for the next half hour I sat there, feeling sick and desolate, my hands clasping a mug of cold tea.

The following days were bleak. I scarcely saw him, and whenever we did meet he was coldly polite and distant. We tended to take care of ourselves when it came to meals, but it was difficult to avoid each other at breakfast and suppertime. I followed my old habit of listening to the news, but I tuned in now to cover the silence. Vince sat with a stony face, scratching away at crosswords.

We'd agreed on a trial period, but I was afraid to raise the matter. The truth is, I was torn. There was now a part of me that wanted him to go, that wanted to be alone again, that wanted an end to the pain. But fundamentally I knew that alone meant pointless, that an end to the pain meant simply the end. People are essential, I recalled; they're the works. So I spoke to Charlie, or at least to the photograph of him that I kept in my wallet. He told me not to do anything rash. Oh yeah, predictable, that. What else to expect from a guy who couldn't let on to his long-term partner that he was terminally ill?

Coda

The Players were having a break before tackling their next production, *Pygmalion*, so I had a week to sit and bite my nails. But on the Friday evening the phone rang.

'Hi, Owen. It's Nick.'

'Nick,' I said.

'Sorry, am I disturbing you? Just thought I'd give you a buzz. I found your number in the book.'

I went silent. To be honest, I wasn't exactly thrilled to hear from him, which I'm sure he realised.

'Anyway, I was wondering if you were free tomorrow night. It would be nice to catch up, and I could whip us up a modest little meal.'

I hesitated. 'Well,' I said, with a tiny cough, 'that would be lovely.'

He lived on the third floor of a block of riverside flats. The spacious lounge was furnished with an arrangement of foam-filled cubes and the floor twinkled with a scattering of oriental rugs. The walls were softly lit, trailing plants cascaded from every ledge and sliding doors led out onto a fair-sized balcony. He took my coat and to my surprise I was instantly at ease. So I settled back and we chatted while he prepared a bowl of pasta. He'd not always lived alone, he told me, but nowadays he liked to have his own space. He worked for a travel firm and was often away from home. Hence his rather tenuous connection with the Players; he loved theatre, but could rarely commit himself for long periods.

It was strange how the evening worked on me. I'd arrived feeling distant and apprehensive, with a plan to leave early on the pretext of having a journey to make the next day. But as the night wore on, I found myself, with the help of some good wine, growing more and more talkative. We had a good chuckle over the snog on

Festival

the stairs, I spilled all the beans about Charlie and his misdeeds, and was amazed to hear myself speaking frankly about my loneliness. Then eventually we got round to Vince. Nick was amazed to hear that he was lodging with me and listened with interest to the tale of the orphanage. But I said nothing about our recent falling out. It was too close, too raw.

We came at last to a pause. I glanced at my watch, and saw with astonishment that it was after two. I drained the wine in my glass, and shook my head when Nick moved to refill it.

'We must do this again sometime,' he said.

At the door he gave me a hug. It was a long, slow hug, and I was tempted to pull away. But then my resistance crumbled and I melted into him. It was the first hug that anyone had given me in years.

When I got home that night, I stood in the hall for a few minutes and simply listened. Don't ask me why. They say we all have a sixth sense, don't they? Anyway, for some reason the house felt weirdly hollow. I don't mean stripped, or burgled, or anything like that – though, to be honest, I'm not sure *what* I mean. All I can say is that the place felt different. I glanced around, trying to spot the difference, but nothing met my eye. I just had this mysterious tingle in the pit of my stomach.

In the kitchen I snapped on the light. Everything was spotless and cleared away, but an envelope with my name scrawled on it had been carefully placed in the middle of the table. I picked it up, lifted the unsealed flap and pulled out some crumpled banknotes. A week's rent. I stared at the money, and the tingle in my stomach flared into a grip of pain. I had to clutch the table to

Coda

steady myself. Then I backed onto a chair and sat gazing through the window at next door's cat prowling in the garden. Funny I should remember that. Funny how scenes imprint themselves at crucial moments. Funny how life goes on when it ought to stop. I can never see that cat now without a residual pang of grief.

After a while I climbed the stairs. The door to Vince's room was slightly ajar. I called to him through the crack, but nothing came back. So I went in. The place was all but empty, stripped to the bare essentials and chillingly tidy, like a room in a guesthouse. The duvet was rolled back, the surfaces were cleared, there was not a possession in sight. In fact, aside from the furniture, the only things in the room were a vase, an ashtray and the copy of *Jane Eyre* I'd leant him. It was lying in the middle of an otherwise empty bookshelf. I thumbed through it and a strip of paper fell out. I bent to pick it up. It was a stub from the local off-licence. Was this all I'd have for remembrance? I stared at it, smoothed out the creases and replaced it carefully. Then I sat on the edge of the bed and wept like a child.

Rehearsals for *Pygmalion* began the following Tuesday with a reading of the play. I went along, partly out of curiosity – would *he* be there? – and partly from a sense that life must go on. I'd mentioned his departure to no one. I was still too upset.

He was not there. Nor was Nick. But Anna was. She kept glancing at me from the other side of the room and then looking away whenever our eyes met. So during the break I went across and tapped her on the shoulder. She turned and smiled with a slight blush, and I went straight in.

Festival

'Have you seen Vince?' I said.

She stared at me. She looked mildly alarmed, and there was a hint of guilt in her eyes. 'Not for a while. Why?'

'He's gone,' I said.

There was a long pause. She looked down at her feet and her mouth flinched. 'We had a row,' she mumbled.

I nodded and waited to hear more, but she just shrugged. Nevertheless, I felt secretly relieved; her admission removed at least part of my own sense of guilt.

Over the next few months Nick and I began to see each other frequently. At first our friendship was no more than relaxed companionship. But then one night, after a large meal at my place, followed by a glass or two of vintage port, we stumbled up the stairs hand in hand. It marked the start of a new phase in our attachment, and some weeks later we discussed the possibility of living together. We decided against it, though. We both enjoyed our own space and the current arrangement was fine, why mess with it? I continued to attend rehearsals, and Nick came whenever his work allowed. I was even persuaded to accept a few walk-on parts, though walking on was all I'd agree to. All in all, these were good times for me. Some of the happiest of my life.

The one pain in my heart was Vince. I thought about him every day. I wondered where he was, what he was doing, who he was with. I remembered the scars on his wrists. He was no longer in town, I was sure of that. There was no sign of him, and the people at the hostel simply shrugged. So did the management at Harrison's, his old firm.

Coda

A year went by. Nick and I took a holiday in Spain, and on our return he dropped me off at the house. There was a heap of mail on the mat and I stared at one of the items before tearing it open. The handwriting was vaguely familiar. I reached inside and pulled out a flyer for a play: *Nights at the Circus*. Venue: Goodwin's Music Hall in the East End. Nearest tube: Whitechapel. There was also a complimentary ticket. I turned it over. The message scrawled on the back read 'With love, V'. I felt a prickling in the scalp and my eyes turned filmy. I had to sit down. I glanced at the dates. Was I too late? No, the run continued to the end of the week. My heart leapt. There was still time.

So the following afternoon I took the train to Liverpool Street. I said nothing to Nick. He was back at work anyway and unlikely to make contact. I had a bite to eat in a sandwich bar and went in search of the place. And after a few inquiries I found it: a tall building with a canopied entrance and a golden cupola. I showed my ticket to a smiling man in uniform and he escorted me to a seat in the stalls. I glanced around. The seating rose in tiers, the walls were crumbling, the seats were worn, the brass was tarnished. 'Victorian,' grinned the man beside me. 'Bit of a ruin, but we're raising money for its repair and, trust me, its glory days *will* return.'

The play was highly fantastic, a riot of colour and action. The central character was Fevvers, the world's only winged woman, whose story emerged in an interview with a sceptical journalist intent on exposing her as a fraud. I loved every minute of it. Most of the actors played multiple roles, singing, dancing, tumbling, clowning, and I spotted Vince instantly. He kept changing costume, but his voice and features were

Festival

unmistakable. I caught his eye too, whenever the action spilled into the audience. The cast got a standing ovation. 'Bravo!' yelled the man next to me, as we stood shoulder to shoulder, clapping till our palms ached.

The audience started to drift away. I sat down and waited. A couple of men appeared on stage and began to shift props, but there was no sign of Vince. Would he turn up or should I go in search of him? I sat a bit longer, and after a while, feeling confused and disappointed, I got up and wandered towards the front. And it was then, as I hung about on the edge of the orchestra pit, that he suddenly emerged from the wings, still shimmering in the sequinned suit he'd worn at the final curtain. He leapt into the auditorium, strode up and we held each other in a long embrace.

'You made it,' he grinned.

'You too – all the way to the sawdust ring.'

'Hey, you're looking good.'

'Well, look at you. What a dazzler!'

'Got time for a drink?'

'Okay, just the one – I've got a train to catch.'

We sat on stools in the crowded bar and swapped news. He was living nearby in a cramped bedsit with dingy tube lighting, a split in the sofa and pipes that knocked. But it was just about bearable and things were looking up. They were taking the play to Edinburgh and he'd been offered a place at drama school. Meanwhile he was temping, taking anything that came along. Money was tight, but he was following his dream.

I pulled out my cheque book. 'Hey no,' he insisted. 'That's not what I meant.'

The talk went on. We recalled old times and I gave him the news of the Players, carefully avoiding any

Coda

mention of Anna or the events that had come between us. I spoke briefly about my friendship with Nick and how happy I was. He smiled and clasped my hand. There was a lot to say and not enough time.

The moment of parting came. We hugged each other again. 'Vince,' I said in a shaky voice, 'you will look in from time to time, won't you? The room's just as you left it.' I spread my palms. 'So whenever you need ... well, you know, a break from the wandering life, a retreat, a bolthole, a refuge ...'

'Hey now, hold on,' he grinned. 'Don't make offers you might regret.'

At Liverpool Street, with just minutes to spare, I flew down the platform, leapt aboard and sank exhausted into what seemed to be the only spare seat on the train. It pulled out bang on time and, dabbing my face with a rag, I settled back with a sigh. Then some way down the line I opened my wallet and spoke again to the Oracle. Any thoughts? Was I managing okay? The response was predictably gruff. 'A fair outcome. That lad's got his head screwed on and you're beginning to acquire a modicum of sense yourself.'

I smiled, closed my eyes, and drifted into a comfortable doze.

Acknowledgements

I am grateful to Phil Bales, Val Scullion, Marion Treby, Harry Goode, Will Tate and members of Cambridge Writers for comments on these stories, many of which first appeared in anthologies prepared by Cambridge Writers, some as prize winners. *You Farzan, Me Duane* first appeared in *A Boxful of Ideas: Poetry and Prose by LGBT Writers*, edited by John Dixon and Jeffrey Doorn and published by Paradise Press.

Printed in Great Britain
by Amazon